BLOOD MOUNTAIN

L. J. Martin

PINNACLE BOOKS
Kensington Publishing Corp.
http://www.kensingtonbooks.com

PINNACLE BOOKS are published by

Kensington Publishing Corp.
850 Third Avenue
New York, NY 10022

All Kensington Titles, Imprints and Distributed Lines are available at special quantity discounts for bulk purchases for sales promotions, premiums, fund-raising, educational or institutional use. Special book excerpts or customized printings can also be created to fit specific needs. For details, write or phone the office of the Kensington special sales manager: Kensington Publishing Corp., 850 Third Avenue, New York, NY 10022, Attn: Special Sales Department, Phone: 1-800-221-2647.

Pinnacle and the P logo Reg. U.S. Pat. & TM Off.

First Pinnacle Books Printing: February 2003

10 9 8 7 6 5 4 3 2 1

Printed in the United States of America

Prologue

Auburn, California
Late March 1864
Mile 36

Two men, both larger than most, both dressed in city clothes with narrow-brimmed hats, strode down Auburn's boardwalk. One man wore a fine ankle-length overcoat, the other a sheepskin three-quarter-length with the wool out at collar and cuff. Last night's light snowfall had been worked into a muddy slush in what passed for a street, and their boots were weighted with a generous supply of muck.

The one in the long overcoat, at least 250 pounds—but a good part of it table muscle—sported a silver-headed walking cane in one hand and a generous cigar in the other. He had the build of a man more than a little comfortable with himself, but his searching, intelligent eyes belied that mistaken observation. At forty-three, he was was still a long way from adorning a rocking chair.

His younger associate was equally tall, but fifty pounds less in weight. The city suit looked out of place on his muscular frame, and under the sheepskin. He was never still, and looked as if he'd be more comfortable swinging an eighteen-pound sledge against a rock drill than carrying the sheaf of papers he'd folded in one hand. Normally, when prowling the job, he carried a pick handle and had been known to back up his demands by freely applying it to hard Irish heads.

As they walked, the sound of a tinny piano wafted from a nearby saloon, and an occasional raucous laugh echoed.

They'd just left the almost-complete construction of Auburn's new depot—a clapboard affair barely ten feet by twenty, housing an office just large enough for its rolltop desk. The larger of its two rooms hosted a waiting area with a roaring potbellied stove and a few hard plank benches. Less than a year ago this was the railhead of the Central Pacific.

A few steps from the station building squatted a single-walled outside privy, sandwiched between the depot and an imposing thirty-foot-tall water tower eclipsing both smaller structures. Dripping icicles graced the water tower, some as large as stalactites hanging four feet long from the tank high above. With the early evening temperature rapidly dropping, they wouldn't be dripping for much longer. But the ice also indicated the slackening of winter—on New Year's Day the water tower had been a labyrinthine ice sculpture, some of the frozen stalactites six feet in length. The station building was the minimum possible to serve the railroad's interests; the water tower was built as heavily as the ramparts of a Saxon castle, to withstand any onslaught.

Charles Crocker had kept the interests of the Central Pacific centered on productive uses of money, not frills, and he considered creature comforts an unproductive, thus unprofitable, embellishment. The man pacing beside him paused and pointed eastward, up into the real mountains that made up the backbone of the Sierra Nevada.

"Charley." His breath showed in the February cold. "We're posed at the mouth of the monster. Right when we should be . . . must be . . . at our strongest. I'm at my wit's end. Just about every damnable time I think we have a tolerable crew, the buggers get a stake and slip off to the hills to see if they can pan up some color."

Both men stopped in their tracks, as a man flew from the swinging door of a whiskey parlor a few steps in front of them and, arms flailing, fell beyond the boardwalk and into the muddy roadway.

James Strobridge pulled his sheepskin coat back and rested his hand on the shiny grip of a butt-forward revolver. But he didn't pull it. As they came even with the door, another man burst through. He paused, and tipping his hat to Crocker, mumbled, "Mr. Crocker," then charged around them and out into the mud, He kicked the first man, who was trying to regain his feet, flush in the face.

Strobridge barely broke stride, or the cadence of his speech. "Hell, we hired two thousand new men last spring, and three thousand through the summer. By rights we should have ten thousand employed, and yet we are still only at five thousand or so."

Strobridge dabbed at his eye socket as he spoke, as it still wept even though it no longer hosted a workable eye. He'd lost it weeks before in a nitroglycerin explosion on Bloomer Cut. They'd tried the new explosive with great success, but also at great cost. He folded the handkerchief and stuffed it back into a coat pocket.

"Every two weeks I'm starting with a bunch of fresh meat, most of whom haven't seen calluses since pullin' on Bessie's tit back on the farm in Ohio . . . or tippin' a bottle in Tipperary."

"Stro." Crocker used the familiar nickname James Strobridge's few friends called him, as he studied his construction manager. "I've been as frustrated as you, maybe more so, but you've done a hell of a job so far . . . and I think I've a solution to our problem." He paused to draw on the big cigar, his cold breath punctuated by a cloud of Cuban-scented smoke as he rested a big hand on the other man's shoulder. Strobridge gave him a skeptical one-eyed gaze, but it didn't faze Crocker, and he continued. "You don't have time to get back to the end of the line before they'll quit for the day, so come on into the Golden Stag with me and I'll stand you to dinner. Those six kids of yours can eat your share if Hannah has yours waiting. We can chew the labor problem up along with a beefsteak, and over a cup of good hot coffee, although you look as if you could use a shot of demon rum."

Stro knew he didn't mean it. Both men were ardent teetotalers by conviction.

"I really should get back—"

"No, Stro, you really should sit with me a while, and supper's as good a place as any. I'll catch the supply train back to Sacramento at ten."

"Yes, sir," Strobridge said, but sighed deeply. He hated to be out of sight of his work, and the lion's share of the work was another ten miles up the line, from where spikes were being driven and rails laid, to where a few small trestles were being built, and on to roadbeds being cut and filled, and rock blasted. And where his private car and family awaited.

But Crocker was the boss, one of four actually.

Four merchants who had never before built anything grander than a hardware store; Charles

Crocker, Collis Huntington, Mark Hopkins, and Leland Stanford were the primary stockholders in what was considered by many to be the world's greatest endeavor—the attempt to construct a railroad tying the East Coast of the United States to the West—at least as far east as the oncoming Union Pacific Railroad, marching westward from Council Bluffs, Iowa, just east of the mighty Missouri River and a stone's throw from the state border with Nebraska and the city of Omaha.

The Transcontinental Railroad.

A Herculean attempt considered a fool's folly by many. But an attempt considered critical by President Abraham Lincoln, critical to the Union in its effort to stem the Great Rebellion. Critical as the country's culmination of Manifest Destiny.

So far the western portion of the railroad, christened the Central Pacific, had seemed a formidable, most times insurmountable, task, for the western road was blocked by the great four-hundred-mile-long, in places fourteen-thousand-foot-high, granite rift—the spine of the West, the Sierra Nevada. Crossing such an impediment with a railroad had hardly been dreamed of, much less done. And the CP was at the toe of that great, heretofore impenetrable obstacle—at least impenetrable by wagon road. Men had crossed it many times, by horse, mule, and shank's mare, but many had left their bones to be ravaged by the bears, wolves, and smaller predators when spring thaw stood testament to their folly.

After the meal, as a fiddler scraped out jigs and reels, and occasionally more sophisticated fare, Crocker lit up another cigar and leaned back in his chair. He eyed Strobridge with some trepidation before he broached the subject that had prompted him to keep the younger man from his work and family. He reached into his coat pocket, drew out a small bottle, un-stoppered it, and took a swig. "Dr. Holstetter's stomach bitters," he offered. "Seems to settle my nervous gut."

He took a deep draw on the cigar and sighed, expelling a cloud of smoke.

"James," Crocker began, uncharacteristically using Strobridge's given name, "I'm going to hire us a crew of Chinese—"

"The hell . . ." Strobridge caught himself, realizing that he was talking to the man who paid his wages. He cleared his throat before continuing. "Charles, if you put the yellow scourge on my crews, every bloody Irishman will take his leave, and I'll be left with a bunch of skinny, stooped, no-account heathens who'll spend their time smoking that evil flower and . . . well, the long and short of it is, you'll be ringing the death knell for the Central Pacific." He added with finality, "I'll not boss Chinamen."

It was just the reaction Crocker had expected from Strobridge, and he was ready. "Stro, we used John Chinaman on the Dutch Flat and Donner Lake road, before your time, and your Irish lads had to bust it to keep up with them."

"That was twenty lousy queue-keepers and probably the best of the lot in California."

Crocker smiled. "I doubt if we were so lucky as to catch the best twenty out of fifty thousand. James, you do know of the Great Wall of China? They didn't do a bad job on that, and it's by far the largest, and most grand construction job in the history of mankind."

As James Strobridge listened, the fiddler slowed the tempo and began playing "Greensleeves." A customer sitting nearby pulled a mouth harp from his vest pocket and joined in. It sounded like a dirge to Strobridge, and he thought it particularly appropriate, given the subject matter under discussion.

The give-and-take raged on until Crocker missed his own work train and had to spend the night in Auburn, but before the head-butting was over, James Harvey Strobridge had agreed to hire a token crew of fifty Celestials, a crew easily obtained right in the town of Auburn, for twenty-three dollars a month, the Chinese to pay their own keep. There would be an Irishman to boss crews of no more than twenty Celestials. Still, he was convinced that he would have one hell of a time holding onto his five thousand Irishmen, even though they were paid at least two dollars a day more and were provided with all the boiled beef, pork, beans, and cabbage they could consume. Strobridge was convinced that the Chinese would last only a few days before running back to Auburn with their long queues between their legs.

In fact, after relenting to Crocker's demands, he bet his boss a box of the best Cuban cigars that that was just what would happen.

And Strobridge had given up the habit a year ago.

Chapter One

When the proud seventy-five-foot brig *China Wind* reached San Francisco Bay late in 1849, the captain was clever enough to lay off a half mile from shore—he'd heard tales of men risking life and limb, and the wrath of their captains, to make for the gold fields.

It took the crew, over half of whom were Chinese, almost twelve hours from the time the anchor parted the quiet bay's surface to totally abandon the ship, helping themselves to every shore boat including the captain's own. They left the captain and first mate to stare at the burgeoning city—a city constructed mostly of Mr. Goodyear's rubber tents and clapboard—and wonder what they would do for sailors, and for a shore boat.

It was another week, and a hundred saloons visited in recruiting attempts, before they, too, decided to try their hand at the goldfields. At that time, over eight hundred ships lay bare-masted, bobbing at anchor in the San Francisco and San Pablo harbors, none of which could muster enough men to swab the decks, much less man the yardarms. Ships were being stripped of any material that could be used to build a city; some were even winched onto shore in one piece to serve as hotels and restaurants, bordellos and gambling halls. Canvas became awnings; lines became handrails and bindings and tack and haul ropes for the mines. One ship was even towed upriver to become a more honorable institution—the Sacramento jail.

The *China Wind* belonged, lock, stock, and scuttlebutt, to Captain Edward Oldman, and, on this voyage, a one-sixteenth share of the voyage profits went to the first mate. When Oldman gave up on the dream of a crew, he sold the ship to the Peninsula Salvage Company and shared the proceeds with First Mate Nolan O'Bannon, just as he would have shared the proceeds of the voyage. Nolan O'Bannon had served him long and well. Oldman then returned their original sums to his voyage investors in Boston, plus a small profit, by way of bank drafts drawn on the Wells Fargo Company.

From that day on, Nolan O'Bannon had become a landlubber, but not one blessed with the beneficence of Gold Mountain, as the Chinese referred to California. He'd mucked his way the length of the Sierras and turned up so little color that he couldn't have made a decent locket for his ma back in Boston.

When his money belt became thin he signed on with the Placer County Canal, ending up as line boss to a hundred of his countrymen. He worked that job until it was finished. When he heard that his old canal boss, James Strobridge, had taken up railroad building again—Strobridge had been well schooled in railroads in the East—he set aside his ax. O'Bannon had been cutting wood for the steam-driven boats on the river, and had a small wood yard on a slough near the Sacramento. When he'd not turned the profit he'd hoped, he sought Strobridge out. Now he enjoyed bossing one fifth of the Central Pacific's five-thousand man Irish workforce. Actually the majority of the men were Irish, but Poles, Welshmen, Cornishmen, Peruvians, Australian Sidney Ducks, and a half-dozen other nationalities were well represented.

It was Sunday morning, with the first sun they'd seen in a month, and it was unusual for Strobridge to call his line bosses together on their one day of leisure.

Hannah Strobridge had made a real home out of the converted boxcar she shared with her husband and their six adopted children. In fair weather the rolling home sported a canvas awning and nested on a small spur off the main line, near a bubbling brook of fine fresh water, a spur it shared with the railroad's work train. But it was still far too cold to enjoy the frill of an awning and outside living, and too early for the blooming houseplants she'd hang there when it was warm enough.

The work train, which normally rested at the railhead, was made up of first a track car, with track laying materials: switches, timbers, steel rods, lining bars, wrenches, barrels, iron plates, cables, etc. The next car housed a complete feed store and saddle shop; the third a carpenter shop and washhouse; the fourth the sleeping quarters for the mule skinners; the fifth a blacksmith shop. The next three were sleeping cars, holding 144 bunks each. Most of the men preferred to sleep outside in tents or in the open when the weather permitted, as the stink in the cars was something awful, as were the bedbugs and the snoring.

The next two cars in line were dining cars, then the cook's car, which shared space with a telegraph office. As the rail line progressed, so did the telegraph line. Then came flatcars with needed supplies. The last car was loaded with two redwood water tanks. During the summer, additional stock cars would carry beef and hogs, which would be butchered for the men, but with the snow-covered meadows, the cold, and the lack of graze, meat was hauled on the daily work and supply trains from Sacramento, and easily kept fresh in the cold.

Five men gathered in Hannah Strobridge's small living area, their hands warmed by cups of strong black coffee. When Stro entered the room from the rear of the coach, Hannah excused herself for the purpose of quieting the children, but actually to let the men get on with their business.

Strobridge wasted no time. "Gentlemen, we have to have more hands on this job of work, and even though they're small hands, the big bosses are hiring a crew of Chinamen—" He didn't have a chance to finish, as the roar of complaint permeated the small space.

"By all that's holy," Liam O'Riley sputtered, "I'll not have the bloody yellow trash on my crew . . . I'll draw me pay first."

Strobridge waited until the initial outrage died down, then extended his hands and quieted the men until he had complete silence, totally ignoring those threatening to pack it up.

"Nolan here has bossed the Chinee for a half-dozen years, and speaks more than one of their dialects. He's volunteered to take the Chinee experiment under wing."

The rest of the men looked at Nolan as if the bats had indeed invaded his belfry, but he merely smiled. He'd sailed the China Sea for many years, and in all that time had only had to apply the cat-o'-nine-tails to one Chinese crew member, and that was a case of theft, not laziness. And even that had proved unnecessary, as the man "fell" overboard a fortnight later in a summer squall. Nolan O'Bannon was sure the man had been the victim of his own Celestial crew members' wrath. Not only would they not tolerate a man not pulling his weight, they sure as hell proved they wouldn't tolerate a thief.

O'Bannon merely smiled at the others, then finally spoke quietly when they settled and waited for him to do so. He'd long enjoyed their grudging admiration, as his crews regularly outperformed all others.

"Gentlemen, and I use that term in its most liberal manner in regard to you louts . . . I'll bet me next week's wages that you'll all be eatin' yer mackinaws when I've had a week with the Chinaman. He'll be lookin' back to gander at yer boys eatin' his dust."

"By the saints, that's a wager," Liam extended his calloused paw, as did O'Bannon's nemesis, Anatole Bochevski, and the other two.

Bochevski shook his large head and scowled. "I guess it will be fine to be able to swing the sledge and bash in a few yellow heads, should the need arise. It will serve as a fine entertainment to the other men."

"I'll handle the Chinee," O'Bannon said, eyeing Bochevski coldly. "You've enough to handle yer louts."

Strobridge merely guffawed, but it was a hollow laugh, as he, too, was convinced that the Chinese experiment, as he and Crocker had taken to calling it, would be an utter failure.

Far up the line, well beyond the end of any rail spiking and over two thousand feet above the elevation of the roadbed where grading and fill was underway, Simon Striker perched on an icy rock outcropping overlooking the valley far below that was soon to be the cradle of the Central Pacific's gleaming iron road. Almost a year ago he'd begun work on what he was then convinced would be the making of his fortune. At great time and effort and with all he'd earned in the goldfields, he'd worked to develop his holdings on the west and north slopes of Blood Mountain, a mountain he'd named himself as he had spilled a great deal of blood in order to claim, procure, and protect it. A name he'd chosen as one that might just serve to keep others away.

The first to feel his wrath had been a small settlement of Norwegians who had carved out a tiny three-cabin village and begun to hand-cut posts and poles from the fine stands of Jeffery, lodgepole, and ponderosa, and to whipsaw timber into planks and haul them all to the valley thirty and more miles below.

Two well-timed fires to post piles and cabins had dashed the Norwegians' hopes of a settlement to call their own, as had a couple of well-placed backshots when Striker found them working beyond earshot of their bohunk chums.

The second and bloodiest of his forays to protect what he considered his was to rout, single-handedly, a settlement of two-dozen yellow dogs who'd been breaking the law by mining a fresh discovery. The law plainly said no Chinese could mine anything other than tailings. He was well justified in setting a charge that caused a landslide, an inundation saving him from any consideration of burying the twenty or so in the ravine they'd invaded on "his mountain." Even the stench of the little yellow men had been covered in rock and debris.

Unfortunately, it had also entombed their discovery in tons of over-carriage, so Striker's thought of jumping the illegal claim was buried along with them. Hell, it was probably a worthless vein nonetheless, and one to which only the Chinee would pay heed.

Yes, he'd gone to great lengths to protect his place here in this paradise.

He considered even the railroad an interloper, but at least it was one he'd schemed to profit from. And he'd invested greatly in order to do so. A herd of twenty prime mules fed on last summer's meadow hay spread in a nearby corral. Striker had hired a skinner, now buried down at the end of the meadow not far from where Striker had built his small cabin. He'd also inherited the animals' fine tack and tow-rigging, oiled and hanging in the small barn out behind Striker's cabin. An unmarked grave was the payment received by the mule man.

The animals were another addition to Striker's growing fortune.

Striker's ownership of the mule man's property was a fitting salute, at least to Striker's way of thinking, to the hard work the man had invested to haul the hydraulic mill over thirty miles up into the Sierra to Simon Striker's Blood Mountain.

The man had even been foolish enough to keep the deposit Striker had paid him in a satchel in one of his saddlebags. Not only had Striker gotten the job done, he'd gleaned the mules, tack and tow gear, and his deposit back.

It was a wonder to Striker what could be accomplished with a simple half ounce of lead, or a pound of black powder placed under the proper rock outcropping.

It had taken him another two months, pushing his own small crew of Chinamen and digger Indians, to build the flume and penstock to deliver the proper amount of water to the mill to drive its foot-wide leather strapping and three-foot-diameter saw blade, but it now spun with enough force and diameter to cut a timber large enough to serve as a railroad tie, at a rate of one every five minutes or so, if his worthless crew humped. Ten to twelve an hour could be produced, less time than it took to sharpen the blade before each workday began . . . and that with a crew of only seven men. Three Chinamen worked on the mill as tie hackers; one served as cook, stock wrangler, and performed some extra duties tending the still, a couple of hundred yards up the mountain just below a sweet-water spring, that had been cooking corn mash for the last three months. The other men were both flume herders and teamsters who wrangled the lodgepole pine down the mountain to be cut.

The mill could handle much more timber than the small crew could deliver.

Striker had a half-dozen hogsheads of whiskey put up, for he knew how the Irish loved their drink.

The Chinese worked for little more than food; the Miwok Indians, one on the mill crew, and two to maintain the flume, were virtually slaves. They worked for beans and the occasional hunk of bacon, and fear of what Striker would do to them should they attempt escape.

The only Chinaman who had attempted to quit Striker had been waylaid halfway down the mountain, and his wages were returned to Striker's pocket long before the crows had begun to feed on his pebble-black eyes.

When the traveling became a mite easier, he would haul the whiskey down the mountain and set up a tent, unseen in a deep dark draw, where the Irish could come and spend their hard-earned. He knew that the construction boss, Crocker, and the superintendent, Strobridge, were dead set against whiskey for their crews, but he'd find a way. There was always a way to get whiskey to the Irish, for they would work as hard as he to see it accomplished.

The best result of the north side of Blood Mountain's fine location was that the timbers could be easily skidded down the mountainside to within a couple of hundred yards of the rail bed. A perfect skid road began in a long, smooth ravine only a hundred yards from the mill, a ravine formed by the Good Lord as an avalanche trough. Thousands of tons of snow and ice had cleared the trough and ground it smooth many times in years past. The tailwater from the mill, when the raceway thawed, would serve to grease the skid road.

All was near ready.

Simon Striker had several hundred ties cut and stacked on the lip of the road, ready to skid, and another stack of timbers a foot square by twenty or more feet long piled nearby, to serve as bents and cross-bracing for trestles and bridges.

By the end of the coming summer, he figured he would be a wealthy man.

The hell of it was, the damned railroad, and that cursed son of a she-dog Crocker and his flunky Strobridge, had proposed a sawmill of their own. Rumor was, if the *Sacramento Union* could be believed, Crocker would soon start construction, not but a few miles from Striker's, with the advantage of being on the railroad line.

Of course, as Striker sat on his rock and surveyed the work far below, he decided these were problems easily solved with the proper application of a little black powder, a sulfur match, or a small pellet or two of lead.

Before the snow melted off, his two younger brothers and a cousin should be here to lend him a hand. Last spring he'd sent a letter to Illinois and ordered them to join him, not long after hearing of the CP's plans to build a mill.

The best of it was that Striker had worked up a scheme, a result of his own farsighted planning. He'd spent many a long hour ferreting out who might benefit from any problems encountered by the railroad, and now he was on the payroll—in cahoots, one might say—with two of the most powerful companies in San Francisco.

Two commodities would severely hurt well-established companies in Frisco if they were delivered by a competing firm, and the CP would be that firm, once it reached the high ground in the Sierras. Ice was a valuable necessity hauled by ship from far up the Pacific Coast in Alaska. Timbers and planking from the great forests of both southern Alaska and Canada's British Columbia filled San Francisco's ever-present demand for construction materials. Striker had made an evil, and very secret, alliance with a pair of companies—each agreement unbeknownst to the other. For each day Striker proved he had delayed the railroad, he was to collect twenty dollars in cash money, and that was doubled as he was on the payroll of both companies. Northern Currents Ice Company and Atlantic-Pacific Ship and Brig were more than willing to invest in the slowing—and would be happy to invest in the complete destruction—of the Central Pacific Railroad Company.

The number of men willing to go beyond the law to protect their own backsides was never a surprise to Striker.

And all he had to do was apply powder to the right locations. Not only would he delay the CP, in the same fell swoop he could guarantee the CP's demand for more timber; every time a bridge or trestle went down, and timber was splintered, more was called for. It was already well known that the railroad would pay almost any price to try to stay on schedule.

Striker would see that prices went sky-high, especially for timbers. He and his tie hackers would be kept very, very busy.

It was a perfect plan. He would be paid for delaying the railroad, and he would be paid by the railroad for supplying timber to keep them on schedule. From his vantage point, he could see a spot where it would be necessary to build a bridge that he'd learned was to be almost nine hundred feet in length and 120 feet above the floor of the water course. He couldn't begin to estimate how many timbers it would require to complete what the railroad had named the Long Ravine Project.

Striker would see to it that Long Ravine required many more timbers than estimated by the CP.

The Long Ravine bridge, at least if the *Sacramento Union* was correct, would consist of three spans of almost three hundred feet each, with a pair of monstrous towers standing proud, but vulnerable, at equal distances from the ends of the length.

The whole thing could be destroyed with a pair of well-placed kegs, if it came to that. But he had a better plan for Long Ravine, should the weather cooperate. A plan that would be much more effective and much more devastating than a mere explosion.

That effort alone should cost the CP several months, and would earn Striker forty dollars—twenty from each company—for each day of delay.

Yes, his time was coming.

Simon Striker scratched his rough chin deep in the black beard he sported, then chuckled as he rose and stretched his large bulky frame, turning carefully on the slippery outcropping in order to make his way back to his cabin. Lee Toy should have supper ready for the camp, and the no-accounts who worked for him would be getting restless, since no one was allowed to eat until Striker had his choice of quantity and quality of the grub.

He liked to run a tight camp.

Chapter Two

Mile 44

Nolan O'Bannon sat on a timber round in linsey-woolsey shirt and Levi's reading a copy of the *New York Illustrated News*, a weekly newspaper that he subscribed to and received over six months after its publication. He also subscribed to the *Sacramento Union* newspaper, and *Frank Leslie's* and *Knickerbocker* and *Arthur's* magazines. He enjoyed keeping up on what was happening in the world.

He noted several things of interest in the paper, primarily the fact that Emperor Maximilian of Mexico had asked that his adopted country be recognized as a monarchy, an attempt that was received with great trepidation in Washington, D.C., and considered self-aggrandizement on Maximilian's part. It seemed, from the article, that Washington would be just as happy if the gentleman returned to Europe and if no European-style monarchies were ever established in the Americas.

Nolan chuckled when he read that the Union Pacific's progress had been stalled in the fall by an invasion of locusts so thick the track had become too slippery for the engines to gain traction. The Indians continued to harass the line, firing into tent camps at random.

It seemed the UP had its own share of unique problems. Still, he decided he'd be happy to trade problems with them. Meanwhile, the work train arrived and blew off its load of steam.

Fifty Celestials piled off the flatbed they'd ridden up from Auburn to the end of the line, to the accompanying grumbles of a group of nearby Irish hands.

Nolan O'Bannon folded his paper and shoved it into a coat pocket, then stood with his rough hands on his hips, shaking his head in wonder. He had the same coal-black hair as the Celestials, but that was where any resemblance stopped. His full head of jet-black hair lay combed straight back, and although more generous in length than it would have been had he had a city job, it never reached his shoulders before he visited a tonsorial parlor. Nolan's blue eyes and light, even complexion were pure Ireland. And he wore an adequate sheepskin coat and calf-high lace-up boots with trousers tucked in against the cold. Although the Chinese dressed in multiple pairs of britches and linsey-woolsey shirts, and in woven reed hats or felt broad-brimmed ones, none wore a coat. Their long queues, jealously protected against the sharp folding knives of the Irish, swung freely behind their backs. A few wore well-scuffed brogans, but most endured simple sandals without any form of stocking. And of course, Nolan O'Bannon was a head taller, at least a hand-span broader through the shoulders, and seventy-five pounds heavier than most of the Celestials.

That morning, the temperature had bottomed out at sixteen degrees and even at this low elevation, snow lay a foot deep. Snow at the summit, a railroad builder's almost unfathomable distance away at Mile 105.5, had been reported in drifts ten feet deep. And many claimed this a mild winter. O'Bannon and the other bosses prayed it would stay that way, and so it should, as spring lay near.

The Celestials gathered near the car, awaiting instruction, standing up nicely to the glares and taunts of the Irish and the mix of other nationalities who came and went from the nearby cook's car. The small Orientals were used to hard looks and rude comments, and kept their own demeanor light and unaffected.

They'd had a taste of what they were in for work-wise as they'd passed through Bloomer Cut at Mile 39, just past the burg of Newcastle. Irish crews had used some five hundred kegs of powder a day for many weeks to gouge a trench eight hundred feet long and up to eighty-five feet deep. It was the line's first major engineering obstacle. Many more were yet to come.

In a gruff voice O'Bannon chided the Irish to mind their work and button their lips, or, he suggested, he would be pleased to find a job to keep them working through supper time. They grumbled as they moved away; Nolan stepped over and welcomed the large group of Chinese. They seemed surprised even beyond his expectation when he spoke in their own dialect of Cantonese, then repeated the message in Szeyup, knowing the origin of most California Chinese near Hong Kong or from the peninsula near the Portuguese enclave of Macao. He ignored the most obvious, Mandarin, spoken by most of the few white men attempting to talk to the Chinese.

"Welcome to your new workplace. Now you will select a leader so I'll not have to instruct each and every one of you."

He stepped away as they chattered among themselves and then obviously took a vote. In moments, one of the older men stepped forward. Nolan guessed him to be in his late forties or early fifties, as he sported a long mustache with ends that hung three inches past his chin on either side of a dot of a fifty-cent-sized goatee that hung the same distance, but with the Celestials it was hard to tell age.

The man bowed, then offered, "I am Ho Chin, elected leader of these worthless Celestials."

Nolan extended his hand, shook, and returned the bow with a slight nod of the head. "And I am Nolan O'Bannon, and it will be me'self who hands you the twenty-three dollars a month each of you will earn, twelve hours a day for the easy jobs, eight to ten or more for the difficult, and believe me, Ho Chin, you and your countrymen will earn every bloody farthing of it."

"Of course, O'Bannon, we Celestials would have it no other way. Now, O'Bannon, it is necessary that we select a pair of cooks and two tea boys. You know of this custom?"

O'Bannon nodded. "I know of it, Ho Chin, and I will honor it and see that it is understood by others." One of the Chinese would be a full-time cook for twenty or more workers, and one would be a tea boy for the same number to deliver kegs of tepid tea, which would be the only break they would take during a long workday.

"Crockerman has promised that we will be cared for should we be injured on this great project. If the gods decide it and should one of us be killed, his honorable remains will be returned to his home province in the Celestial Empire. Is that also to your understanding?"

"It will be so," O'Bannon said, knowing the Chinese belief that they must be buried on their home soil so that their spirits might dwell with those of their ancestors. He had cautioned Crocker of this before he'd left their hiring to Crocker back in Auburn.

"Ho Chin, please make your men understand that you will personally receive the payment each week for all of them, and you will arrange for the food and necessities for your men. You and only you will be responsible for seeing they receive a fair division of what money is left." Crocker and Strobridge had concocted this plan, as they knew they wouldn't be able to tell one Chinaman from another, and this was the only practical means of getting them paid.

Ho Chin nodded, satisfied, and started to turn, but was stopped by O'Bannon's additional comment. "You know that you will not be welcomed by many in this camp, although Mr. Crocker . . . Crockerman and I are depending upon you and your countrymen to assist in all you are capable of."

Ho nodded, and O'Bannon thought he caught the hint of a knowing smile. It went without saying that they would be unwelcome by most. Hell, they'd been beaten and murdered and run out of camps up and down the Sierra. Chinese moving day, as the rout of the Chinese was called, was common practice. In fact, it was considered to be an entertainment. Still, O'Bannon thought the potential problem must be broached.

"If you believe you are wronged, or if you have needs, you are to come to me with your problems. All of these men you see here, other than Mr. Crocker . . . er . . . Crockerman, and Mr. Strobridge, who you will meet soon enough, are in my employ, and it is up to me to judge them. There are four other crews in other locations who have different bossmen. It is also up to me to deal with the other bosses. I will not tolerate any misbehavior on their parts, or on the part of your men . . .

although I know and respect what you can and will do, and know you will act honorably."

Ho merely nodded, as if that went without saying.

O'Bannon continued, his voice a notch lower and harder. "So do not disappoint, or I will lose much face with Crockerman and the other bossmen."

"As you say, O'Bannon," Ho said, then to Nolan's surprise, offered in very good English, "I have heard of the great decision it was for CP to hire Celestials. We not disappoint O'Bannonboss, or Crockerman."

"Not only will you not disappoint, Honorable Ho, you will surpass even what you think you can do."

"As you order, O'Bannon." He nodded, then started to turn away, but hesitated. "For this ignorant Celestial, would you explain the rank of those you mentioned . . . Crockerman is as a general?"

"Ah," O'Bannon said, smiling slightly and hesitating as he was wondering how to put it. "No, Ho. Charles Crocker is the emperor, James Strobridge is the warlord, and I am one of five generals. You are my lieutenant, and those"—he motioned to the group of Chinese—"are our soldiers. Now let us begin the battle."

"I understand," he said with a nod, then returned to his soldiers to explain the order of things.

Nolan smiled to himself as the little man moved away. He had come to truly admire the Chinese culture, and knew that even though his Irish would make this employment of the Celestials a crisis on a daily basis, as the Irish so loved to do, their attitude would only stimulate the Chinese to rise to the challenge. In fact, when the word *crisis* is written in Chinese, it is done so in two characters—one representing danger, one opportunity.

With that, Nolan O'Bannon had a crew of Chinamen, and along with them, he feared, he also had the wrath of the CP's thousands of Irishmen.

And now he had the wager of forty dollars, a week's line boss wages, to protect. In the morning it would be time to get the Celestials up the road, showing their tails to the Irishmen.

The Irish God, and the many Chinese gods, willing.

The next morning, Saturday, after being presented with his first problem by Ho Chin, and conferring with Strobridge, O'Bannon decided to move his Chinese a dozen miles up the line, three miles past Colfax. It was near O'Bannon's own campsite, and would give the Chinese a day—Sunday, a supposed day of rest—to find cover, pitch their tents, and build the rough shelters they'd require for their cantonment.

Colfax was a primary goal of the spikers of the railroad as it was a hub of wagon roads and trails to the mines, and it was hoped the new business there would help offset the terrible debt the road had incurred, and was continuing to incur. Even though President Lincoln offered his full support to the Transcontinental effort, he and Congress had the war to deal with, and prying funds out of them was worse than prying a tick off a sheep's back.

One of the great engineering challenges to face the CP was the proposed slash in the face of the hard rock cliff-side known as Cape Horn. If the Chinese were to prove themselves, it would be there. Five hundred Irishmen had been kept on the mountain's hard shoulder in one eight-hour shift through the winter, when weather allowed, making little headway. Two thousand feet above the valley floor, the granite face had to be hacked and blasted for three miles into a precipitous cliff overlooking the North Fork of the American River. The mountain plunged away at a seventy-five-degree slope—barely even goat country, with birds nested on its ledges—with no trails offering the security of a flat foothold. In many places a misstep or frayed rope would mean a two-hundred-foot plunge to a broken and blood-splattered death, and that was only the first bounce. To add insult to the great potential of injury, the curved roadbed on the rock face had to move both upgrade and down.

The problem Ho had earlier brought Nolan had been easily solved. Already Ho Chin had dispatched two of his countrymen—his younger and much larger brother, who displayed the same mustache and goatee, and a young, tall, but smooth-faced, helper. With a cash advance of three dollars a man from O'Bannon, they'd ridden the last work train down the mountain to Auburn to fetch food the Chinese would tolerate. Almost all of the Chinese had refused the boiled beef and fat-soaked beans offered them by the Irish cooks that morning. They had slept the cold night under a pair of flatbed cars, wrapped only in light blankets, and made do with tea and barely a mouthful of rice and boiled cabbage each—the one foodstuff they did accept from the cooks' car to add to their rice.

The Irish had been at work on the ledge for most of the winter, lowering their fellows in bos'n's chairs—little more than canvas strapping around the waist, with a sling enclosing a butt-wide board to support the buttocks—to strike rock drills, place black powder charges, fix and light fuses, then be hauled away with a block and tackle from above—hopefully before they were blown away by their own handiwork. It was one of the few skilled jobs they felt happy to turn over to the Celestials, as they'd already lost three men to jammed ropes, bad communication, and a fast fuse. They would be more than pleased to go back to felling trees above the cut to keep them from falling across the rails when future storms weakened them, or moving ahead of Cape Horn to Mile 55 to begin work on the great bridge known as Long Ravine. The masons were already building the foundation structures and landings for the timber edifice.

But the weather had everything held up. Mortar froze before it could be lathered into place, and water had to be thawed to mix the sludge in the first instance. Nolan prayed for springtime, when he could work two crews for a minimum of eight hours, and three in eight-hour shifts in Tunnel One, which they would begin at Mile 77.

Iron track had brought his crew of Celestials as far as it would take them toward Cape Horn; now it would be stomping through the snow, pulling handcarts loaded with tents, personal belongings, and what little food had come with them. As they passed the gandy dancers laying track, they again withstood the derision of hoots, howls, whistles, and insults. The spike mauls the men used quieted, and the constant rhythm of two solid strikes, iron on iron, and the flatter final ping of iron on wood, spike, and rail, still echoed, but faded.

Anatole Bochevski, one of the five line bosses and the only Pole among the Irish, stepped forward from his hard-shouldered gandy dancers and guffawed. He was not a man favored by Nolan O'Bannon as friend, but he did his job and used his bulky, barrel-chested, exceptionally strong frame to drive his men to exhaustion each day. The Irish referred to him as Bo-shit-ski behind his back, but none would dare voice the insult to his face.

"Hey, O'Bannon," he shouted, shaking the broken sledge handle he carried in the direction of the group of Chinese, "where you going with those hundred-twenty-pound sacks a' mule dung?" His men enjoyed a hearty laugh.

Heat flooded O'Bannon's backbone as he strode along beside the much smaller, but very proud, Ho Chin. Ho—although Nolan was sure he understood every one of the Polack's words—never cut his eyes the huge man's way. Rather, he actually seemed to walk a little taller than his five feet two inches.

Nolan paused; derisively he hocked a wad of spittle onto the newly filled roadbed near Bochevski's feet. He could see anger flare in Bochevski's cold blue eyes, and his already ruddy face flush even more, but all O'Bannon received in return was a smirk. Bochevski had long seemed to be weighing how far he could push O'Bannon before the two of them would become the evening's entertainment for the other men. Deep down, Bochevski believed that the smaller man would offer little competition in a rough-and-tumble, but there would be a better time to find out—a time when the first blow, preferably with the sledge handle, would be unsuspected, unexpected, and deadly efficient.

Chapter Three

Nolan O'Bannon centered dark eyes on the wide-shouldered Polack who easily had fifty pounds on him, and tried not to snarl. It took all he could muster.

"I'm off to move aside a bunch of louts, some of which have lard arses almost as grand as yours, Bochevski. My crew here is ready to tame Cape Horn so yer flatland babes can have an easy time of it."

"Ha! We will run over you and those tiny insects with our rails."

"As I said, we'll do the hard work, you and yers keep a-comin' along on the road we cut for you."

Bochevski merely guffawed again, and was joined by his crew, who stopped work to taunt the passing Celestials.

When the big Pole realized his men had paused, he slapped his palm with the sledge handle he carried, emulating the big boss, James Strobridge, and shouted, "Back at it, you flea-infested no-accounts. It's rail we're paid to lay, and by the gods we'll get a mile of it today or I'm not Ana Bochevski."

With three solid ringing swings of the sledge to each spike, they quickly took up the steady cadence of the CP spiking ahead, marching onward and upward.

And the Chinese continued their shuffling trek to the deadly cliff face known as Cape Horn.

Not all men remained in camp on Saturday night, even though it was the preference of both Crocker and Strobridge. Many hiked to the railhead in time to catch a flatbed on the last work train down the mountain to visit the saloons and brothels in Auburn, Newcastle, or Sacramento.

Anatole Bochevski found it unnecessary to travel any further than Auburn to satisfy his carnal desires. He was not particularly picky when it came to female companionship. It was nearly midnight Saturday when he descended the narrow stairway inside Miss Melissa Dearborn's Ladies' Boarding House, his broad shoulders barely clearing the flocked and paint-striped walls, the best Miss Melissa could do to imitate the fine silk wall coverings of a high-quality San Francisco establishment.

The sitting room of the brothel offered a short five-seat rosewood bar with backless stools—the bar being Miss Melissa's pride and joy—and a pair of claw-footed tables, each fenced in by six ladder-back oak chairs. Chinese silk carpets lay below each circle of table and chairs.

Gas had not yet come to Auburn, so single candles flickered in wall sconces around the room, and a dozen adorned each of a pair of fine crystal chandeliers hanging high above each table.

A full complement of men were scattered at bar and tables. The place featured half-a-dozen girls, from a skinny hundred-pound freckle-faced Scottish redhead to an ample two-hundred-pound blond German lass. Bochevski had just left the latter sobbing with a red welt across her face—even as a whore she'd refused to perform some of the ministrations demanded by the Pole.

It was the girls' calling to entice the men upstairs. It would be a good long time before the German girl worked up her courage to return to the sitting room to try and earn another of Miss Melissa's brass tokens. She would at least wait until she no longer heard Bochevski's gruff voice among the customers.

One table had a poker game in progress, and the play was in deadly earnest with several men already having committed a week's wages.

The second table hosted only one man, a large black-bearded mountain man with dirt-colored canvas trousers adorned with the grease of a dozen butchered animals, and worse, broadcasting their rancid odor. The knife he wore at his waist would fell small timber, and a fine English Whitworth .45-caliber long-range rifle, with sights adjustable for windage and distance, rested within easy reach, leaning against a windowsill. He leaned on the table, resting both ham-sized forearms, cradling an empty glass, which was almost unnoticeable in his large hands.

The man's company suited Bochevski just fine, and he moved to the table, shouting over his shoulder at Miss Melissa, who tended the bar. "Bring me a bottle, woman."

She eyed him with distaste, but a dollar was a dollar, and she got a dollar for a bottle that brought only fifty cents in Auburn's less civil establishments.

Bochevski paused at the table, and the black-bearded man centered dark eyes on him.

"I will sit," Bochevski said, more of a demand than a request, staring back with ice-blue eyes, not awaiting an invite. And he spun a chair around, straddling it, and did so.

The rough man in the canvas britches shoved his empty glass forward when Miss Melissa brought the bottle. Bochevski was amused by his brashness, as they were men of equal size, by far the most imposing in the place.

"I will pour, you will owe me," Bochevski said with a slightly evil smile, really a tight liver-colored gash across his broad ruddy face.

"I'd rather owe you than cheat you out of it," the man growled, without returning even the tight smile. Then as soon as the Pole poured, he upended the glass and drained it. He placed it back on the table as if expecting it to be filled again.

"Before I pour you another, I'll be expecting an introduction," Bochevski said.

The man eyed him coldly for a moment. He studied the empty glass as if making up his mind, then extended a rough hand. "I be Simon Striker, the owner of Blood Mountain Ranch and Timber, with a crew of tie hackers that know no equal . . . and keeper of a fine whiskey still. And you?"

Bochevski grasped the other man's hand, each clasping with iron grips, neither able to cower his adversary, until reaching an unspoken but mutual understanding. They broke apart as if two bulls had unlocked horns.

The man in the canvas britches looked slightly amused, but he didn't speak.

So the big Pole did. "I am Anatole Bochevski, boss of bosses on the great Central Pacific Railroad. The only royal blood," he lied without a blink, "a prince of Poland, among five thousand common Irish trash and fifty newly employed worthless yellow heathens. You wouldn't be Irish, now would you, Striker?"

With this, Striker finally guffawed. "By God, I'm as English as Queen Vic's broad backside. I may be paying back that drink before this night is over. You're the first railroad man ever to talk sense to me, speaking of Irish trash and the worthless Chinee. Now pour me another, and tell me about this 'royal' business."

They talked well into the morning, finishing that bottle, then another bought by Striker.

Much later, under a cold, flat, overcast, starless sky threatening another snowfall, they left the establishment. Bochevski, his stride wavering a bit, followed an equally inebriated Striker out to his horse and his full saddlebags. There the Pole tested a jug of what Striker claimed to be California's finest whiskey, and agreed that it was tolerable, if not the best he'd tasted. They haggled for a few moments, then again clasped hands, only this time in agreement.

Fires were no stranger to any railroad, and the CP had already had its share.

When the work train headed back up to the railhead on Sunday morning, engineer Harold Pettibone, in control of the beautiful shiny new C.P. Huntington locomotive, released the dead-man throttle and applied full brakes when he spotted the first wisp of smoke, only a tendril, barely noticeable around a curve at Mile 39, where a small forty-foot trestle crossed Dog Creek. And it was a good thing he didn't hesitate, as the trestle lay destroyed in a pile of smoking embers and the rails angled sharply away to the frozen creek bed a dozen feet below.

The engine slid to a stop no more than an arm's length from the potential derailment.

Tok Lo, the younger brother of Ho Chin, and

one of the largest and most able of the Chinese workers, had been entrusted with the 150 dollars in gold coin advanced by O'Bannon, and sent to Auburn to purchase supplies for the men of the Chinese experiment. Tok Lo, his young helper, Lu Ang—one of the two selected as tea boys—and fifteen crates loaded with rice, green vegetables, fish, other Chinese delicacies, and two dozen fat ducks, rode perched atop a carload of ties. Tok Lo and the youngster had spent the night hidden beneath the train, guarding his precious cargo, and he was more than merely panicked when he, one of the crates of ducks, and a crate filled with dried oysters, dried cuttlefish, dried bamboo sprouts, dried mushrooms, peanut oil, and four kinds of dried fruit, did a header off the car to the hard roadbed below. The young helper had managed to stay astride the car and protect the other crates from a similar fate.

Almost a hundred Irishmen, and Anatole Bochevski, all sporting well-earned hangovers, all riding atop the cars ahead of the one that carried the Chinese, also had kept their perch. They managed to overcome headaches long enough to laugh and hoorah the two Celestials as they made a fine sight, scampering after wing-flapping, quacking, ducks . . . but did nothing to help them.

As fast as Tok Lo could limp with a severely twisted leg, he and his young helper only caught three of the half-dozen ducks that had bolted to freedom from the smashed lath cage. The escaped birds and a broken crock of peanut oil was not the worst of it for him; the worst was the fact he would be delayed until a temporary trestle could be built and the rails re-spiked. And forty-eight waiting men would again be without decent food.

The two Chinese extracted some silent revenge, as it was the Irish who were put to work replacing the trestle by Charles Crocker, who happened to be riding in a new blacksmith's car at the rear of the five-car work train.

But again that Sunday, and the following Monday morning, the forty-eight remaining Chinese each subsisted on a handful of rice, a half cup of boiled cabbage, and tea.

They were already at work on Cape Horn by the time Tok Lo and the young boy, who had been selected to be a tea carrier, arrived at the railhead, and it was well after supper time Monday night when they finally made the makeshift camp at Cape Horn, each towing a handcart. At that, seven of the crates had to be left at the railhead.

While the Irish crew had been rounding up the necessary materials to repair the trestle, Charles Crocker had carefully inspected the fire, and wondered about its source. It seemed strange to him that a trestle would catch ablaze, no matter how many glowing embers passing engines expelled, particularly when it was as cold and damp as it had been.

Only one train had passed the trestle on Saturday afternoon and evening, going to and coming from the railhead.

That, the prints of a horse nearby, and the fact that he sensed, more than smelled, the odor of coal oil in the air.

It was surely odd.

Then again, he was tired to the bone, and his mind could be playing tricks with him.

Nolan O'Bannon had long had the habit of living near his crew, even though the rest of the line bosses elected to stay at the railhead, near the comfort of the cooking and baking car and bunk cars.

Half of Nolan's thousand men were ahead of

Cape Horn; cutting and filling roadbed, or attempting the masonry work on the landings and foundations for Long Ravine Bridge, foundations that would support a trestle 120 feet high and nine hundred feet long, and half were on the face of the cliff or behind, grading and smoothing the finished roadbed to the engineer's specifications. A couple of weeks before the first snowfall, Nolan had selected a tent site only a hundred yards shy of where the cliff face began, in the center of his work crews. His tent was a good bit fancier than most, and consisted actually of two tents. One a ten-by-ten wall tent with four-foot high sidewalls as a living and meeting area, with the same size tent nuzzled up immediately adjacent and to the rear, which served as his personal living space.

The front tent housed a small table and a few rounds of logs serving as chairs. It also enjoyed the smallest of potbellied cast-iron stoves with a standpipe passing through a tin fitting in the rubberized canvas roof. A stove so small it would only accommodate two-inch-diameter branches eight inches in length, but one which would nicely seat a single blue twelve-cup porcelain-covered tin coffeepot on its surface. The cast iron glowed red, and the enticing odor of coffee permeated the close air.

Each Monday morning O'Bannon's habit was to meet with his five straw bosses, each with a one-hundred-or-more-man crew, just after sunup to discuss the week's labor, and to share a pot of coffee with the men.

On Monday morning a new man was added to the roster. It was a very self-conscious Ho Chin who sat with legs folded Indian style on the canvas covered ground in O'Bannonboss's tent—as the Chinese had begun to refer to Nolan O'Bannon—even though O'Bannon had offered him his own timber round as a chair. Ho took coffee from a tin cup, even though he considered it an inferior drink.

After the men had groused for a while, O'Bannon got their attention. "As you can see, there's a new man among us. Gentlemen, meet Ho Chin, the straw boss of the new Celestial crew."

He gave them a moment to silently chew on the fact that Ho was among them, even though he know that the Chinese work force had been monopolizing the Irishmen's conversation ever since they'd arrived. Only Troy O'Shaughnnessy extended a hand to the man. O'Shaughnnessy was a diminutive man, no taller than Ho, but had served the Union well as a colonel until losing a left forearm at Shiloh. He'd been a railroad man before the war began, and had worked to keep the Union trains running while serving, even after his amputation.

He had an infectious grin under a full head of red hair. Ho shook without rising, seemingly surprised that even one among the straw bosses had greeted him.

"Okay," O'Bannon continued. "You've all had plenty of time to complain about the Celestials. Now it's time to forget about what they're up to, and worry about your own work. I've worked with them for many years, and have come to respect them just as I do all of you. I don't give a damn if *you* do or not, but I do give a damn if you or the men on your crews interfere with them. Stay well shy of them, and have your men do the same, and you'll have no trouble with me.

"I'm going to have the Celestials do the shovel work today to clear what snow needs removing. We had little more than a dusting yesterday, so it should be no-hill-for-a-stepper. As soon as your men can get at their jobs, send the Chinese back to Cape Horn.

"Tolliver," he said to the man in charge of the crew actually working the face of Cape Horn, one of O'Bannon's own crew chiefs, "you pull your men off the up-line end of your job and concentrate them down this way. The Chinese will work the far end as soon as the spadework's finished."

The man guffawed quietly, shaking his head. But then he relented. "You're bossman, Nolan."

"That I am. Ho, you'll divide your men into five crews, and have them ready to go with each of these bosses. Each of your men will draw an Ames shovel from the tool tent."

Ho merely nodded.

"Now let's get some chow, then get to work."

One of the Irishmen's most hated jobs was clearing the snow each morning after a storm, before they could attack the road grading or masonry. Nolan knew he would gain the favor of the Irish if the Chinese were given this task. It would make accepting the Celestials much easier for the Irishmen if their presence made Irish lives a little easier.

With grunts of grudging acceptance, the men drained their coffee cups and headed for the cook tent, where beans, biscuits, fried side pork, and all the coffee they could drink in thirty minutes awaited them.

O'Bannon motioned to Ho Chin to hold up a minute. "Ho, I'll join you in a half hour after I bean up, and we'll go inspect the Horn together while your men are working the snow under these other bosses." Nolan hesitated a minute, then with his voice an octave lower, said, "I noticed that your man didn't return from Auburn with your foodstuff. It is unlikely that he has taken your money?"

"Not unlikely, O'Bannonboss, impossible. Tok Lo is of my own blood, and he would die before he would dishonor."

Nolan nodded, satisfied. "I suspected such. By the way, knowing he wasn't yet back, I took the liberty of having the cook tent boil up a big pot of extra cabbage."

"Thank you, O'Bannonboss. I will send some men over to carry it to our humble encampment, and we will repay the cooks after our next trip to Auburn."

"It is unnecessary. Repay the CP with your good work."

"As you wish."

At Nolan's suggestion the Chinese had set up camp, eight to ten men jammed in an eight-by-eight tent, not far from O'Bannon's own tent site. He knew of their habit of bathing daily, and he was near a free-flowing creek that had not frozen over except for two weeks in the coldest of the winter. He suspected that the creek was fed by a hot spring, even though it was so cold near his tent you couldn't leave a hand in it for long. He'd wanted the Chinese camp to be nearby for another reason . . . so he could make sure they weren't bothered by his own crew of hooligans.

Besides, he found them to be good neighbors when he'd bunked not sixty feet from them on board the *China Wind,* he aft the mast, and they before. If he knew the Chinese, half of them would be wanting to do chores on the side even after a twelve-hour workday, and he could stand to have his laundry and mending done, his firewood hauled and stacked, and would be happy to enjoy some of their cooking. He'd learned to be a fan of pressed duck, and many other dishes. It would be a pleasant change from boiled beef, boiled pork, beans, hard biscuits, and cabbage.

As Ho walked away, O'Bannon stepped from the tent, spread his arms wide, and took in the beautiful sunny morning. God willin', they'd about seen the last of winter.

"Glory be, the Good Lord has smiled on us this day," he said aloud, more to himself than to any of the men passing on their way to the cook's tent.

He was halfway to the chow tent himself when the echo of a man screaming at the top of his lungs reverberated down the valley.

Chapter Four

O'Bannon trotted toward the source of the scream, his eyes searching the roadbed ahead. A group of men 150 yards up the graded path moved from the pile of logs they'd been using for stools and tables while finishing their breakfast, to the edge of the embankment, where it fell away fifty or more feet to a copse of trees.

They were standing, staring down, with hands on hips, when Nolan trotted up. "What the hell's going on?" he snapped, and one of them pointed down the grade to where the new-turned earth toed out and stands of buckeye and digger pine again reclaimed the hillside.

A man, obviously a Celestial, lay in a heap in a patch of snow.

"Get a stretcher," Nolan commanded to no one in particular, then began side-sliding down the steep slope. When he reached the man's side, he realized he was conscious. He lay with his bruised and bleeding face, with both hands at the back of his head, embracing the stump of his queue, which had been sawed away.

Nolan helped him sit up. One eye was swelling

to half-egg status and his lip was broken and bleeding, but otherwise he seemed all right. Nolan offered him a hand and helped him to his feet. "You all right?" Nolan asked in Chinese.

"My queue, my queue," he mumbled in Chinese.

"Who did this?" Nolan asked.

"White devils . . . white devils. Many white devils," the man said.

"They will be punished," Nolan offered, but it seemed to be no consolation to the man.

A group of Chinese had arrived on the edge of the slope above. Nolan looked up and waved them down. When they arrived, he merely said, "Take care of him." Then he began the climb back up.

When he reached the top, a group of men stood with the stretcher standing on end, still folded and tied. "That won't be needed," he said. "A little soul-searching might be in order for you louts, but not the stretcher. Get back at yer picks and shovels." O'Bannon's voice rang with derision, but it was probably to no avail, as the men who'd attacked the Chinaman had been long gone before Nolan had arrived, and he doubted greatly if they had been among those standing at the top of the slope staring down. The tracks of two men had led away in the snow and into the copse of trees. Nolan was sure it merely circled back to the roadbed, and the tracks would disappear among a thousand others.

He went to the cook's tent for his breakfast, but his mood had soured. *God, I hope this stupid kind of thing is the worst of it,* he thought, but knew in his heart it probably wasn't. And he knew the loss of a queue wasn't stupid to the Chinese; it was just short of devastating.

A good portion of the men had already begun to move away to wherever they were working, so when Nolan finished his plate of food, he went to the head cook and had a few words with him, before he went to seek out Ho and move out for the newly designated Chinese section of Cape Horn.

Back at the railhead, Simon Striker leaned against a stack of ties and waited as James Strobridge, a few steps away, finished giving some instructions to Simon's new friend and partner, Ana Bochevski. When Strobridge started to stride away toward the big bay gelding he rode, Striker yelled out to him, "Mr. Strobridge, a moment of yer time?"

When the tall man turned and paused, Simon moved over and extended a grizzled hand. "I'm Simon Striker, and you'll be a happy man when you hear what I've got to say."

"Is that so, Mr. Striker. It'll take a great deal to make me smile this morning." He paused, then lit a cigar, a habit he'd taken back up. Then he eyed Striker, a gaunt-faced man equally his own height, with skin drawn tight across his cheekbones and face scarred with the remnants of some long-ago bout with the pox. "So," Strobridge said, "make me a happy man."

"You'll be able to stock a fine pile of timbers, both ties and trestle material, up line, only a stroll from yer Long Ravine trestle site."

"Of course I will, as soon as the rail reaches there."

"You can do it now, if you please."

"And how am I to do that without rail, short of a long arduous freight-wagon haul?"

"With the proper amount of gold in my hand, you can start stockpiling as soon as the snow lets up."

Strobridge's patience wearing thin, he demanded, "And how is that to be done?"

"I've a thousand or more timbers up the mountain, and a fine skid road to within a hundred yards of your rail bed. My tie hackers are hard at work up the mountain. We've got hundreds of thousands of board feet of lodgepole pine up the mountain from our mill, just waitin' for a contract. I've got a fine mill hydraulically driven, and teamsters with the best mules to slide 'em down to the saw."

Again Strobridge eyed the man, only this time with increasing interest. "And what would be the cost of these timbers?"

"I would think fifteen cents a foot a fair price."

Strobridge guffawed, and shook his head before he replied. "Maybe a fair price for you, Mr. Striker, but far too proud for the CP. Are these timbers the same quality as those you were leaning against?"

Striker had no idea Strobridge had even known he was in the neighborhood. Then again, he'd heard the man missed little. "At least that fine, and better."

"A nickel a foot would be more along the lines of what we've been paying."

"Aw, but you've had to stack, store, load, and haul. No, sir, fifteen cents is more like it."

"You've a small point there, Mr. Striker. Would eight cents be to your liking?"

They haggled for another ten minutes, until a price of ten cents a foot was agreed upon, with the caveat that Charles Crocker must approve the deal, and with delivery beginning as soon as the snow allowed, which should be within the week the way water was coursing off the hillsides.

As Strobridge mounted the bay, Striker managed a hint of a smile and a wave, and called after him. "It's a fine bargain you've made today, Mr. Strobridge."

"That's yet to be seen, Mr. Striker. Deliver me good timbers, and you'll get your ten cents a foot,

Crocker willing. Check with me in a couple of days and I'll let you know what Mr. Crocker says."

As he rode away, Striker pulled the makings from the pocket of the soiled canvas pants he wore, and rolled a cigarette. *And what you don't know, Mr. Strobridge, is that it'll take you two or more timbers and ties for each use, at least twice than it might have taken, as I'll make damn sure your trestles come down in flames or rock slide.* He laughed, then walked back down the line to where Anatole Bochevski held a track gauge, the tool used to make sure the tracks were set the proper distance apart, shaking it like an ax handle and cursing his crew. He stepped away from the men when Striker approached.

Striker spoke in low tones. "About a mile back down the rail there's a small trestle. There's a nice clearing two hundred yards up the creek and it's an easy walk. Even these Irish louts should be able to find it. I'll set up there."

"As good as any. I'll find a reason to send a couple of men, who I know to be so inclined, down that way just before day's end. You be out by the track so you don't miss 'em."

With that, Striker touched his hat in approval, then ambled away to his own mule to return to his small pack string. He'd left two loaded mules to graze well out of sight of the roadway.

Ho and O'Bannon stopped and studied the Irish work crews on the face as they moved up the proposed roadbed. Occasionally they had to find cover when the yell "Fire in the hole!" rang out.

When Ho and O'Bannon reached the portion of Cape Horn that had been assigned to the Chinese, the most easterly and most difficult slope, they began a treacherous climb up to the head of the cliff, where a stand of Jeffery pines lorded over the digger pine and buckeye eight hundred feet below. A hawk screeched from where it passed below them. The cliff itself harbored little soil to support trees, even if saplings could find a spot level enough to gain roothold. It was so steep only the occasional spot of snow offered relief to the monotonous granite gray, although the Sierra peaks in the distance were still white, cold, and deep. Trickles of water were finding their way down the cliff face—a new impediment for the workers to contend with.

"May I speak freely?" Ho asked after they reached the relatively level slope above and rested on a pair of boulders.

"Of course," O'Bannon replied. He stretched his arms wide, enthralled with the view up and down the American River Valley on this clear and marvelous day. A Clark's nutcracker perched on the very top of a nearby Jeffery pine, sassing them.

"I see," Ho offered, "that your crews are using block and tackle, and pulling the drillers up and away from the blast when a charge is ready."

"That's correct."

"I should not be presumptuous," Ho said, obviously hesitant to speak.

"Ho, when it comes to making my job, or yours, easier, don't ever hold back."

"Please have your man in Sacramento contact Low Choy in San Francisco, and arrange to have twenty bundles of stiff reeds delivered to our camp. They are inexpensive, and will make the work go much faster."

"Basket reeds?"

"Yes, basket reeds. Tell Low Choy they are for Ho Chin, and he will know what to send."

O'Bannon studied the Chinese man for a moment, then shrugged his shoulders. "This won't hold up your beginning work on the slope?"

"We will begin as soon as I have enough men to make up a crew. What we do with the reeds will be on our own time."

In the background, the occasional blast shocked the peaceful morning.

Lu Ang was tall, but slight. His queue was much longer than most, hanging to his narrow waist. Carrying the two powder kegs that had been converted to tea kegs, one on each end of his shoulder stock, was all the tea boy could manage. Tea was boiled, poured into the kegs, then hauled to where the Celestials worked and either delivered directly to the crews or placed in hogshead barrels where the crews could use a spigot to fill their cups at their leisure.

Lu had just set out to deliver two brimming kegs, and was passing a crew of two joint-tie men, when Mickey Sullivan looked up from setting a tie. These were control ties, set in precise locations fourteen feet from the last. His hangover was raging, and it was liquid he needed . . . any kind of liquid.

"Hey, you Godless heathen," he called out, but Lu Ang knew little English, and kept plodding along. Mickey recovered a rock, half the size of his fist, and flung it. It struck Lu between the shoulders, knocking him to his knees. Sullivan guffawed. Lu managed to recover his feet, and turned to see his attacker.

Sullivan waved him over. "You weak-kneed tea sop, get your heathen ass over here with that slop!"

Again, Lu did not understand.

"Now, you yellow heathen!"

Lu did understand the motion of Sullivan's calloused hand, and with great hesitation, moved back to where Sullivan and his crew led the tie gangs, setting a guide tie every fourteen feet.

"Give me a dollop of that slop," Sullivan demanded.

Lu set his load on the roadbed and folded the lid back. Taking a cup from where it hung at his belt, he handed it to the big Irishman.

Sullivan dipped it, gulped deeply, then spat. He paled, then raged. "It blistered me bloody tongue. It's boilin' hot."

He slung the tin cup at the tea boy, who was trying to resettle the load on his narrow shoulders.

Lu tried to duck, but was impeded by his load, and the cup clanged off his forehead.

Sullivan took two strides and drove a slamming blow to the boy's upper chest, knocking him flying down the shoulder of the grade. Unsatisfied, the big Irishman scrambled down, driving kicks into the boy's back and side. Lu, screaming a loud feminine cry of pain, abandoned his tea kegs and tried to scramble away, but Sullivan stayed after him, finally grabbing him by the collar before he could scamper into the trees. Managing to turn him, he smashed two blows to the boy's smooth face with cracks that echoed up and down the track, cutting an eyebrow deeply, and knocking him limp and unconscious.

"Sully!" The second joint-tie crew member yelled down at him, his tone demeaning and disgusted. "That's a wisp of a boy yer beating to a pulp."

Sullivan came to his senses, giving the boy a shove and another kick for good measure, then turned and began the climb back up the slope.

"Bloody worthless scum, tried to burn me tongue from me head," he groused under his breath. His head ached worse than ever, and now his tongue was scorched and wouldn't taste for days.

The boy remained unmoving in a pile of rocks, his limbs askew and his kegs spilled and cast aside at the bottom of the slope, as the two joint-tie men moved quickly, chasing a grading blade pulled by a team of four mules. They moved in precise fourteen-foot increments, a mule-drawn cart, tended by a skinner, moving alongside.

Following them, a much bigger crew of tie setters filled in the ties between.

Then the iron men, five each side to a 560-pound rail, moved in a careful rhythm to pull rails from a cart astride the rails just set, gandy-dancing with stiff strides to move up and drop their load into place. When empty, the back iron men would tip the cart off the rails so the next loaded cart could be pulled into place.

The spikers had passed, with their percussion overture, before Lu Ang began to regain consciousness.

That evening, at the supper hour, the crews found the doors of the cook car closed. The serving tables, set up just outside those doors, were empty of food pots.

They milled around, the noise of their complaints rising and falling.

As the hungry crowd swelled, Nolan O'Bannon approached and mounted the ladder at the car's end. Climbing to the top, he moved to the center of the car and stood over the closed sliding doors. Roiling steam from the roof vents and smoke from low stacks framed him, and he appeared somewhat like an apparition from Hell itself.

He raised his hands until the crowd silenced.

"You know, me old da used to tell me that no man stood so tall as when he stooped to help a boy. Some of you here are not so tall; in fact, some of you are lower than a snake's belly. I know many of you men well"—he began to pace back and forth as he spoke—"and I think I know what you'd think about a lout who'd beat a boy a third his size."

He slowly eyed each man in turn; then his eyes centered on Mickey Sullivan. He glared for a moment, then spat a wad of phlegm to the cook car roof with a disgustful glare. "I personally would be hard put to *sully* my hands with such a man." Then he turned his attention back to all of them.

Mickey Sullivan reddened, and he stood with fists balled at his sides, but he said nothing, and O'Bannon continued.

"I've asked little of you men, other than to do your work. Now I've asked you to leave the Celestials to do theirs, without being harassed. One of my Chinese crew was beaten this morning, and another, a slight wisp of a boy, this afternoon.

"This has got to stop." He turned to leave, then had an afterthought and turned back. "You know, some of you beggars are no better than bloody English landlords."

The crowd had silenced, but now the murmur of dissension began to rise. It was almost more of an insult than they were willing to stomach.

O'Bannon extended his hands to silence them, and they did quiet again, but reluctantly.

"You can rest assured, me fine lads, that if this happens again, it'll be Nolan O'Bannon who comes callin', and we'll see if a shillelagh will convince you to mind yer manners."

Anatole Bochevski, who ran the crew of which Sullivan was a member, pushed to the head of the crowd. "Hey, O'Bannon," he yelled up, derision in his tone. "It's up to us bosses to discipline our own crews. You take care of your heathens and dirt muckers, and we'll watch out for our own."

Nolan moved to the edge of the car. Placing his hands on his knees, he glared down at Bochevski. "Then I'll be tellin' you, Ana Bochevski, and the other bosses. If yer men continue to harass my Celestials, then I'll be holdin' you bosses responsible. And it'll be me a-comin' to have a little talk—"

"Wit shillelagh in hand?" Bochevski's face was reddening.

Nolan's tone dropped ominously lower. "Whatever it takes, darlin' boy."

"And that'll take more than the likes of you, and your pissant shillelagh, Nolan O'Bannon."

As the last of this exchange took place, James Strobridge rode up on his bay. He eased the big horse through the crowd, until he could be heard, then yelled out. "What's going on here?"

O'Bannon straightened. "Just a difference of opinion, Mr. Strobridge."

"Let's get these men fed, and forget our differences."

O'Bannon stomped on the car's roof, and yelled, "Open it up, Cookie."

The doors slid aside and the odor of boiling beef roiled out as three servers jumped from the car and began to receive the big pots, and baskets of bread, handed out to them.

O'Bannon and Bochevski exchanged hard looks before Nolan turned and headed for the ladder to dismount from the car.

As Nolan climbed down, he decided that if he wanted his crews to be able to do their job in peace, it would be himself that would have to stand between them and his Irish countrymen—and face-to-face with a big ugly Polish boss—no matter what Strobridge or Crocker had to say about the subject.

The time would come, and it must be soon.

Chapter Five

The next few days saw the weather change. The sun and a warm wind went to work on the snowfields, and the rivers and streams began to rise.

A Sunday had come and gone, and the Irish had staged a clogging contest to the serenade of fiddle, banjo, mandolin, and a trio of mouth harps.

Things seem to be going well, too well, O'Bannon surmised. *Too damned well.*

When the new week began, rivulets of water coursing down the face of Cape Horn became streams and waterfalls, but the Chinese seemed unperturbed. A dozen baskets, each large and strong enough to hold two men, appeared in intervals on the face of the cliff, some suspended from movable swinging booms shaped from the Jeffery pines on the head of the cliff. Not only could the men working in the baskets be hoisted with block and tackle to escape the wrath of their hard work, but they could be swung aside. And more importantly, the men could hunker down in the basket, which helped protect them from flying rock.

James Strobridge stood with reins in hand at the foot of the slope, a hundred yards down the proposed roadbed from where the Celestials worked, and Nolan O'Bannon walked over to greet him.

Strobridge shook his head in wonder. "I'm glad I didn't bet Crocker more than a box of cigars . . . these little men are moving much quicker than I ever would have believed. And this boom-sling method is much better than a mere block and tackle."

O'Bannon smiled. "They have a way of working that looks as if they're not getting much done, but they are as steady as drops of water worrying a rock. Things get accomplished, far faster than it might appear."

"So I guess I eat some crow, and tell Crocker to hire some more of the little yellow men?"

"Mr. Strobridge, I'd hire every Celestial I could get my hands on."

"And you don't think we'll pay double by losing our Irish crews?"

"I may have to take an ax handle to one or two, but lose them? No, so long as we pay more than the next company, have plenty of work, and have good vittles, we won't lose a mother's son."

Strobridge paused a moment, then mounted the bay. Before he reined away, he cleared his throat, then added, "Nolan, it looks to me like you and Bochevski are on a collision course. It's not much of an example for the men."

"Maybe not, Mr. Strobridge, but I don't see either of us sashaying aside."

"Then take it away from the crews. And be careful, he's a hard man." He paused, then a light shone in his eyes. "No, Nolan, I've got a better idea. How about taking it into a boxing match. It might be a good diversion to have a Queensbury boxing challenge, crew against crew . . . say, five men from each crew. These men need some diversion, and it wouldn't surprise me if you and Bochevski wound up in the same ring."

"Nor me."

"After you, that only means four more from your crew of a thousand drovers and graders. Of course, you can always enter a Chinese or two." Strobridge chuckled as he gigged his horse.

Strobridge reined away just as Lu Ang, his young, smooth face still badly bruised, the cut in his eyebrow covered with plaster, passed with tea kegs dangling from his shoulder cross-brace. O'Bannon watched him begin the slow climb up a rift in the cliff face, marveling at the ability of the slight boy to balance the kegs, and ascend the steep slope at the same time.

Nolan turned, and had begun to return to his grading crews when he heard and felt the shock of a blast from above. An explosion dwarfing those small rock-shattering blasts of the dozen crews of Celestials hanging on the cliff face.

He'd learned long ago not to duck when an explosion blew rock into the air, as one could not dodge effectively unless he knew the trajectory of falling debris. He held his ground and looked for the attack of descending rock, but the blast reverberated from far up the mountain.

Far from where any railroad crews worked.

What the hell was happening?

Simon Striker stood across from a small ravine, two hundred yards from a rock outcropping high above Cape Horn. His hands rested on his hips; his eyes shone with satisfaction. The huge outcropping across the rift was beginning to wane. Not just the rock that had been blown and shattered away from its base, but fifty or more tons of overhanging granite was beginning to follow gravity's compelling pull as its natural foundation had been blown away with a keg of powder.

"I hope you bloody fools are at a dead run." Striker chuckled as he spoke. Then he yelled, "Run, boys . . . don't let yer shirttails hit yer ugly backsides," knowing that no one would hear. "For the wrath of Simon Striker is a-comin' down on ya." He began to guffaw, then to slap his thighs and do a little jig, as he cackled aloud.

Tons of rock rapidly gained momentum, wrenching Jeffery and ponderosa pine out by their roots, scooping snow and brush, bounding and crashing down the steep slope.

O'Bannon realized that the horrendous roar was emanating from far up the slope, far above Cape Horn.

Avalanche!

He began to scramble toward the base of the slope, at the same time yelling at the men suspended above, two-dozen men spaced a quarter mile along the cliff face. But they had no time to ascend the cliff, not that ascension would put them out of harm's way. All they could do was hug the rock face and hope against hope. . . .

It was only moments before bounding rocks began to careen over the men trapped in the baskets and crash far below into the semblance of a roadbed.

Lu Ang had also moved back toward the cliff face, shedding his load of tea kegs, his eyes wide, questioning, fearful, his face still a mass of bruises from the pummeling he'd received.

"Against the wall!" O'Bannon shouted, now barely heard over the growing roar of cascading mountainside. But the lithe Chinese boy did not understand; either that or fear overcame reason, and he bolted, obviously hoping to run clear of the onslaught.

O'Bannon glanced up, cringing, seeing two of the baskets and four men swept away with the increasing barrage of rock and timber.

When O'Bannon turned back, Lu Ang had bolted right into the path of peppering fist-sized boulders. He went down, and immediately was being covered by earth and trash from above, at risk of being crushed by the tons following.

O'Bannon sprang from the momentary safety of a rock overhang, grabbed the boy, and tugged with all his might, freeing the youth and jerking him back to the cover of overhanging rock.

Luckily, the preponderance of the landslide was up the roadbed, fifty yards from where O'Bannon and the unconscious boy cowered beneath the slight protection.

Almost as quickly as it had begun, it was over. But the rough-cut roadbed, for almost two hundred yards, had disappeared under tons and tons of rock, uprooted trees, and debris. O'Bannon glanced at the unconscious youth with some self-satisfaction. He seemed bruised and beaten, but otherwise unharmed. Then O'Bannon realized the boy was bleeding from a wound in his back. He pulled the boy's shirt up, and removed a shard of rock the size of his palm, a portion of which had penetrated the boy's lower back. When he applied his kerchief as a compress, the bleeding began to wane, but he could do little more as he studied the scene ahead while the dust began to clear.

Then he heard the muffled cries of panicked men. He jerked his belt off and wrapped it around the youth, using it to hold the compress in place.

An Irish crew from below them was beginning to arrive with Ames shovels in hand. Teamsters and mule teams were moving quickly toward the scene, and teams were unhooked from haul wagons, ready to be used to tow away debris.

O'Bannon left the boy and moved up the roadbed to begin directing the rescue operation. As soon as they began to dig where they thought a basket and a pair of Chinese might be buried, Ho Chin arrived from where he'd been directing work at the head of the cliff.

"Twelve men are missing, O'Bannonboss," he shouted as he approached.

"We'll do our best, Ho," O'Bannon said encouragingly, then turned to the Irish crew. "Dig, men, as if it was your sainted mother under there." But the men needed no encouragement. Chinese or not, these were buried men, with only moments to live, if any were left alive.

Ho moved up to work beside O'Bannon, who was heaving what rock he could move aside. Strobridge returned, having reined and spurred his horse down the roadbed and away from the onslaught. He joined the men, working with his hands to remove debris.

As Ho paused to catch a breath, O'Bannon informed him, "Your tea boy is hurt. Took some rock trying to beat the slide. I was barely able to drag him out of the rock fall. I left him down the roadbed aways, with my belt and kerchief binding a wound in his back."

"Thank you, O'Bannonboss," Ho said, then moved to help move a keg-sized rock away. "We will tend to him," he said, gasping with the effort of the load.

As the day wore on, only one of the twelve men who'd disappeared off the cliff face was found alive, and he was injured so badly it was doubtful if he'd live to see his homeland again.

It was dark when O'Bannon stumbled into his tent, and without bothering to eat, or remove anything other than his boots and mackinaw, fell into his bedroll.

He had been down for only a moment when he heard Ho's voice announcing himself from outside the small meeting tent.

"O'Bannonboss, I have your belt."

Nolan struggled to his feet and padded through the tents to fling the flap aside.

"And I have problem," Ho said.

"Come on in," O'Bannon managed, letting the little man pass.

O'Bannon seldom drank during the week, but this seemed a good time to make an exception. He dug a small bottle of Black Widow whiskey out of a satchel where he kept his shaving strop and razor, and wiped out two tin coffee cups.

"I don't know if you're a drinking man, Ho, but after today maybe you'd like to become one."

Ho took the cup with a grateful look, and both took a deep draw.

"Now, what's this about a problem, as if we haven't had enough today?"

"It is about Lu Ang."

"Not hurt too badly, I hope," O'Bannon said, his look anxious as he'd begun to like the spunk of the young boy. "He's a willing boy."

"No, O'Bannonboss, Lu Ang is not too badly hurt. A week or so . . . The problem is, he is not a willing boy, but it appears, as we discovered when we removed his clothes to dress his wounds . . . he is a willing girl."

"I beg your pardon?" O'Bannon's jaw dropped.

"Yes, O'Bannonboss, Lu Ang is a youthful lady."

"By all that's holy . . ."

"So you see, O'Bannonboss, I have a problem. I must treat her wounds, and of course, I must dismiss her. But I cannot send her down the line until she is recovered enough to take care of herself."

O'Bannon shook his head in wonder. "How could she . . . I mean, how could a woman . . ."

"Many of our people are very modest, particularly when young. We thought he was a very modest youth. He kept to himself—"

"Herself."

"Yes, herself. We had no idea. But what is now to become of Lu Ang?"

O'Bannon scratched his head, staring out the tent flap, then turned back to Ho. "Bring the girl here," he offered. "She can use the front tent until she's recovered and can go back to Auburn. So Lu Ang is LuAnn." He chuckled.

Ho seemed to be searching for words; finally he spoke tentatively. "It would not be proper—"

O'Bannon interrupted him, not angrily, but rather slightly amused. "Then you, too, shall bring your things to my meeting tent until such time as Lu Ang can return to Auburn. You can become a chaperon to go along with the rest of your duties." He chuckled again, then turned serious. "How badly hurt is she?"

"She had barely begun to regain consciousness when I decided to come here. I think her head has been struck, as well as her back. No bones appear to be broken unless she has received a crack in her skull."

"A possible concussion?"

"As you wish. A crack, possibly."

"Bring her here, and you and she can bed down on opposite sides of the meeting tent."

"As you command, O'Bannonboss," Ho said, but he didn't seem particularly pleased.

"It won't be for long," O'Bannon encouraged. "Only until she can travel." With that, he returned to his bedroll in the rear.

When he lay back down, he recalled for the first time the roar of an explosion from high up on the mountain.

A roar that preceded the avalanche.

A roar that had nothing to do with his crews.

"Some low-life son of a bitch," he mumbled.

He would deal with it in the morning.

In the morning he'd get a horse from the wrangler, or better yet a surefooted mule, and work his way up the mountain to see what he could find. The last thing they needed was someone working against them. Hell, there was enough going against them.

He fell into the deep encompassing sleep of the totally exhausted.

When Striker got back to his camp, he was pleased to find that his brothers and cousin had arrived from Illinois.

Simon had been more like a father than a brother to his two younger siblings. When their father was killed working a deep rock mine, Striker had no choice. At only twelve years old, he went to the coal mines himself, working as a mucker. At seventeen, he became a mine hostler, handling the mules, but soon he'd had enough of Cousin Jacks getting all the good jobs, and made his way to St. Louis and found a job on a river flatboat. For the next five years, he worked the river, in the light and clean air, down to Cairo, back to St. Louis on steam paddle wheelers.

He learned plenty of rough-and-tumble, and could kick, elbow, bite, and gouge with the best of them.

His brothers, at twelve and thirteen, were old enough to work the mines, and with what he was able to send home, his family was able to keep body and soul together.

Then the news of gold in California crossed the country like a lightning bolt. For over three years, Simon worked to get enough money together to head west. Then his ma died of consumption, and it was no longer necessary to send money home. He was able to save far more, but it would still be years.

Working as a deckhand on a paddle wheeler, he watched as a gambler relieved a half-dozen men of their hard-earned, and Simon saw his chance.

When the gambler disembarked at a St. Louis quay one moonless night, Simon followed. The gambler made the mistake of turning into an alley to relieve himself, and after the application of a cobblestone to the back of the gambler's head, Simon had his heavy purse. And the gambler never awoke.

With over a thousand dollars in hand, Simon headed downriver to New Orleans, then across the Isthmus of Panama and north to California.

The bloom was off the goldfields, but other opportunities awaited. Some of them legal.

But he never forgot his brothers, and as soon as his finances allowed, and he had work that needed doing at Blood Mountain, he sent for them. They wired him back that a cousin also wanted to come, and Simon arranged for a Wells Fargo draft, sending them enough money to buy a wagon and four-up of oxen. They were on their way.

It took them almost a year, as they had to lay up at Washoe Meadows on the east side of the Sierras until winter passed.

But they were here now.

Simon was so happy he broke out a bottle of his own good whiskey, and they all got drunk and toasted his old ma and pa.

One thing they were sure of: None of them would ever return to the deep, dark, dank hole that had sucked the life out of more than one Striker.

Milo Stark, the cousin, was a good man with a rifle, having made his living as a hunter and trapper. He was the closest to Simon's age, the lightest in coloring with a Dutch woman for a ma, and the tallest of all the Striker clan. Simon was surprised to learn that his brothers had broken Milo out of jail just before they all headed west. He had backshot the man who'd bought Simon's old homestead at a sheriff's sale.

Efren Striker, Simon's youngest brother, was a humorless man, with a brooding brow, a head that seemed to sit on his shoulders neckless, and a body like a tree trunk. He was the slowest of the bunch, but good enough with a gun or Arkansas toothpick.

Jedidiah was the middle brother, slimmer than than Ef but still on the stocky side. One eye had gone pearl from being stuck with a flying rock in a mine blast. His attitude was always as sour as the day he'd found himself blind in one eye.

All of them were capable men, each in his own way.

And now, the Striker camp was far stronger.

In fact, Simon believed there wasn't much they couldn't handle. Not now, not together.

Chapter Six

O'Bannon awoke angry.

He dressed warmly and carried a slicker with him even through the day appeared clear and bright. He'd enjoyed long experience with the Sierras' fickle high country weather. Before leaving, he dug deep into the satchel holding his belongings and found his Colt revolver and holster. Pleased it exhibited no rust, as he hadn't laid eyes on it since this job had started, he wiped it down nonetheless. He strapped on the belt with its small leather container of paper cartridges, caps, and wads, and a flapless holster. He made sure the small thong that looped over the hammer was tight, as he anticipated a steep climb and probably having to dismount several times, then inspected the paper cartridges to make sure they were sound and dry. His attention would have to be centered on the trail, and what he might find, and not on worrying about his belongings.

It wouldn't do to find whoever had blown that shelf of rock high up the mountainside, then reach for an empty holster.

O'Bannon was no oiled-holster shootist, but he

was an accurate shot, his aim perfected off the aft quarterdeck of many a ship, and utilized more than one time against South Sea pirates. Maybe even more importantly, he possessed a calmness in the face of danger that had surprised even himself at times.

Ho's bed pallet lay smoothed and empty, but on the other side of the outer tent the girl lay quietly with her back to him. He wondered how the wound in her back fared, but she seemed to be hard asleep and sleep would do her far more good than his awakening her to inquire.

Without even bothering to make coffee, not wanting to bother the girl he now thought of as LuAnn, he strode out of the tent and walked the three hundred yards back to a small relatively flat meadow with its own trickle of water, and some grass beginning to peek through the snow. The wrangler had erected sturdy but temporary corrals of lodgepole pine to contain his hundred head of mules and horses. Scatters of hay had already been forked over the fence, and the horses and mules were all head-down.

"A surefooted saddle animal, with plenty of heart," he instructed Orvel Jenkins, the wrangler who was stoking up a fire and pumping a small bellows to reshape the shoe resting in the glowing charcoal. Jenkins had a hard angular face softened by a wispy baldness, but his eyes were crowfooted and always kind; more importantly, he was an all-round saddle maker, blacksmith, and hostler. He'd long ago earned O'Bannon's respect.

"Where you off to, Mr. O'Bannon?" the wrangler asked.

"Got business up the mountain, Orvel. Appears to be a hell of a climb, and I don't know if there's a trail."

"I got a big sixteen-hand bay molly mule that come

out of a Percheron mare. She got hindquarters sired by a locomotive. That mountain will be no hill for this stepper."

"I'm no vaquero—"

"She's sweet as mother's milk, got her own head, and won't abide you gettin' her into trouble. I'd trust her with my grandbabies, had I a gaggle. She'll be pleased to be out of the traces. She's been on a grading team, but I noticed the collar was a-gallin' her. The saddle rig will be no bother . . . she's well acquainted with the saddle. Point her and give 'er her head."

"Is there any kind of a track?" O'Bannon stared up the mountainside, wondering if he'd bitten off more than he could chew.

"I was up there, probably halfway to the summit, last Sunday, working a couple of rank mustangs we got. Nothing like a hard steep trail to calm a hotheaded horse. There's a pretty good set of plateaus that you can work your way up, if you back-trail down the line about a half mile. You might still pick up my track if'n you look close."

O'Bannon knew Jenkins was a master when it came to his animals, and he trusted the man completely.

Jenkins gave a wave toward the fire. "There's a pot near that pile of charcoal. Wipe out a cup and help yourself while I find some tack that'll set her easy."

O'Bannon did so, and the coffee seemed to settle his nerves.

When he mounted the fine-looking dappled gray, Jenkins noticed the firearm on his hip.

"Ain't no snakes out this time a' year," Jenkins said, eyeing the piece.

"I'm not so sure, Orvel. Some snakes know how to build fires to keep warm, and set off black powder charges."

When O'Bannon reined away, he headed straight to the cook tent. With a half loaf of bread and a hunk of boiled pork tied in his slicker on the back of the saddle, he and the mule Orvel called Perch headed back to find the trail up the precipitous mountainside.

It had been a quiet, relatively dry night, and any sign left by whoever had set the mountain down on his crew should still be there.

And maybe, just maybe, he could find it and follow it.

After O'Bannon had left, Charles Crocker rode up to where James Strobridge was surveying the damage and repair work.

"Where's O'Bannon?" Crocker asked.

"Up the mountain, or so the head wrangler told me."

"On top the cliff?"

"No, way up the mountain, on some damn-fool mission."

"His place is here, particularly now," Crocker groused.

"Agreed, but we're gettin' on just fine. We'll have this back to where we were before the slide—"

"In a week's time?"

Strobridge nodded. "That's probably a close estimate."

"Damn the flies. If it's not one thing it's another. You chew O'Bannon's backside when he returns. This is no time . . . ."

"Yes, sir," Strobridge agreed.

LuAnn awoke and managed to sit up on her bed pad. She was dying of thirst, and didn't know where she was. The last thing she remembered clearly was O'Bannonboss dragging her from under the hail of rocks, then nothing until she awoke in his tent.

She reached around and rubbed the bandage over the wound in her back, then realized the white cloth serving as bandage encircled her body, just under her breasts—the same cloth she'd used to tightly bind her breasts to keep her fellow workers from discovering her womanhood.

She'd been unbound . . . and found out!

What was she to do now? Was she to be punished? What was she doing in O'Bannonboss's tent?

Her life had been in turmoil since leaving China. She arose shakily to her feet and peeked out the tent flap. Things were going on as usual. No one was paying attention to her.

She found a keg of water in a corner, glanced around tentatively, then helped herself to a dipperful.

She thought about escaping, but she felt so terribly weak, and her head reverberated as if a palace guard was pounding a giant gong in its confines.

She would sleep some more, and escape later.

Carefully she eased herself back onto the sleeping pad, and was soon in a deep repairing slumber.

High up the mountain O'Bannon nudged the big molly mule along. Each step was now the careful placement of a big hoof, and a careful bearing of weight. The game trail they followed wanted to give out, becoming only a trace. The snow was slushy and the hillside only devoid of snow where the sun was able to heat it for several hours. But that portion was always muddy and slippery. Shaded portions were still deep in snow and ice.

After two hours of slow but steady moving, O'Bannon dismounted and let the mule blow. She truly was a willing animal, and so long as he didn't hurry her she was surefooted, never missing a stride.

He could see Cape Horn in the distance far below and to the east. Estimating he had two miles to go before he reached the mountainside, high above where he could see the men at work, he remounted and again let the dappled gray mule find her way.

It took almost another two hours to cover the two miles, as each step was a potential danger.

He came upon a stretch of mountainside that looked like an avalanche trough, but it wasn't in even a remote hint of a ravine. An unusual spot for a natural avalanche. He moved back to the edge of the steep clearing and studied the slope, picking a way the mule could manage, then spotted an out-of-place piece of new wood; he dismounted to take a closer look.

It was only three inches in length, but finished on two sides and blackened on one of those. Even more interesting, it had a portion of a letter stenciled on what remained of its outer surface, in black ink.

It looked like a shard of a powder keg to O'Bannon.

He slipped it into a roll of the slicker on the back of his saddle, then remounted and began to work his way up the mountain.

Fifty yards above where he'd come upon the slide path, he found where it had begun. Dismounting, he loosened the saddle cinch and dug into the small saddlebags on the skirt of the saddle, and was pleased to find both hobbles and a lead rope and picket pin. He didn't think the mule would wander far, so he hobbled her front legs and let her graze on what little grass poked its way up near the edge of the slide, grass that had been uncovered by the avalanche.

He was more than an hour circling, studying,

kneeling to closely investigate, when he decided he had a trail. It was only the possible scraping of a metal shoe on a rock outcropping, but it was out of place.

Retrieving the mule, he tightened the cinch and remounted, then moved slowly, studiously, where he thought the trail might be leading. Finally, in the snow, he found a set of hoofprints, then in a muddy bottom, dismounted to study them closely. He wasn't much of a tracker, but it didn't take much of one to see that one of the animal's shoes had a notch dug into its upper left-hand side at, say, ten o'clock. He doubted if another shoe would be trail-marked in the same way.

He could see the trail stretch out to the west, and the valley bottom far below. As it was, it would take him most of the remaining daylight to descend the mountain and get back to his tent.

But the sky was gray. What if it snowed again? Even if not, what if the spring and warm wind melted the track away? He would probably never again find the trail if he didn't pursue it now.

Had he any idea this would have been the outcome of his search, he would have told someone where he was headed, and why. Well, Jenkins would report to someone that he'd ridden off up the mountain, and Strobridge was smart enough and knew him well enough to know he was on some kind of mission.

Even if he was gone well into the next day.

Which looked very possible at the moment.

Strobridge made his rounds of the three crews working on and beyond the end of the rail. When he returned to where the spikers were ringing out their melody, he spotted Bochevski and waved him over.

"Ana, how goes it?"

"Smooth as a whore's backside," the big man said with a guffaw.

"I've been thinking, why don't we schedule a little entertainment for this coming Sunday."

"What you have in mind, Mr. Strobridge?"

"I'm thinkin' a boxing match, bare-knuckle, crew against crew."

Bochevski smiled broadly. "Crew against crew. And we bossmen? How about us?"

"Sure, I don't see why not. Pick five of your best, and yourself if you think you're among 'em—"

"There's no doubt of that!"

"—and I'll have the other crews do the same. We'll work up a progressive ladder of the five crews. Let's see, that'll be twelve matches and a bye, then six or so, then three, then two and one. Twenty-five matches at nine minutes, or less, each. We should be able to do that in a Sunday afternoon with no problem."

"And will there be a prize, when we knock those other louts into the hereafter?"

Strobridge hadn't thought about a prize so he rubbed his chin a moment, then offered, "How about a shiny fifty-dollar gold piece to the winner . . . and I'll have the company buy a fine yearling pig to roast. It'll be boiled beef, beans, and cabbage to the losers, and roast pork and stewed apples for the winning team . . . boxers and bosses only, of course. I'll be the judge. Let's see, it'll be three intervals of three minutes each; most blows landed, most knockdowns, or a knockout determines the winner."

"Only three intervals?"

"With at least a minute of rest in between, and more if I deem it's needed. I want these men to be able to work come Monday morning."

"There's some I'd like to pound for longer than

three intervals; then, of course, they probably won't be standing at the end of one. . . ."

He guffawed again as Strobridge shook his head in wonder at the man's audacity. Then again, he didn't really doubt him. He was as hard a man as Strobridge had ever known.

Bochevski continued. "Then I'll be earnin' a double portion of pork and apples, as boxer and boss. It sounds a fine idea to me. None of those laggards can match the iron muscles of my spikers and gandy dancers."

"I guess we'll see, won't we." Strobridge touched his hat brim, gave Bochevski a tight smile, and reined away.

Then he thought about the Chinese, and wondered if O'Bannon would dare include any of the Celestials on his team. Not that he imagined Celestials were adept at the manly arts.

However, that would make things doubly interesting.

It was damn near day's end. Where the hell *was* O'Bannon?

On his way back to Ireland?

O'Bannon straddled the mule high on a ridge, where a sluiceway worked its way down the mountain—a wooden sluiceway devoid of all but a trickle of water in the winter freeze. It would be running soon, judging by the way the snow was melting. O'Bannon presumed it originated at a creek or big spring high up on the mountainside. He'd lost the track of the nicked shoe a half mile back, when a rocky ice-covered slope obliterated all sign. But he'd gone on, thinking he might pick it up again.

He wondered where the sluice went. Where it went could be where the horse with the nicked shoe was to be found, and the blackguard who'd set the powder and brought the mountain down.

Then again, why would men making an honest living want to interfere with the CP? The CP would bring prosperity to all of California. It didn't make sense.

Then again, there'd been many times when men didn't make sense to O'Bannon.

Giving heel to the molly, he urged her down the mountain, alongside the sluiceway.

If the nicked shoe was down the hill somewhere, he would find the man who'd brought the mountain down.

It was getting dark quickly.

He looked for dry wood, but found none. It would be a cold camp. The bread and hunk of pork tasted as fine as a meal at Delmonico's in San Francisco, but he wished it had been hot. At least he had the slicker to roll up in.

The canvas did little against the bite of the cold as he bedded down in the small protection offered by the root ball of a blown-down ponderosa, the molly hobbled nearby.

It looked to be a long night.

Chapter Seven

O'Bannon was up and gone with first light. He hadn't slept more than a wink as the cold kept him changing position to seek warmth, and even the molly mule seemed irritated with their circumstances.

She moved at a steady pace down the mountainside along a ridge overlooking the American River Valley. The sluice was only yards downhill from them. They found a trickle of water, and O'Bannon allowed the mule to drink, and dismounted himself to take a deep draw of the shockingly cold water. It wasn't hot coffee, but it would do to wash away the cobwebs of a cold night.

Before the sun was on the mountainside he glanced to the south, away from the river valley, and caught sight of a pair of smoke tendrils working their way skyward out of a thicket of ponderosa and lodgepole. It looked to be no more than a hundred yards off.

He dismounted, tied the mule, palmed the Colt, and began to pick his way through the trees.

In moments he found himself overlooking a permanent log cabin camp consisting of two cabins, a small barn, and a mill. One of the two columns of smoke he'd seen snaked its way upward from one of the cabins. The other came from on up the hill, its source out of sight from where he now stood. Probably burning garbage or slash from the mill. The mill was the terminus of the sluice he'd been following, and had a three-foot-diameter saw blade driven by a water wheel and set of leather straps and gears.

Two men worked in the barn, mucking out a pair of stalls and a corral containing some fine-looking stock, mules as handsome as the big molly he'd been riding.

It looked like an enterprise of hardworking, if rather slovenly, men. He approached closer, and the two dark-skinned men working the barn noticed him and stopped their mucking. He kept the revolver out of sight behind his leg. They tentatively waved and nodded, then returned to their endeavor.

O'Bannon holstered the weapon and moved closer. He was almost doused by a man who slammed open a cabin door—making O'Bannon grab for the Colt—and slung out a pan of wastewater. He barely noticed O'Bannon. Turning back around again he realized a stranger was among them, then slowly turned around again to face him.

"You want somethin'?"

"Coffee wouldn't be refused," O'Bannon said, carefully eyeing the man.

"That we can do, then you'll be moving on. We got work to do."

"Sounds right," O'Bannon said.

The man disappeared into the cabin and O'Bannon kept a careful eye, wondering if he might reappear with a scattergun in hand, but he returned with a steaming tin cup.

"Obliged," O'Bannon said, reaching for the cup and taking a welcome warm-up sip.

"You just passin' through?" the man asked.

He was a hatchet-faced man, as tall as O'Bannon, with oil-slicked black hair to match his dark inquiring eyes.

"O'Bannon's the name. Workin' the CP, down in the valley. Came up the hill to see what caused the landslide we suffered yesterday."

"I wouldn't know nothing 'bout that. This here's the camp of Simon Striker, my kin. I just come here late yesterday. Simon's down in the valley, headin' somewheres to do a bit of business."

"You got a name?" O'Bannon asked, risking being offensive.

"Milo . . . not that it's business of your'n."

Two other hard-looking men appeared in the doorway behind the one speaking.

"Looks like you're cutting timber," O'Bannon said, still working the hot coffee. It was an obvious observation, as a growing pile of ties and trestle timbers were perched near a ravine that cut its way down toward the valley far below.

"Cuttin' ties for the railroad. Simon's got a contract," the man who called himself Milo offered.

It seemed unlikely that folks with a CP contract would be wanting to harm the railroad's progress.

Still and all . . .

O'Bannon motioned with the coffee cup toward the enclosure. "Fine-looking corral full of mules. You inclined to sell any of that stock?"

Milo shrugged. "Don't know what Cousin Simon has in mind for them."

"Mind if I take a closer look?" O'Bannon asked, finishing the coffee, handing the cup back.

"You can take a gander on your way out, if you like. Most everything Simon owns he's inclined to sell. Like I said, we got to get back to work."

"Obliged for the coffee. You might ask your cousin . . . Simon you said. You might ask Simon to stop and give me a howdy should he get down to where we're carving the road."

"I'll do that," Milo said, then slammed the door in O'Bannon's face.

Nolan walked to the corral, giving the two men, who he now surmised were Indians, a nod.

"Gonna take a look at your stock," he said, but they merely nodded and continued their mucking.

Nolan slipped between the rails and went from animal to animal, checking each of their forefeet for the telltale nick. None of them showed a sign of one.

Damn, he thought.

There seemed nowhere to go from here, and more importantly, no time to get there.

He returned to where he had the mule tied, then headed down the mountain.

It was early afternoon before he arrived. Returning the mule to Jenkins, with a compliment as to the animal's demeanor, he made his way back to Cape Horn at a brisk pace.

Strobridge stopped from directing a crew, still removing debris, when he saw O'Bannon approach. He stood with hands on hips until Nolan got close enough to hear.

"Where the Billy Joe hell you been, O'Bannon?"

Nolan fished the shard of wood out of his back pocket and handed it to Strobridge.

He eyed it a moment, then looked up. "So, what's this mean?"

"It means this catastrophe was an unnatural man-made event. Some low-life son of a bitch placed a keg of powder under a rock ledge a half mile or so up there." He pointed up above Cape Horn. "Sure as spring's coming, he murdered those eleven men we dug out—"

"Twelve," Strobridge stated. "The twelfth man died this morning."

"Those twelve men. A by-God dirty deliberate act."

"Any sign of anyone up there?"

"Long gone. I followed a trail with a cut shoe for a while, but it'd take a better tracker than me."

"Any chance of someone else trailing him."

"I doubt it. Tracks are all but gone with the melting snow. By the end of the day, by the time we could get back on them, what little's left will be wiped out. But I'd sure as the devil turn it over to the law."

"Yes, I'll do that. You get back to work and I'll smooth things over with Crocker. He was on the warpath this morning when you didn't show up here."

Strobridge started to walk away, then turned back. "Nolan, you did the right thing. We needed to know if we're going to have this kind of a problem . . . what we might be up against. Hell, this could be one of our own who did this, seeing as how it seemed to be the Chinese who were targeted, and only the Chinese injured."

O'Bannon merely nodded.

"By the by." Strobridge had started away, but paused again. Then he explained the upcoming boxing match before leaving.

Nolan worked the day away, but headed straight for the tent when it ended. He'd managed to overeat with a late lunch, and sleep sounded a lot more attractive than supper.

LuAnn had awakened at midday, her head still banging away and her back aching terribly. But she arose and straightened the tent, then walked to the Chinese camp and borrowed tea, rice, eggs, a hunk of chicken, a dried cuttlefish, and vegetables, and returned to O'Bannonboss's tents.

She had time to think while awaiting the courage to arise and face the day, and the pain.

She could not bring herself to try and escape. If she was to be punished, she must face what fate would bring. The reason she couldn't run was that O'Bannonboss had saved her life, dragged her from the jaws of certain death.

Her life was no longer her own. Her life now belonged to O'Bannonboss.

She would serve him, even if he scorned her. How could it happen that she owed her life to a heathen white devil?

By the time she heard approaching footfalls, she had tea, a fine thick broth of vegetables, cuttlefish, and eggs, and a dish of rice, vegetables, and chicken prepared. Steaming, wafting a wonderful aroma, and awaiting him.

If he was to punish her, perhaps he would be more accommodating with a full stomach.

When O'Bannon whipped the tent flap aside, he was surprised to find the place spotless, his small stove ablaze, and a couple of tin pots steaming and emitting fine smells. He was even more surprised to find the girl up and about . . . and looking like a girl. She'd combed her long hair out of the braided queue, and it hung full and shiny black down past her waist. Wherever she had been hiding what now bulged under her simple cotton shirt, he couldn't imagine.

Still bruised and swollen, her fine features were less than appealing, but the potential was obvious.

He sat on a log round and removed his boots, watching closely as she poured him tea, handed him a cup of broth, then served a bowl of vegetables and chicken on a bed of rice.

He was pleased to see that the fine meal was for him. "Thank you," he managed in Chinese, and she nodded and backed away. He took a long time to eat, savoring each bite. It was the best meal he'd had in months. As he ate, he studied her. It made him smile to think that now that he knew she was a girl, her every movement seemed feminine. She moved with a grace and economy of motion that belied her being male. Maybe it was the fact that she was now in what passed for a kitchen that made it so obvious.

He, and every other man she'd worked with, had been made fools of. He laughed again under his breath. What would Mickey Sullivan think when he found out he'd been beating a young girl? If he was half a man, he'd be flabbergasted.

Ho arrived moments afterward and, having already eaten, refused the bowl she offered him with a haughty wave of the hand. It was obvious he was still offended that she'd fooled him. He packed a carved jade pipe, retired to a log round outside the tent, watched the sun set, and smoked.

LuAnn watched O'Bannon closely as he deftly utilized the chopsticks. Maybe he wasn't quite so much the heathen white devil she'd imagined.

Keeping her eyes lowered whenever he glanced her way, she sat on another log round and waited until he'd finished, then took the cup, bowl, chopsticks, and cooking utensils, cleaned them, and went to her pallet and lay down. He thanked her and she nodded, her back to him, the only real exchange between them. In moments she was fast asleep.

O'Bannon felt guilty for a moment, accepting

her labor when she obviously felt as bad as she looked.

Nothing he could do about it now, he decided, and found his way into his sleeping tent, then collapsed on his cot and slept.

Simon Striker had ridden down the mountain to Auburn astride the same hammer-headed tall dun gelding he'd taken up the mountain. He put him in the livery, then caught the train to Sacramento. On arrival he went straight to the waterfront, found a packet about to leave, and paid a dollar for a ride down the ever-widening Sacramento, across San Pablo Bay, then San Francisco Bay to the city. It was late evening before he arrived in the bustling burg of over fifty thousand inhabitants, now grown from a hovel of tents and ship remnants to a fine city with more than its share of brick and stone buildings.

It was dead dark when he arrived, too late to call upon the two companies that owed him for his service from the day before, but it wasn't too late to call upon a fine San Francisco brothel.

But then again, why spend a day's wages in the city center when he could spend a half day's up on Grant Street. Feeling flush, he waved down a hack and directed the driver up to Grant. As they climbed the hill away from the waterfront, then through the shantytown section of Chinatown, the populace became more and more yellow-skinned.

Grant Street was lined with tent shops and shacks, with only the occasional finer clapboard structure. Paper lanterns glowed in Mandarin-red splendor, and shops and stalls hung with flattened ducks and geese and every variety of critter, including reptiles, most processed into some kind of edible.

None of it was of interest to Striker.

He was stopped by the sound, then the procession of a Chinese funeral. A long line of men, all dressed in white, weaved from boardwalk to boardwalk, carrying placards and paper incantations and images of dragons and other creatures. A Chinese band plucked resonating stringed instruments and beat brightly decorated drums. All of them followed a body, the subject of their attention, which was wrapped in white linen and carried by eight men, who from time to time hoisted it on high.

Finally, tired of his short wait, Striker shoved his way between the mourners and crossed to the other side of the street, continuing on to his destination with purpose aforethought.

The only building of interest to him was Su Lee Chan's, Chinatown's most famous house of ill-repute.

Much to the chagrin of the girls he met, he spent the whole night there.

Whisky-sodden and bleary-eyed, his head hurting, wincing from the yelling of dray and hack drivers and the clattering and clanging of their wagons and buggies, Striker waited outside the Northern Currents Ice Company offices for Mr. Juston Wellington to arrive. Northern Currents hauled both ice and sawn timber from the southern coast of Alaska to San Francisco, and was desperate to protect a very profitable trade.

Striker intercepted the well-dressed but generously rotund company vice president on the street before the man could reach his waterfront office.

"Wellington," he said, without the usual niceties, "you owe me for what will be at least a two-week delay."

"Striker," the man mumbled in surprised recognition. He placed the end of his walking stick against Striker's chest, and tapped it. "How could we owe you for a two week's delay, when we struck our bargain less than a week ago?"

"I dropped half the mountain on the bloody CP."

"Let's get a cup of coffee."

"I don't need no damned coffee, Wellington. I need my gold."

Juston Wellington shook his head, keeping the walking stick between himself and the wild-eyed man, already regretting the bargain he'd made.

"Look, Striker, would you pay a man in advance for a bit of work?"

"My work's done, and I want my money."

"But we can't judge the results of your work, now can we? As soon as we can verify that the CP was held up a week or more, then you'll get your money. Come back in a couple of weeks—"

"The hell you say," Striker said, his tone rising, the spittle beginning to fly. "I want my money now." He reached for Wellington's lapels, but was held off by the walking stick.

"You'll get your money when we verify the results."

Striker didn't want to spoil a good thing, but he also was not going to be cheated by this dandy in city finery.

His voice dropped an octave and he spoke slowly. "A week, then I'll be back. You have someone verify what I'm telling you. . . . But I'll warn you here and now, Wellington. I'll see you in the dark of the night, and that skinny walking stick will do you no good, should you cheat me."

"I honor my bargains, Striker," Wellington said, backing away from the hulking man.

"You'd better," Striker called after him as Wellington spun on his well-polished heel and entered the building.

Striker had no better luck with Morris Ackerton at Atlantic-Pacific Ship and Brig. Their coast-to-coast, around the Horn trade would be totally ruined by the railroad. But they, too, were businessmen, and they, too, informed Striker that they paid for work completed, not promised, or only half-proven. Again Simon Striker advised them, in no uncertain terms, that he was not a man to be cheated, and that the wrath of God would descend upon them should they try.

Dejected, he caught a steam-driven packet back to Sacramento that night, his pockets empty, his head aching from the whiskey, his attitude reflected in his clamped jaw.

He would wait another week.

In the meantime, he would make sure they had results they could measure.

There would be no doubt.

Chapter Eight

The sabotage of the line was not the only problem faced by Strobridge and O'Bannon. Whiskey was the bane of a working crew of men, particularly Irish men. The brew was not allowed in the CP camps, even though it was common knowledge that most of the men, even the bosses, kept a ready supply for "medicinal purposes."

But it was getting out of hand.

The men were appearing for their shifts bleary-eyed and sluggish, some having to take breaks to lose their breakfast, most having to visit the water casks far too often.

Strobridge and O'Bannon stood outside O'Bannon's tents, sipping coffee, discussing the day's work. O'Bannon had suggested to LuAnn that she stay out of sight until such time as she was well enough to leave, and on Strobridge's arrival, she'd retired to the rear tent.

O'Bannon had seen no reason to mention to Strobridge Ho's embarrassment that he'd had a woman working on his crew.

"I'll be on Cape Horn all day," O'Bannon said, "Maybe up the line as far as Long Ravine." He finished his cup and turned it upside down, draining the dredges into the mud where snow had been only a week before.

"There's another hundred or so Celestials comin' in on the work train, and more every week. Crocker has a labor contractor in San Francisco hard at work hiring them."

O'Bannon smiled. "The way these are workin' out, it seems a good piece of business."

"You could'a knocked me over with a feather," Strobridge said. "I think you should plan on putting half the new men to work on Cape Horn, and the other half can begin hauling ties and trestles up to Long Ravine, or grading the approaches there.

"That fella Striker should be sliding timbers down the mountain all this week. I'll send the Celestials on up the road when they get to line's end."

"Good enough. Can I get at it?" O'Bannon asked.

"You bet." As O'Bannon started away, Strobridge stopped him. "Hey, how's the boxing match coming along? The other bosses have their men selected and are giving each other pointers every night after work."

O'Bannon had given it little thought. He'd been much more concerned about the abundance of whiskey in camp—although his Celestials were little affected by it—and the potential of sabotage. Many of his Celestials would spend Sundays smoking opium, but by the next day they were back at work seemingly without aftereffect.

"I'll get on it today," he said.

As he moved on up to Cape Horn, he contemplated who he might have on his boxing team. Most of his non-Celestials were surveyors who spent their time laying out the slope and grade of the roadbed, or teamsters and graders. Hardworking men, but not like those who were driving spikes or gandy-dancing rails.

One of his surveyors, a man O'Bannon barely knew, was walking nearby with a bundle of stakes on his shoulder.

"Hey," O'Bannon yelled at the tall young fellow.

He looked over.

"What was your name?" Nolan asked.

"Peterson, Mr. O'Bannon. James Peterson. What can I do for you?"

O'Bannon smiled at the man's heavy English accent, but motioned him along without comment and took up stride beside him. "We're having a little entertainment this coming Sunday. Any of you boys ever do any boxing?"

"As a matter of fact, I did a lot of club fighting back home. . . ." He seemed to think a minute, then the light came in his eyes. "Taggart, an Aussie chap who's a chainman on the second crew, he's always running his mouth about fisticuffs. This is Wednesday, Mr. O'Bannon. That's not much time to get ready—"

"Good," Nolan smiled, ignoring Peterson's apprehension and patting him on the back. "I know who Taggart is." The Aussie was, even taller than he was, and Nolan could imagine him being a rough-and-tumble sort, but he eyed the young Englishman questioningly. "You're a mite on the small side, but you seem a willing lad."

"Small, sir . . . but quick as a whip, if I do say so me own self."

"Then it'll be you, me, Taggart, and I'll see if a couple of the Celestials are of a mind to take some knots."

"That'll be a sight," Peterson said, shaking his head in doubt. Then he said, "With your permission, I'll check with the other boys on the grading crews. I know MacTavish would if you asked him, but he's a little long in the tooth."

Arnold MacTavish was a crew chief with a hundred men working under him cutting the final grade, and he was as old as or older than O'Bannon. Nolan smiled at the young man. "Aye, he's a bit on the old side for such as this. Leave him be, but you go ahead and ask around the others, and get the word out to the graders. But nonetheless, you and Taggart be at my tent after you get some supper."

"Yes, sir, it'll be my pleasure."

O'Bannon smiled tightly as the young man strode away. He was willing and tall enough, but slight of build compared to some of the bulls on other crews. *I wonder how he'll do three minutes times three, against the iron arms of Bochevski's men. Hell,* Nolan thought, *I wonder how* I'll *do.*

It was the midday break when the new crew of Celestials arrived. O'Bannon called Ho down off the top of Cape Horn, and had him give the new men an orientation as to what they'd be doing, where they could set up camp, and how they would be paid. After they broke into five crews of twenty or so, and selected their tea boys—O'Bannon hoped they *were* all boys—and cooks, he sent them off to make their camps. They would start work in the morning.

As they began to move away, O'Bannon couldn't help but notice one of the Celestials who was not only taller than his countrymen, but, O'Bannon estimated, a half head taller than himself.

He waved Ho over and explained the upcoming boxing match to him.

Ho smiled. "It has been the talk of the camp, O'Bannonboss. We will all be on the hillside to watch you white devils beat each other senseless." Ho smiled sheepishly, as he'd never tested O'Bannon as to his tolerance of the belief of the Celestials that all whites were "devils."

But O'Bannon merely guffawed. Then he pressed Ho. "I think one of your people should join in the fun. Do you think one might be willing to step into the ring with a white devil?"

Ho shrugged, obviously not taken with the idea. The Chinese had enough trouble with the whites, and certainly going looking for a fight held little attraction.

"In fact," O'Bannon said, pointing at the retreating mountain of a Chinese man, "how about that little fella?"

Again, Ho shrugged. "I can only inquire, O'Bannonboss, but if I may talk plainly, I think it will only cause more trouble."

Nolan weighed that. So far, other than a couple more incidents, trouble had stayed at bay. He certainly didn't want to antagonize it.

"You're right, Ho. Let's let it well enough alone."

"As you wish, O'Bannonboss." With that, he hurried back to climb to the head of Cape Horn. O'Bannon had barely gotten clear of the rough roadbed below Cape Horn when the cry of "Fire in the hole!" rang out, and the quiet morning was shattered with the roar of black-powder blasts.

Late that afternoon, when he arrived back at his tents, LuAnn had his laundry done and hanging to dry on the tent stays, ropes tied to nearby trees. Socks and shirts, trousers and long underwear hung from the lines.

Her facial swelling was beginning to recede and more and more she was looking like a girl, disturbingly so.

And she had dinner prepared for him. He'd purposely passed the chow tent, secretly hoping she'd been hard at work, and he wasn't disappointed.

After he'd eaten, while she was cleaning up, he posed a question. "Miss LuAnn, when do you think you will be ready to go back to Auburn?"

She eyed him, then went back to her cleaning, not answering him. He presumed she didn't understand, so he asked in another manner. "LuAnn, you seem much better. It is not fitting for you . . . a young woman . . . to stay here with Ho and me. You will go down the mountain as soon as you're well enough."

This time she didn't even turn, but continued to work.

Oh, well, he thought, *she isn't well enough yet to leave, so when she is, I'll have Ho explain it to her.*

For the time being, he was enjoying having her around. In fact, he probably enjoyed it much too much.

Almost as soon as he'd finished his meal, he heard a commotion outside, and walked to the flap of his tent to see a dozen of his crew there with James Peterson, Grady Taggart, and Arnold MacTavish among them.

He laughed as he held the tent flap aside, then moved out among them. "I take it you're all here to join in this Sunday's festivities?"

There was a boisterous concurrence from the rowdy group.

"Then let's get at it. I'll draw a circle. MacTavish, bust up some straws and we'll draw to see who matches who."

As soon as he had two men who'd both drawn the short straws, he'd figured out how he would eliminate them. His circle was drawn in the mud, and he pointed at it. "Since I'm the boss here, I'm appointed by me own self to be one of the fighters. You're trying out for the four remaining spots. And

I'll be the one and only judge of who goes or stays." There was some quiet complaining, but it ended quickly. He pointed. "That'll be our ring. You will go at it openhanded, one minute by the watch, so there's enough of you left in one piece to get into the rope ring on Sunday."

The men groused, but not seriously, and before long, he'd cut it down to five, including himself.

James Peterson was not among those remaining, having been felled twice by the old man, MacTavish, a tall, lanky, raw-boned, redheaded Scotsman. Peterson had been right. He was fast, and slapped the old man a half-dozen times for every blow he took, but the few he took knocked him wobbly-kneed, even though they were struck openhanded. Grady Taggart, the Sidney Duck, made the cut. He was truly a rough-and-tumble fighter, who concentrated on the other man's nose with a vengeance, and ignored the blows that fell upon him.

So it was to be MacTavish, Taggart, O'Bannon, a big Welshman named Troy Tallman, and a stubby pug-nosed Irish lout with a chest like a beer keg, carrying the handle of Paddy O'Houlihan.

They scheduled an evening practice for every night after work until the competition.

The next morning, when Nolan arose, he was both saddened and relieved to find LuAnn, and her small bundle of belongings, missing.

Ho shrugged his shoulders when asked about her whereabouts.

"I gave her the few dollars she had coming before we retired last night. I suspect we have seen the last of her, which is for the best, O'Bannonboss. In which case, I will move back to my camp, with your permission?"

"Of course," Nolan agreed.

He would miss them both—he enjoyed Ho's company—but particularly he would miss LuAnn, who he imagined he'd never see again. He'd liked her as a boy, and wondered about her as a woman. Even though he selfishly felt abandoned, he wished her the best, then decided he would put her out of his mind.

It would take some concentration.

But he had a boxing match to get ready for, not to speak of a railroad to build.

Chapter Nine

With the new morning, while walking the length of Cape Horn to inspect the progress, Nolan spotted a man stumbling up out of the brush at the top of the slope.

He waited until the man reached the roadbed, then stopped him.

"You drunk, bucko?" Nolan asked.

"Wa' the hell do you care?" the man growled back, and started to walk away.

Nolan reached out, grabbed him by the shoulder, and spun him back around.

The man turned, but did so with a wild roundhouse left.

Nolan stepped back, and the blow swished by his face. The man almost fell with the effort, then tried to come at him with another roundhouse right. Nolan slapped him hard, snapping his head, and the man reeled back but didn't lose his footing, then focused as he caught his breath.

"You'll be a sorry sort that you smacked Alec Flynn," he growled, then seemed to center his intent on Nolan, focusing not only his eyes but his anger. He charged forward, windmilling arms trying to connect.

Nolan stepped inside, blocked his wild punches, slapped him hard again, then followed him as he backed away, slapping him again and again, snapping his head back and forth like a flapping flag, until the man went hard on his back in the rough scrabble of the roadbed. Placing a knee in his chest, Nolan pinned him to the ground, grabbing him by the throat with a steel grip.

"Now, bucko, where's the bottle?"

"Down in the weeds," he slurred.

"And where might you have come by it?"

"Wit' my bloody six dollars a day, that's where."

Nolan eased up on the pressure on his chest, and relaxed the grip on his throat. "Before I let you up, and before I decide if you get your walking papers here and now, I'll ask you again. Where did you come by the whiskey?"

Flynn hesitated for a moment, then reluctantly mumbled, "Whiskey drummer."

"They're not allowed on the job, or anywhere near. Where is this 'whiskey drummer'?"

"You'd not fire me for a little taste now and again?" he asked, his demeanor completely changed, his voice taking on the hint of a pleading tone.

"Yes, I would. There's no bloody drink allowed in the camps, and you know that. Where's the drummer hang his hat?"

"In the woods, different places. The boys on the spike crew always know where he'll be, of a given night."

Nolan arose, let Flynn stumble to his feet, then put a finger hard against his chest.

"You go back to your camp and sleep it off. Leave the bottle in the bush, or sure as dog-shit stinks, I'll give you the boot. Come see me at my tent tonight, and come sober or don't let me see you on the CP again."

"Yes, sir," the man managed, then spun on his heel and stumbled away.

It seemed Mr. Bochevski should be paying more attention to his crew's recreational habits. He decided he had to have a talk with Bochevski.

After Nolan checked the Horn, he moved on a mile up to the bottom of the skid road where Ho had taken half the new Celestial arrivals. They were well beyond the railhead, which was still two miles short of Cape Horn, yet well short of their job site, so the timbers would have to be loaded on wagons and hauled another mile over the rough road to be stored near the location of the pending Long Ravine trestle.

Ho had things well under control, with men receiving the timbers at the bottom of the skid road and stacking them where the road flattened and they would no longer move under their own power, still others hand-dragging them down the ravine to the first place that could be reached by wagon and stacking them again.

There they were loaded on wagons, and Irish teamsters moved out with heaping loads pulled by their six-up rigs of big mules, to the storage clearing at Long Ravine. Other Chinese crews unloaded the wagons and stacked the timbers, where they would await being moved into place for the erection crews. While this was ongoing, two more Celestial crews worked grading the approaches to the trestle, and three dozen skilled Irish and Welsh masons slapped mortar to stone erecting the foundations and diversion structures from native stone.

It was all coordinated so the trestle would be complete in two months, the scheduled arrival of the spikers and the track.

A hawk-nosed man O'Bannon didn't know sat on

a log above the bottom of the slide road, seemingly keeping track of the numbers and lengths of timbers gathered at the bottom of the slide road. A big dun gelding was tied near where the man sat.

O'Bannon concluded that this was Striker, the supplier Strobridge had mentioned, and the man whose camp O'Bannon had visited when he'd made his sojourn up the mountain after the avalanche. O'Bannon walked up the ravine, then climbed up to the log where the man sat tallying timbers, and stuck out his hand.

"You Striker?"

"That I am."

"I'm O'Bannon, division boss for this part of the rail."

With this, Striker arose and took the offered hand.

But his brows furrowed and dark eyes deep in his hatchet face peered skeptically. "I been dealin' directly with the big bossman, Strobridge."

His tone was a little condescending, but Nolan ignored it. "Actually, Charles Crocker is the big bossman. Strobridge is the general foreman, and my boss. So, it appears your timbers are coming down the mountain in good stead."

"Sound as twenty-dollar gold pieces and faster than a French whore," Striker said, his tight lips in a semblance of a smile. "You want to check my count?"

"We'll pay by what arrives at the job site, Striker. We'll count 'em there and check the numbers against your invoice." O'Bannon's tone became less businesslike. "I was up at your camp not long ago—"

"My crew done tol' me someone from the CP was up there . . . so that was you. Quite a climb."

"That it was. This your dun?"

Striker ignored his question, but the horse was

obviously his. "You inquired about buying some stock, or so said my cousin."

"I did. You've got some fine-lookin' mules up on the mountain."

"I use 'em every day, they be as good as mules get, but like ever'thing, they are for sale."

O'Bannon climbed the few steps up to where the dun was tied. This horse had not been in Striker's camp when he was there. "You seem to take good care of your stock."

As he spoke, Nolan lifted the horse's hoofs and checked his shoes for the telltale nick, but his shoes were clean. "Good shoeing job," Nolan said offhandedly.

"I do my own. Shoed this ol' boy just yesterday."

So there's no way of telling.

"Well," Nolan said, touching his hatband and moving away, "keep 'em coming. We'll be placing timbers at Long Ravine by the middle of next week."

"As long as the CP is payin', they'll be comin' down the mountain."

"Well, Mr. Striker, keep it up." With that, O'Bannon strode away.

Charles Crocker and James Strobridge sat in folding chairs near Strobridge's private railcar; his wife had just warmed their coffee cups.

"We're going to try this new nitroglycerin again," Crocker announced.

"It's got a bad reputation, Charles, and it's already damn near cost you one general foreman," Strobridge replied, worried.

"I've checked and checked on it. If it's handled correctly, it'll make our blasting a lot easier and a damn sight cheaper. It's much lighter than powder, and much more powerful. It detonates much easier—"

"I've noticed it detonates whenever it damn well pleases," Strobridge said.

"Not so, James. Your accident was a fluke. You build a ten-by-ten building somewhere very near Cape Horn. I've got a man coming up to mix this concoction right on the spot. We'll need another location a good ways away for storage . . . a cave maybe, with some kind of constant temperature."

"As you wish, Boss, but I'm not convinced." He subconsciously rubbed the eye patch he wore; the loss of the eye a result of their first attempt at using the volatile explosive, when a workman's pick struck near an undetonated load. A stray spark from iron striking hard rock did the rest.

"It'll be fine this time," Crocker assured him. Then he continued, changing the subject. "James," he said, "we've got a hullabaloo to put on in a couple of weeks."

"How's that?" Strobridge asked.

"Stanford will be here with a whole entourage of heavyweight politicians to show off the line."

Leland Stanford, one of the original four and a partner in the CP, had just been elected governor. Collis Huntington, another of the partners, stayed in Washington, D.C., cajoling money out of the federal government and handling the politics of the line; while Mark Hopkins, the fourth partner, handled the books and day-to-day financial operations in California from their Sacramento headquarters.

"So, what can I do?" Strobridge asked.

"As we get closer, I'll know more. But I'm sure we'll have a fancy lunch at the railhead, then we'll horseback on up the line at least as far as Long Ravine, and maybe a good bit farther. There's nothing on the road, at least yet, that will impress them like Long Ravine. . . . You *will* have some timbers up—"

"Hell, I have high hopes that we'll be half done in two weeks. We'll at least have a goodly number of timbers standing, God willin' and the creek don't rise. And I mean that literally in this case."

Crocker shook his head. "I can't tell you how important this is. These are both California and Washington politicians, and the blackguards owe us a pile of money."

"We'll do our best."

"I know you will, James. This man Striker, he's fulfilling his contract?"

"So far so good. We've got a pile of timbers growing at Long Ravine. If he keeps this up, he can supplement our own mill for months."

"I know you haven't been back to Auburn for a while, but our company mill's coming along in good order. The millwrights will begin setting the steam-driven sawing equipment this week. I'll see you tomorrow as I make my weekly pass with the payroll; then I've got to head for San Francisco."

Strobridge smiled. He hadn't mentioned the upcoming boxing match to Crocker, knowing that his boss would not approve of any activity that might interfere with the work, or the men's ability to do their jobs. It was just as well that he'd be out of the area.

Crocker made note of his pleased expression. "Does that please you, James? That I'll be gone?"

Strobridge laughed. "No, sir, I was pleased to think that you might be taking a day off for a change."

"Not a day off, James. A load of rail is due in from the East, and I'm going to meet the ship and make damn sure it gets off-loaded and barged up here. You keep making roadbed, and I'll make damn sure we've got material at hand to fill it with railroad."

"Yes, sir. I should have known."

This brought a hint of a smile to Crocker's wide face. "I'll take a hell of a lot more than a day off when we tie up with the Union Pacific, which I hope will be somewhere in Wyoming if we can ever get over these damnable mountains."

"Yes, sir."

"You gentlemen need more coffee?" Hannah Strobridge was at Crocker's elbow.

"No, thank you, Hannah," Crocker said, this time with a genuine smile.

"And I've got to get up the line," Strobridge said, handing her his cup. "See you at supper, Missus." With that, he headed for his horse and Crocker strode away to the work train.

That night after supper Strobridge showed up at O'Bannon's camp to watch the men exercise and train for the coming boxing match, with only two days left to prepare. He was not the only spectator. There were a number of other men, including Ho and the big Celestial O'Bannon had mentioned to Ho as a possible fighter if the Chinese wanted to join in the competition.

Ho and the man, who was called Chang, stood far back and watched as the men in training feinted and blocked, ducked and punched without contact, and counterpunched the same light way.

Strobridge sat on a timber round, sipping coffee, gnawing a cigar, watching with interest, as Simon Striker walked up and settled down on his haunches alongside.

"It appears your timbers are up to snuff," Strobridge said with a nod.

"As I said they would be."

"We're moving up our schedule, so keep them coming."

"What's this I hear about you fellas building your own mill?" Striker asked.

"Down at Auburn, but there's plenty of timbers needed and we won't be able to keep up. We plan another mill when we reach the east side of the mountains. Even then, when we begin the march across the desert, we'll need all you can supply and more."

Striker nodded as if he agreed, but he was convinced the new mill would mean they'd stop buying from him, or at least they'd try and chisel the price.

Well, he'd see about that.

Maybe he'd stop by and check out the new mill on his way to San Francisco.

Hell, a sulfur match was much cheaper than a keg of powder.

Chapter Ten

That night, when O'Bannon had finished his boiled beef and cabbage, and the men's workout, and he approached his tents, the man who'd called himself Flynn sat rolling a smoke near the tent flap.

He rose from a timber round and cast the half-made cigarette aside when O'Bannon walked up.

His tone sheepish, he began. "Mr. O'Bannon, I'm here as you ordered. I wanted to apologize for getting into that bottle while on the job—"

"Forget it," O'Bannon said. "That's behind us. You do your job from now on and you'll keep it. What's in front of us at the moment is getting this whiskey drummer out of our hair."

"I walked on down to the spike crew while you fellows were getting ready for the boxing and having your supper, and found out where he was set up. It's in a meadow just a hundred yards or so below the line, back twixt here and the railhead."

"Hold on a minute, then we'll head down that way. It's time I had a chat with the old boy."

O'Bannon turned to enter his tent, but Flynn stopped him with a pleading tone. "Mr. O'Bannon, if I show you the way down there, my name will be mud on this crew. The men won't—"

O'Bannon extended a hand, palm out, stopping him, then eyed the man a moment. Flynn had been fairly square with him so far. "You just walk me back as far as where I should head down the mountain, then you can keep on walking."

"Thank you, Mr. O'Bannon. I'll not forget—"

"The best thanks you can give me is to keep doing your job, and doing it sober."

O'Bannon went to his satchel and got his holstered Colt and strapped it on his hip, then returned and started down the roadbed afoot with Flynn at his side.

At just over a mile's walking, they came to a small trestle with a trickle of water under it. A spot that was normally dry, except during runoff time.

"This is it, Mr. O'Bannon," Flynn said, and O'Bannon dropped down the rock escarpment without comment. Flynn turned and strode quickly back up the roadbed, which at this spot was finely graded, finished, and awaiting the rail.

The place lay thick with buck brush and within a dozen yards of the freshly graded roadbed, it was dark with a heavy stand of lodgepole pine. By keeping to the streambed, Nolan was able to work his way down making little noise. He was only a few yards into the trees when he heard voices. Moving up out of the streambed a few yards, he waited out of sight while a half-dozen men, each carrying a bottle, passed him while laughing and hoorahing each other and the night.

Nolan waited until they were well up the hill, then continued on his way. The talking and laughing filtering through the trees now resonated up from down the mountain, and the sound and streambed showed him the way.

It was just growing good and dark when the

stream flattened out and widened, and he saw the flicker of a campfire up ahead.

He made his way to within a dozen paces of where twenty or more men were lined up at a makeshift table made of a couple of lodgepoles lying across two granite rocks.

Four mules, looking familiar to O'Bannon, grazed nearby. One was still saddled with a riding rig, but three had packsaddles, packs, and pack ropes resting nearby, and six wooden panniers rested in a semicircle around the back of the makeshift table.

O'Bannon palmed the Colt and toed forward. As soon as he reached the men, those who recognized him began to quiet, and in a heartbeat or two, all had stopped their boisterous revelry and were staring as he quietly walked past and rested his Colt and both hands on the lodgepoles.

The man serving as clerk was digging into a pannier, then turned with six quart bottles, three threaded through the fingers of each hand.

He realized that the men had quieted. He had one of the latest in weapons, a shiny new Spencer repeating rifle, resting on a downed log near his work, and glanced at it when he saw his latest customer with a revolver, resting a hand on the bar.

The whiskey drummer was the man who'd given Nolan a cup of coffee in Striker's camp.

With a quick nod of his head, O'Bannon motioned to the men lined up, now behind him.

"You fellas get back to camp. If you've got a bottle, leave it here or you'll have to deal with me later." He took his eyes off the whiskey drummer long enough to glance at the line of men. "I know most of you—"

He heard the movement from the bartender, the bottles dropping to the muddy ground, and quickly turned back to see him grasping for the Spencer.

With the Colt raised and cocked, and the man

with only one hand on the resting Spencer, O'Bannon stopped him with the addition of a little advice. "Mister, if you want a third eye centered in your forehead, you go on with what you're doing."

The man blanched, and rose, leaving the rifle still at rest on the logs.

"Get on up the hill," he snarled at the line of men, most of whom were already moving away. Three bottles rested in the stream-side grass where they'd been dropped.

"This is none of your affair," the whiskey drummer mumbled.

O'Bannon spoke in deadly earnest. "You're about to see just how much of my affair this is."

He motioned to the man with the barrel of the Colt. "You start breakin' bottles, friend."

"By God, I'll not—"

O'Bannon dropped the muzzle level a couple of inches, and the Colt roared. One of the bottles resting near the man's brogan exploded, and he backed away with arms flailing, almost tripping. He recovered and glared, wide-eyed.

"As I said," O'Bannon repeated. "You go to bustin' bottles."

There must have been over a hundred quarts of whiskey, unlabled, in the panniers at the man's feet.

"My boss will have your head—"

"Striker?" O'Bannon asked.

The man stared out into the woods for a moment, then turned and gave O'Bannon a weasel glance. "No, I don't work for Striker anymores. This paid better."

"Not anymore, it doesn't. Break bottles, friend, and you might live to see another sunrise."

The man began to work his way through the supply, and was more than half done when O'Bannon realized, with the crack of a twig, that someone was behind him. As he spun to meet the threat, he caught the flash of a whiskey bottle at the end of a rapidly swinging arm.

Then his face was in the mud, he fought to clear his vision, but another blow drove him deeper into the muck, and all faded to black.

A full moon greeted O'Bannnon when he awoke, lighting the empty camp with eerie shadows. He was afraid to move quickly, afraid his head was broken and what little brains he had would leak out into the already slushy ground. He reached back and felt the goose egg on the back of his head, and brought the hand back to see it covered with drying blood.

God, his head hurt, throbbed, a drum pounding a constant reverberating cadence. Very slowly, he managed to sit up; with the effort the drum's cadence hastened, and a hint of bile soured his throat.

He also felt as if he'd been trampled by the mules as they left. Carefully, he felt his side, and wondered if a rib or two was broken.

But thanks be to God, his eyes would focus.

The mules were gone.

The whiskey drummer was gone.

The only remaining sign of the drummer's camp was a scatter of glass shards, spikes from bottle necks and bottoms that threatened the unwary passerby.

His Colt was gone.

Had he felt better, he'd have chastised the night and his inattention with a few curses, but he knew he couldn't stand the pain if he tried to do so with any fervor. Even speaking was beyond the question.

That revolver and holster had cost him the better part of a twenty-dollar gold piece.

He tried to rise, then decided he'd better sit back down as the stand of lodgepole proceeded to do a swivel-hipped war dance around him, keeping time to the staccato drumbeats.

That couldn't be quite right.

Lying back in the mud, with a shiver in the cold night air, he decided he'd rest a while before he jumped up and went after the no-account lowlife who'd backwhacked him.

For the moment, that would have to wait.

When he awoke again he noticed that the moon had crossed the night sky. Cold to the bone, he managed to sit, then carefully stand. It was hard to catch his breath, his side hurt so badly. The camp was empty, except for the diamond-flash moon reflection of broken bottles strewn over the area. Getting to the little trickle of water, he splashed his face and washed his mouth out, then began to work his way up the streambed, up the mountain, back to the roadbed, back to his own bed. Pausing just as he reached the little trestle that marked where he should ascend the bank, he soiled the water that marked his path by placing his hands on his knees, and retching up what was left of his supper, which caused a pain in his side that almost made him pass out again.

It was much farther returning to his tents than it had been coming.

He awoke at first light, and as usual, tried to sit up, but his head swam too much and the tent mimicked the dance the trees had done the night before, and he had to get flat again. If it was possible, his side hurt even worse, hurt with every breath. Trying to remember what happened, he finally recalled a vision of the flash of the whiskey bottle, then awakening and splashing water on his face. He couldn't remember the walk home, nor pulling off his boots and falling into his cot.

It was midmorning when James Strobridge shook him awake. "Nolan, you bled all over your bedroll. One of the surveyors was a hospital aide before he lost half a hand at Pea Ridge, but he can still sew. I'll get him over here to put a few stitches in that. What the hell happened?"

"How about a slug of water?" Nolan managed, his voice shaky.

He kept a cask of water in the outer tent, and Strobridge located it and handed a dipper to him, then seeing how much trouble he was having, lifted his head and helped him drink.

"Now, what the hell happened?"

"No-good . . . dirty dog . . . of a whiskey drummer. Last night. I rousted him down the road . . . a ways, and had him under the muzzle of my . . . my Colt." He paused a moment. "Son of a bitch stole my Colt. Anyway, I . . . I had him bustin' his bottles up, after I ran . . . ran our men off, somebody busted me across the head. Whiskey bottle, if I recall. Must'a been a thick one."

"It's a damn good thing your head's a thick one." Strobridge laughed quietly. "Rest easy. I'll have someone bring you something to eat."

"Hell, I'll be up in a few minutes. Just let me get my bearings."

"You'll stay in the sack, and that's an order. I'll get you something to eat, and don't you even think about trying to get up."

"Yes, sir."

Sounds like a hell of an idea, Nolan agreed to himself, and rested his head back down. When he awoke again, he could see by the light on the tent that it was late afternoon.

He thought he'd been knocked completely senseless, or maybe this was redemption for his few good deeds, and he was awaiting his turn to get through St. Patrick's golden gates, for there was a heavenly vision at the foot of the bed. A vision unlike anything that should be miles up the CP, among thousands of sweaty dirt-stained men.

"You would like some water?" the vision asked.

A beautiful vision. Long hair, ebony eyes, cheeks the color of summer red plums on the high cheekbones. A red silk dress with black trim, and buttons all the way down the front, buttons shaped like lions' heads that must have been carved from black jet. *Chinese dogs, that's what the buttons are,* he thought. *And besides all of this, she is beautiful.*

No, more than beautiful, a vision.

Without asking again, she rose, approached, lifted his head, and brought the dipper to his lips.

"Your soup has gotten cold," she said. "Lu Ang will seek some hot for you."

"LuAnn?" he said, then realized that the girl had returned. This could not be the same girl, but then again . . .

"You came back," he ventured.

"Yes. I merely took a small journey to Sacramento, where I invested my earnings to become as a woman again."

He merely stared. It was an understatement. When he didn't reply, she continued.

"It has been two years since I was able to be as I was born."

"Why?" Nolan managed. "Why were you here as a man?"

"It is a long story, and you must rest, and I must get you some hot broth from the cook's tent. Strobridge has asked them to make you broth. He left a man here to watch over you, but I ran him from the tent."

"I like your broth better than ol' Cookie's," he managed.

This time it was her turn to smile. "I will cook for you from now on. I brought many things to cook for you. But Strobridge said broth from the cook tent, so I obey."

He was in no condition to argue, so he laid his head back down and rested. Confused, but happy she was back.

Someone entered the tent, and he presumed it was she, until a man's voice cautioned him, "This is gonna smart a mite." He opened his eyes to note that the surveyor's helper was at his side with a wet rag in hand. Scrubbing the wound, then stitching it, then dusting it with sulfur powder, he attended to Nolan until LuAnn returned.

"You were right," he managed to say to the man, his brows deeply furrowed, "it did smart a mite, but maybe it won't weep now."

"It'll be good as new in a fortnight," the man said, then he handed LuAnn a bottle that he'd removed from his pocket. "This is Peruvian Syrup, should make him feel a lot better. A teaspoon a couple of times a day." He left the way he'd come.

Lying quietly with his eyes closed, Nolan let her spoon a teaspoon of the bitter medicine between his lips. He gagged trying to swallow it. "You can do better than that from the bottom of the privy." She quickly spooned soup into his mouth and made the taste of the medicine go away. She fed him like he was a small child again, not that he could do much about it.

He could see it was dark outside when he awoke again. Some distance from the tent he could hear the men working out for the boxing match.

Tomorrow, the match is tomorrow. I have to get up and get ready.

But his body wouldn't yield to his mind, and he continued to rest. He rubbed his side, sore as a boil. Hell, one blow to his side and he'd probably pass out. He was in no shape to fight this little girl who was waiting on him hand and foot, much less some burly spiker.

In moments, he opened his eyes to see three men standing at the side of the cot.

"Mr. O'Bannon, Ho here wants a Chinee boy to take your place tomorrow."

It was the redheaded MacTavish doing the talking. Ho stood back a ways. Paddy O'Houlihan, the barrel-chested Irishman, stood at MacTavish's side, his thick legs spread, his hamlike hands on his hips defiantly, a scowl on his face.

"What do you think, Mr. O'Bannon?" MacTavish asked.

But it was Paddy O'Houlihan who answered, with bridled anger in his voice. "No damned way, is what we boys think."

Chapter Eleven

Nolan again wondered about the repercussions of having a Celestial fight against the whites. It could be disastrous. Then again . . . .

"Can he fight?" Nolan asked.

"Well," MacTavish answered, a little sheepishly, "we haven't had a Katy-bar-the-door brawl, but he has not backed up a step to the best I, or O'Houlihan here can give openhanded. He blocks damn near ever'thing thrown at him, and gives back as much as he gets, and smiles like a monkey playing with his personal self all the time he's up to it. It becomes a bit irritatin', to give you the God's honest truth, and you want to knock his bloody smiling head off."

O'Bannon couldn't help but show a tight smile, even through it was only in the eyes.

"Ho," he asked, "what do you think?"

"I think we Celestials receive less trouble from white devils after he is allowed to do battle."

O'Bannon's eyes again hinted at a smile, even if his lips did not.

"Well, that's a change in attitude."

"I did not think we should have a Celestial do battle, until I found out where Chang had been."

O'Bannon didn't ask, and the other men only looked on curiously.

Nolan closed his eyes and waved them away. "Chang it is," he managed to mumble.

If Chang was good enough for Ho, he was good enough.

"Ho, you're as changeable as a spring wind. Hell, it don't look like I'm worth spit"—his voice was weak and verified what he said—"as much as I'd like to give it a go." He cleared his throat, then winced with the effort. "So, we have damn near five hundred Celestials on our crew, and it's only right one of our five fighters should be Chinese. O'Houlihan, I guess there is to *be* a damnable way. Let him fight."

Ho seemed to stand a little taller.

"We'll never live it down," O'Houlihan mumbled, but there was resignation in his tone.

"An' put a ten-dollar gold piece on our team for me," Nolan said, his voice again tinged with humor, "now that Chang's into the fray." He bit his lip to keep from laughing out loud, which would kill him the way his ribs felt, then closed his eyes again.

As soon as the men left, he felt a cold wet cloth, gentle on his forehead and opened his eyes to see the same vision kneeling at his cot's side.

He closed them again. "You didn't have to come back, you know," he said quietly. "This is no place for a woman. . . ."

"Ah, but I did," she said, without explaining. "Besides, if I lived here as a man, I can certainly live here as a woman. A woman will have some small advantage. . . ."

This time the hint of an actual smile lit his face, even though he didn't open his eyes.

Small advantage? he thought. *Hell, this woman would have a damned big advantage damn near anywhere in the world.*

Sunday morning dawned with a sky as blue as wild morning glory, and with a bright sun warming the shoulders, or so LuAnn told Nolan when she saw his eyes open. Yet, although he felt much better, O'Bannon still felt as if his head was part of the cot, rather than part of his body. Even though he again awoke angry, it took him fifteen minutes to manage to sit up, and then thirty more to get his trousers, shirt, socks, and boots on.

When he finally managed to get into the meeting tent, LuAnn was smiling, but it was a concerned smile. The odor of tea boiling on the stove wafted through the small area, and it calmed him. He managed to negotiate himself onto a timber round, his head as if in a vise, his throat dry and raspy.

"You should not rise for many days, O'Bannon," she chastised him with the tone of a mother shaking a spatula at an errant son.

"We are not always able to do what we should," he said with a slightly sheepish smile, his anger having fled with the sight of her.

"Aw, that is so. Still, I wish—"

"I cannot participate in the boxing, so the least I can do is sit quietly and lend my support."

"Then you must quickly return to rest," she said with finality.

This morning she had on a shimmering-green silk dress, demurely buttoned up to her neck, but not so demurely split up the side above the knee. There was a rent in the dress the width of an index finger, stitched at its borders with lighter green thread, only six or so inches long, but it found its way from her throat down to the cleavage in her ample breasts.

"How many of those fine dresses did you manage to find, LuAnn?" he asked as she handed him a mug of the boiling brew. After she did so, she closed her fists self-consciously, and he realized she was embarrassed about her hands.

"Why do you hide your hands?" he asked.

"They show the misuse I have put them to. I am shamed."

"It was honest labor."

"I will be proud of my hands and my fingernails again, but it will take many weeks." She ducked her head. "I will never rid my face of the scars."

O'Bannon studied her. She did have some redness where her eyebrow had been cut, even under some female concoction she'd applied to make her complexion smooth and her cheeks and lips rosy red; otherwise, her face was flawless. She had high cheekbones, wide-set large eyes of glimmering ebony, and fine features—much finer than most Celestials. Her teeth were well formed as if by an artist, perfectly aligned, snow-white, and shone beautifully against a flawless almond complexion when she flashed a rare smile. Her hair was pulled up tightly and rolled in a bun on top of her head, and a tortoise-shell comb staked it in place.

"You are very beau—" he started to say, then bit his tongue. She was beautiful, but he didn't feel it appropriate to tell her. "The hint of a scar will disappear soon enough," he said, and returned his attention to the cup.

She, too, seemed anxious to change the subject. "I was fortunate to negotiate for one dress, O'Bannon. A shop run by Celestials in Sacramento has three seamstresses at work. They finished the red one in only two days. Had I worked more diligently, they would have fine embroidery . . ." She cut her eyes with embarrassment. "I am wasteful, I know, but it has been so long." Then her voice lightened. "The other three were packed away at the shop of the only friend I have in Gum San."

"So, you had them when you came here?"

"Yes, O'Bannon. But I have not worn them for two years."

"And why is that, LuAnn?"

He sipped his tea, washing the taste of the long night away, and he felt somewhat better.

"I have some rice, and some dried fruit. Do you desire?"

"I desire," he answered, realizing that she was still not ready to talk about how she came to be a tea "boy" on the CP.

Every step on the way back to where the work train now rested sent a jolt of pain through his head, but he walked the mile there, with the help of a long stout walking stick Ho had fashioned for him. He had peeled and polished the piece. O'Bannon's fighters walked with him in a group, slowing their stride to accommodate his. Due to LuAnn's ministrations, he carried a clean white wrapper on his head to protect the wound.

The dirt-floored ring had been erected of poles and ropes in a natural basin just below the track. By the time he arrived, the slope of the roadbed and the banks of the basin were already lined, packed solid, with men.

A new spur had been built here and the base camp moved over two miles forward. Strobridge had relocated his house car, and all the work cars were moved up. Men satisfied with a more distant view sat on the car's eaves with legs dangling.

This would be their camp for many, many months.

In a very few days the continuous rail would be blocked by Cape Horn. The tie setters and spikers would skip the Horn and move on and begin again just past it, where the road had again been graded.

The good thing was that they could continue; the bad was that the rails and materials would have to be hauled from this campsite by teamster over the rough grade that was being blasted at Cape Horn. It would slow the delivery of the six-hundred-pound rails, spikes, and joint plates, and would slow the progress on Cape Horn.

One problem compounded the other, and both crews would suffer additional endangerment.

LuAnn had insisted she accompany him, and he felt too bad to argue. But she walked at least twenty paces behind his group, her shimmering-green silk dress under a wrap of Mandarin red that kept the chill from her shoulders.

Her silence did not keep her from the attention of over two thousand men gathered to enjoy the match. The laughter and betting and hoorahing quieted as she approached. None of them had any idea such a strikingly beautiful woman was anywhere near the end of the line. She had been spotted by a few and recognized as a woman, even though she'd worn her work clothes, when she'd returned to O'Bannon's tent from Sacramento. Rumors had flown. But none but Ho and the grading crew boxers had actually seen her in polished and pampered full silk splendor.

The grading crew boxers had to shove their way through the crowd to find their position near the ring, but as LuAnn approached, the crowd opened as Moses had parted the Red Sea. Hats were snatched from heads, language cleaned up, and the tone was reduced to a more respectful low roar, rather than resembling the cackle of a disturbed flock of crows.

It seemed the men did not mind a beautiful Celestial woman at the railhead, a view diametrically opposed to having the Celestial men there.

As soon as they arrived, a list of their fighters was handed to Strobridge, who tore it into individual names. The scraps joined another twenty and were mixed well in a high-crowned hat. Strobridge had carefully studied LuAnn as she made her way down near the ring and was offered a timber round to sit upon, almost at ringside. It was the second time Strobridge had been made aware of her presence, and he wondered where she'd come from, and what she was doing there. And why she had been in Nolan O'Bannon's tent. When he saw her there the day before, he'd deemed it an inappropriate time to confront O'Bannon.

He'd worry on that later.

Strobridge had advised his own wife, Hannah, that it would be better if she remained at the house car, and she'd done so, although she took up a position perched in a folding chair on top of the car where she could see the ring, over a hundred yards downslope. She, and the six children, had prime, if distant, seating. The important ingredient was that she and the children were out of earshot; neither the gentle gender nor the children's young ears would be scalded by a careless slip of the tongue.

Strobridge shook up the hat, looked around, then walked to LuAnn and asked her to draw, until the names were gone. Numbers one and two were paired up, and so on, until the slots were filled, with no consideration of weight or size. Strobridge posted the matches at the rear of the ring, and the fighters crowded around to see who was first up, and whom they were matched with.

In the distance, on down the hill a few paces, a hundred-pound pig rotated over a bed of coals, and

Cookie himself muscled the skewer, made from an iron pry bar, around and around with the help of an eighteen-inch pipe wrench. The pig had been on since early morning and had taken on a golden brown color. The odor wafting over the crowd made all wish they'd become fighters so they'd have at least a chance to share in the bounty.

Bochevski pushed his way through the rest of the fighters and strode around the ring to where Nolan had perched himself on a downed log.

The big Pole guffawed as he approached, then snarled, "I see you have decided it unwise to meet your betters in the ring."

Chapter Twelve

Nolan sighed deeply, and Bochevski had to bend close to hear him as he replied.

"I had a little accident a day or so ago, Anatole." Nolan tapped the bandage wrapping his head. "But I'll recover soon enough, and I'll be happy to meet you in the ring or out."

"Talk is cheap, O'Bannon. When you see what we do to your mud-rakers, you'll probably pack up and go back to sea."

He snatched up Nolan's two-inch-diameter walking stick and snapped it like a twig across his knee, then roared with laughter, slapping his tree-trunk thighs as he started away.

"Yet to be seen my friend, yet to be seen," Nolan called to Bochevski's back. The heat rose in his neck, but he remained on his seat.

"Ha," Bochevski said over his shoulder. As he walked away, Nolan overheard him speaking to one of his fighters. "He's cowerin' behind some scratch on his head."

This time the heat caterpillar-crawled slowly up Nolan's spine until he began to see red.

LuAnn glanced at him, then crossed the few feet

separating them and perched ladylike with knees tightly together, her hands folded in her lap, on the log beside him.

"The angry warrior becomes careless, and is the one who falls first; the clever warrior prevails and lives to return to his home and loved ones."

He glanced at her, studying her serene face before he replied.

"Sometimes anger drives a man beyond his normal capabilities."

"And blinds him to all else. Blinds him to other more dangerous enemies. Sometimes the anger itself becomes his most ferocious adversary."

"Okay, okay," he said, and the anger began to fade. "There will be another time."

"It is said by those wiser than me that there are few times when it is not wise . . . to live to fight again."

He smiled. "You're full of them, aren't you."

"I observed and heeded many wise teachers in China."

Strobridge announced the simple rules. No eye-gouging, no blows to the privates, no beating a man when he's on the ground. Then he called the first fight and the battles were on. Two of Nolan's men, Troy Tallman, the Welshman, and Grady Taggart, the Australian, were eliminated by a Strobridge decision during the first half-dozen fights.

The betting between the crews reigned hot and heavy during the prefight activity, with a couple of the more enterprising souls acting as bookmakers. Even Ho took a few bets.

Bochevski knocked his man out in the first interval. His opponent was a tall rangy mason, long and lean with rock-hard hands and muscles well developed from lifting native rock into place. But his strength had been no match for the Pole's.

The next-to-last fight in the first group saw Chang paired up with a much smaller, but stout and rock-hard, Irishman from the spikers. One of Bochevski's men.

Chang met him in the middle of the ring with a big smile on his face.

Before the Irishman closed with him, the smaller man spoke with a snarl and heavy Irish brogue. "Ye bloody pagan gargoyle, what do ye have to smile about?"

Then he charged with roundhouse punches. Chang took a hard blow to the side of his face, but it didn't wipe away the grin. He chopped to one side of the Irishman's neck with his left hand, then followed to the other side with his right hand. The spiker went down as if he'd been hit with one of his own sledges.

Chang bowed to the crowd on each side of the ring. The chorus of boos did not wipe away his grin.

He climbed from the ring and watched closely as Paddy O'Houlihan, the barrel-chested Irishman, won his fight against a cook with a steer's girth who outweighed O'Houlihan by at least a hundred pounds. He won by decision, but he'd knocked his opponent down in every interval.

Arnold MacTavish, the redheaded Scotsman, drew a bye in the first group.

There was a twenty-minute waiting and resting period before the second group was to begin.

This time MacTavish was the first man to fight, paired against Anatole Bochevski. The older MacTavish fought gallantly, and it was seconds before the beginning of the third interval, with MacTavish pounded until it seemed he bled from every opening in his rawboned face, when Nolan O'Bannon made his way to the side of the ring and insisted to Strobridge that he stop the fight. Much to MacTavish's sputtered complaint. Sputtered because his mouth was full of blood. He'd proved his mettle, but was no match for the much younger and much bulkier Bochevski.

Bochevski managed to glower at Nolan when he came to ringside, and cast him an insult. "Had that been you, O'Bannon, I'd have knocked your bloody head clean off your shoulders."

This time Nolan merely shrugged and returned to his seat beside LuAnn.

"It is said," she said placatingly, "that dogs bark when a bull walks by. His snapping does not prove him the most brave or capable, only the loudest."

Nolan again smiled, convinced that there would be a far better time, and more private place.

Chang again felled his man in the first interval. This time the boos rose to a crescendo that deafened. Strobridge raised his arms in the center of the ring until he silenced them. Then he announced, "If you gentlemen cannot conduct yourself as such, then we'll end this match here and now, and never know who the best man is."

There was a palpable silence, until he called the next fighters.

The quarterfinals found Paddy O'Houlihan paired with Bochevski, and Chang against Bochevski's control-tie setter, Mickey Sullivan.

Before Chang's match began, LuAnn walked over and whispered something to the huge Chinaman. He nodded, then bowed slightly, as she moved back to take her seat beside O'Bannon.

"And what was that about?" Nolan asked.

She merely smiled demurely.

This time the match went the full three intervals. Sullivan managed to back Chang away more than one time with hammering blows, but each time he did so he came away with another knot on his head, another bloody cut on his face, or clawed his way back up from a knockdown.

Chang seemed to be toying with him until very near the end of the last interval. A vicious poke with a stiff open hand to the Irishman's solar plexis bent him, then a smashing knee to the face dropped him as if he'd been hit by one of the CP's locomotives. Strobridge called time before Sullivan could regain his feet, and he slunk back to the ground, defeated. His teammates carried him from the ring as he gasped for breath.

He'd gone the distance, but Nolan wondered if the match was allowed to do so only so Chang could punish him for a morning's transgressions against a tea boy, who turned out to be a girl . . . a girl not above retribution.

But this time Chang's bowing and boos were accompanied by rocks and dirt clods. As fast as they were thrown, Chang snatched them up and returned them, until they rained down on him twenty at a time and he couldn't possibly react quickly enough.

Still, Chang never lost the grin.

Again, Strobridge made his way to ring center and raised his arms. When he got them quieted, he said in a low voice that had to be repeated up the basin's slope. "If I see any manjack of you cast a stone, or anything other than a cheer, you'll be drawing your pay." Then he lifted his voice to a withering shout. *"Do you damn well understand!"*

There was dead silence for at least the count of ten, until the men began quietly speaking to one another. They'd never heard James Strobridge raise his voice.

Strobridge walked to the ropes, which were now dangling loosely and were no longer worth much more than a marker, and tipped his hat to LuAnn. "You'll pardon my language, young lady."

LuAnn nodded to him. He ordered some nearby men into the ring to clean up the mess, then called the next fight.

Bochevski against Paddy O'Houlihan.

Bochevski had the height, reach, and weight advantage, but Paddy O'Houlihan was all heart. Although he fought like a bull, and shook off punches that would fell a small tree, he could not prevail. By the end of the second interval, he'd been pounded unmercifully. With tears of frustration diluting the blood on his face, he couldn't get up for the third.

There were only three men left in the competition. Bochevski, Chang, and a huge lummox of a man who, it was rumored, could carry a small horse, should the horse not be able to carry *him.* He had at least fifty pounds on both Chang and Bochevski, and stood six inches taller.

Chang drew the short straw to fight the man, allowing Bochevski to sit out until he faced the bout's winner.

For the first time during the entire day of fighting, Chang lost the smile as the huge man knocked him from his feet. He arose quickly, harboring a great deal of anger. It seemed he'd never been knocked down before.

Like a falcon after a pigeon, Chang seemed to focus all concentration on the huge man. He stalked and dodged with grace belying his size. Every blow he threw landed. Wicked cuts of his rock-hard hands found the man's beefy neck and the sides of his head, and stiff-fingered blows were driven deep into his solar plexus, until blows seemed to fall whenever and wherever Chang willed. The man grasped for Chang, hugging him to ward off the blows, but Chang shook him like a bear shaking an old apple tree, wiggling free, and when at arm's length again, pummeled him with bone-deep blows. Finally, the larger man was driven to his knees. He managed to regain his feet, but Chang threw a straight blow, driving his heavy palm into the man's nose, snapping his head back on the thick neck. His nose was a spigot of blood as he struck the ground with his back. Gamely he tried to regain his feet, but only managed to clamber to his knees.

Chang stood over him, his massive hands resting on his hips, the grin having returned to his broad face, waiting for the man to rise; but it didn't come.

This time dead silence greeted him. No boos, no rocks, no dirt clods. Only seeming disgust. It settled over the crowd like a black wool blanket.

Strobridge called for a half-hour rest period, until Chang had to be back in the ring to meet Bochevski.

While they waited, O'Bannon's curiosity overcame him, and he insisted LuAnn tell him about Chang.

"You seemed to have known Chang before."

She studied O'Bannon for a long moment, then seemed to decide to trust their budding relationship.

"Chang is my friend, although he is the disgraced guard of one of China's mighty warlords. It was Chang who rode at the great lord's right hand, into many battles. Chang trained with China's great war leaders for many years before he came to this position of trust."

O'Bannon was only temporarily satisfied. "Then what brought him to California?"

"Fate. He found himself the subject of the warlord's great displeasure."

"That's not enough, LuAnn. Tell me why he's here."

She glanced away as she spoke. "It is not wise to cuckold the master of the house, no matter how beautiful his concubines, particularly when the master is a powerful warlord . . . when the master has had the ax man separate hundreds of his enemies' heads from their unworthy bodies. Chang was fortunate to escape to the coast, where he could catch a ship to Gum San."

"And then what?"

"He met me on the road, and I gave him shelter and sustenance. As I was also being sought by my master, I well understood his predicament. Chang deemed he had a debt to me, and he helped me find a ship here, a ship he took himself."

"Now I understand. And LuAnn . . . why did she find herself on her way to Gum San?"

She smiled and cut her eyes back to him. "It was certainly not because of cuckolding, O'Bannonboss."

He laughed. "I didn't suspect so." Then his tone became stern, even though it was feigned. "I am Nolan. You will call me Nolan."

"As you wish, O'Bannonboss." She blushed. "Nolanboss."

"No, not Nolanboss, just plain Nolan."

"Thank you, Nolan."

As soon as it was determined who the final fighters would be, Ho had become the busiest man in the crowd, taking bets and recording them, until he could afford no more. A spiker was assigned to him by Bochevski's crew, a constant guard to make sure he didn't abscond with the several hundred dollars in his possession.

Strobridge called for the championship fight, Bochevski against Chang.

Chapter Thirteen

Simon Striker was missing from the festivities.

It wasn't because he didn't enjoy a good row as much as the next man, but because he had business to attend to.

He arrived in Auburn late in the afternoon, about the same time Bochevski was to fight Chang.

The business he was to undertake couldn't be concluded in the daylight, so after he made a careful survey of the town, he decided to while away the afternoon at one of his favorite places—Miss Melissa Dearborn's Ladies Boarding House.

He was not welcome, but neither the girls nor Miss Melissa had to the courage to tell him so.

Chang stood quietly in his corner, the grin again in place.

Bochevski crawled through the ropes to an ovation that echoed throughout the American River Canyon, and it increased to a crescendo as he made a circle of the ring with his big arms raised in feigned triumph, giving Chang a lion's snarl as he passed.

Strobridge directed him to a far corner away from where Chang stood, then raised his arms to quiet the throng. When they had quieted down, he addressed them.

"So far, this has been a good day, except for some lousy, low-life chucking of rocks. Let's keep it that way, so we can have other Sunday activities.

"I'm proud, and Charles Crocker is proud, of the way you men have done your jobs, and attacked this great enterprise. No matter who prevails in this championship match, for the boxing championship of the great Central Pacific, let's celebrate what we all have in common. The iron road, a future iron wedding when we join with the Union Pacific . . . the joining of the country, coast to coast across this great land. And it's you men who will have accomplished it.

"Now, let's see who's the best man."

He was barely able to get out of the ring before they were at each other.

Barrel chest to barrel chest in the center of the ring, blows fell and the sounds, like an ax handle hitting a side of beef, rang over the crowd. The fighting was so intense that even the crowd quieted in wonder.

Chang was backed into a corner with vicious fists; then he in turn backed Bochevski across the ring with chops and kicks.

With Bochevski's back to a corner post, Chang closed until he was snapping elbows to Bochevski's body and head. The Pole wrapped the huge Celestial in a bear hug, then brought a vicious head butt down across the bridge of Chang's nose, and the blood-fountain sprayed across both their chests. Chang spun away, bending low and side-kicking as Bochevski tried to close in for the kill. Then the time was up.

Strobridge had to charge into the ring to separate the men for the few seconds they'd have during the break.

Chang waved Ho over and had him tear some cloth off his trouser legs, then made small wads and shoved them up his nostrils to stem the faucet of blood.

Then he spun back to face Bochevski, and smiled broadly.

Bochevski roared with anger, and again, Strobridge barely managed to get out of the ring.

But Chang feinted as if he was about to flee, then met Bochevski's charge with a wicked kick to the Pole's midsection, Bochevski backed up with wide eyes, then went down. On his knees, he took another kick from Chang, and the crowd went crazy. Strobridge had to charge to the center of the ring and protect Chang from a shower of rocks, and the possibility of worse.

Many of the men in the crowd carried side arms.

Strobridge eyed the screaming crowd, and suddenly thought he'd made a mistake by not banning arms from the match, but no shots rang out, nor were any weapons brandished.

But the crowd quieted when Bochevski regained his feet and managed to stumble back to his corner.

Strobridge chastised Chang for hitting while the other man was down, although O'Bannon was sure the big Celestial had no idea what Strobridge was talking about. Ho moved to Chang's corner and spoke to him in his dialect, interpreting, and the big man nodded in understanding.

Then they were at it again.

Now Bochevski was more cautious, staying at arm's length and showing some skill at boxing rather than the brawling he'd begun the match with.

He managed to avoid some of the Celestial's chops and kicks, and even managed to get in a couple of clumsy kicks himself, before Strobridge again charged into the ring and stopped them for the break before the last interval.

The previous fight, while Bochevski had rested, seemed to have had a great effect on the big Chinaman, and his blows were nowhere nearly as quick and precise as they had been in the early fights—but Bochevski was also gasping in deep breaths, trying to recover for this last effort.

Two of Bochevski's spikers were at his corner, one giving him a swig of stout Monongahela whiskey, even though Strobridge looked on, and the other man, low and through the ropes, passed him something while attempting to conceal it from onlookers.

Bochevski smiled and nodded at his man, and O'Bannon wondered what was going on—and knew he didn't like it, whatever it was.

Again both men charged to the center of the ring, and again Chang drove Bochevski back with chops and kicks until he had him pinned against the corner post.

But a vicious roundhouse right connected with the side of Chang's head. It seemed a strange blow to O'Bannon, as Bochevski had his hand twisted so it struck the Celestial on his balled fist's side, rather than with the knuckles. Chang staggered as O'Bannon jumped to his feet with the rest of the crowd.

Chang reeled to the side, with Bochevski hot after him; another and another of the strange side-slice blows, forehand, then backhand, pounded into the side of Chang's big head, until he crashed to his knees. But Bochevski didn't stop, and he brought a vicious blow down directly to the top of Chang's head, as if he was pounding a spike with a sledge, and the big Celestial's eyes rolled up in his sockets as he collapsed to his side.

This time there were no disparaging screams from the crowd, only cheers.

Bochevski made his way back to his corner as Strobridge charged into the ring to make sure the punishment was over, and the front rows followed suit until the ring was bulging with cheering railroaders.

But O'Bannon didn't charge to the center of the ring; he moved as quickly as he was able to the corner, near where Bochevski was being lifted to the shoulders of his spikers and gandy dancers.

There, lying in the dirt outside the ring, was a short piece of iron pry bar, the length of a man's hand-width. A wicked fistload.

"Cheat!" O'Bannon yelled, but he could not be heard over the cheering, crazed crowd.

He gathered the inch-plus-thick piece of iron up and carried it back to where LuAnn sat.

"The low-life cheated," he told her, holding the chunk of iron for her to inspect.

"What?"

"Bochevski." He again held the heavy fist-load out so she could see it. "He cheated. He used this fist-load to beat Chang senseless. He might have well as struck him with a hammer."

In the ring, Ho was bent over his fallen countryman, trying to keep him from being trampled by the raucous crowd.

Then he was besieged by those who had bet. O'Bannon managed to get through the ropes to Ho's aid.

"Stand back," he commanded. "You'll all get your money."

The men growled and groused, but waited.

O'Bannon waved to a half dozen of his graders, who climbed through the ropes and willingly picked Chang up and got him out of the ring to a patch of grass, then laid him where he could be tended to. It was a good twenty minutes before the crowd began to disperse. The boxers and bosses moved to where the pig was being carved, alongside a huge tub of baked apples, baskets of bread, a huge crock of mustard, and two kegs of San Francisco's finest ale. Strobridge had consented to allow beer in camp for this Sunday only.

O'Bannon and LuAnn made their way back up the slope to the roadbed, and moved slowly back to his tents.

Nolan's jaw was clamped tightly, too tightly to enjoy the roast pig and the company of his non-Celestial compatriots.

He was deeply ashamed of them, and fiercely angry with Anatole Bochevski.

When they reached O'Bannon's tents, he went straight to his cot and collapsed.

The day had been too much for him, in more ways than one.

In the early evening, just after the sun was well down and the bats had begun to replace the birds, LuAnn brought him a plate of food. For the first time since he'd been struck down at the whiskey drummer's camp, he ate with gusto, then promptly fell asleep with the hope that he'd feel like himself the next morning.

Monday morning, and the iron road would have to move on. The westerly foundation of the Long Ravine trestle was complete and it was time to begin construction. Nolan felt well prepared for Long Ravine; after all, rigging a ship was not unlike rigging a bridge. He'd been responsible for the construction of the CP's first engineering feat, the great two-tiered span of the American River, just outside of Sacramento. It was no small task, although it stood only a dozen feet over the river surface, and Long Ravine Bridge would be ten times that high.

* * *

Simon Striker finished with the girls just before midnight. He had only one drink before he left, wanting to have his wits about him.

He swung up into the saddle and headed out of Auburn, making sure to speak to a couple of local merchants who he'd traded with in the past, and who knew him by sight. He continued back toward the roadbed's end, but when he was a mile out of town, he reined his horse off the rail-side road and doubled back.

Just a quarter mile out of Auburn was the CP construction job that would result in a mill to cut ties and trestle stringers. A mill that would result in the CP's no longer needing the able services of Simon Striker and family, as least as Simon had convinced himself.

He dismounted in a grove of sandpaper oaks not fifty paces from the mill, tied his horse to a tree, and settled down to lean against an oak and wait.

He entertained himself with the notion that this night's work would not only result in his own mill producing more and more timber for the CP, but would also result in his being paid a goodly sum for causing a long delay in the road's progress—at least if those highbinders in San Francisco paid up. If not, he knew just how to handle them as well.

The moon set a couple of hours after midnight. He dug a can of coal oil out of his saddlebags and made his way to the dark mill building, constructed of planking with a new wood shake roof just completed. The building itself was basically finished, and the only work left before milling could begin now seemed to be the installation of equipment. A half-dozen or so pieces of equipment were tarped and under the cover of a porch on the building's side, and a few were inside, being installed by millwrights, all of whom were having sweet dreams in town at this hour.

He spread the coal oil alongside the mill building in the construction trash still there, dragged a sulfur head across a strike plate, and dropped it carefully.

The quart of coal oil did not flash, but the flames grew steadily as Simon made his way back to the horse.

He was well down the trackside road when he reined around to watch the flames grow. They reached forty feet into the night sky before some late-night citizen noticed and Striker heard the distant clanging of Auburn's fire bell.

There would be no saving the mill building, and he was sure the equipment would be destroyed also. Equipment that had to survive a six-month voyage around the Horn before it could reach here for any attempt at replacing this night's work.

He whistled as he and the horse plodded their way back to Colfax, where he would spend the night.

The talk of the tiny town the next morning, as Simon took his breakfast at a boardinghouse, was of Ana Bochevski's victory over all the fighters the CP could produce, and particularly of his defeat of the huge heathen Celestial. Simon chuckled to himself. It was good to have partners, and he hoped this one would not begin to believe he was tougher than himself, tougher than Simon Striker.

Simon Striker considered himself as close to indestructible as a man could be, and not only tougher, but cleverer than any he'd come across.

And he'd proved it again last night.

He was due to meet his partner, the toughest man employed by the Central Pacific, after the day's work was over, as he had to settle up with him.

Simon considered it an investment, and one that he'd honor for a while longer.

Nolan awoke to the smell of rice and fruit, and with only a dull aching in the back of his head.

He dressed and got his boots on without feeling like he'd pass out at any minute. It was going to be a much better day.

When he moved to the adjacent tent, LuAnn handed him a plate of food, but the furrow in her pretty, well-plucked brows did not convey anything but deep concern.

He found a timber round and accepted the plate with a smile.

"You're going to spoil me, LuAnn."

"That is my pleasure," she said, but still had no smile for him.

"Why are you here, LuAnn?" he suddenly asked.

"I owe you my life, Nolan."

"I did what any man would do."

"That is of no matter. You saved my life, and we Celestials believe that our life belongs to the one who saved it. I am yours to do with as you may."

He pondered that a moment. He knew of the Oriental belief that a life saved was a life owned, but it was not his belief. Truly, he believed she owed him nothing more than a thank-you.

"LuAnn, your life is your own. I have no claim on it and you will stay here only because it is what you wish to do." She smiled tightly for the first time this morning. "Do you understand?"

"I understand, Nolan. I will stay."

"I can't pay you much. . . ."

"You owe me no pay."

"That's not how it's going to be," he stated with

finality, then dropped the subject. "What's troubling you this morning?"

"Ho just stopped here to inform you that Chang has still not awakened from the blows he received."

"My God, it's been hours."

"It has been more than one half a full day," she said, wringing her hands.

He seemed to study the problem for a moment, then offered her a small smile. "LuAnn, if he doesn't awake before the day's out, then we'll take him to the hospital in Sacramento. Maybe they can do—"

"I fear no one can do anything."

"You may be right, but we'll have to try."

"Nolan!" He heard the shout from someone outside, and set the half-eaten plate aside and walked through the flap. It was James Strobridge, who also looked as if his best dog had died.

"Yes, sir?" Nolan said.

"Some son of a bitch burned our new mill down."

"The hell you say."

"They found an empty quart can of coal oil near the ashes, and boot tracks moving off to a stand of oaks, where a horse had been tied for several hours." He shook his head. "Crocker is mad as a hornet."

"I can understand that."

"He's on his way to San Francisco to contract for more timber. I want you to find that fella Striker and see if he can step up production. He's got some other fella at the bottom of his slide road. You're the only one who's been up to his camp. I'll watch over your crews while you're gone . . . you feel up to it?"

"Of course, if it needs doing, I'll do it."

"I hope this doesn't mean we've got some enemies dead set against the railroad."

"Hell, Boss, we've had that since it was a gleam in Judah's eye. Long before it was a fact." Judah was the engineer who had first found the route over the Sierras, and had died not long afterward. He'd been laughed at and ridiculed, but he'd been right. At least, so far he'd been right. The CP followed his route.

"That's true, but those critics were politicians and such, and these seem to be proving themselves to be men with a purpose, backed by torches and blasting powder." Strobridge sighed deeply, his frustration showing.

Then James Strobridge cut his eyes to the tent. His tone softened. "You still got that Chinese woman with you?"

Nolan had already worried about this coming conversation. He cleared his throat. "She was staying here while she got well."

"She looks well enough to me, and the way the other men were eyeing her, I'd say she looks better than, well . . . in fact damned good . . . to them."

"True, she is well enough, but then I wasn't in such good shape from the rap on the head I took, and she was taking care of me. Said she owed me."

"Well, you just said you're well enough yourself. Isn't that true?"

"Right as rain, or damn near so." He smiled a little sheepishly. "But now I've taken a shine to her."

"We'll have to talk about that, Nolan O'Bannon, but it'll wait until you get back from up on the mountain."

"As you wish," Nolan said, and Strobridge spun on his heel and marched to his horse.

"You want a cup of tea, James, before you ride off?"

Strobridge paused and looked back, exasperated.

"She makes a hell of a good cup of tea," Nolan offered.

"I don't doubt it," Strobridge said, and mounted his bay. "We'll talk on it when you return." He tipped his hat, and O'Bannon waved as he gigged the horse away, then called out behind him.

"Say hello to Mrs. Strobridge for me."

Strobridge reined up and glared at him, without a word. Then again reined away.

When Nolan returned to the tent, LuAnn handed him his unfinished plate.

"Do you desire I warm it?" she asked.

"It's fine," he said, retaking his seat on the timber round.

"Nolan?" she asked, and he looked up.

"Nolan, what is it, 'to take a shine'?"

He laughed, and merely shook his head, dismissing her without a reply, but he was worried about the coming conversation with Strobridge. Not to speak of the fact that he had to climb that damn mountain again.

What would he do if Strobridge insisted he run LuAnn off? He was becoming very attached to her, maybe too much so.

What would he do if he found the same fella at Striker's camp, the fella who said he was no longer working for Striker, but was now working for a whiskey seller? A fella who'd almost caused him to meet his maker, by way of a full whiskey bottle across the pate.

For the first time since he'd come back down the mountain, he remembered the second tendril of smoke rising up out of the woods. A column of smoke that came from a source he hadn't investigated.

That was one of three things he had to accomplish while he was up on the mountain.

He finished his meal, and went to the rear to his

personal tent and recovered his slicker, and wished he had his Colt, but he didn't. He cursed himself for losing it, and the whiskey drummer for stealing it. He felt naked, embarking on this mission without the Colt.

Moving to a corner of the tent, he removed some turf, then dug some soil aside, recovering an Arbuckle's Coffee can he'd buried there. Pocketing some gold coins, he reburied the can.

With some regret he told LuAnn he would not be back until the next day, and said she should find Ho and get him to accompany her to take Chang down the line to Sacramento, if need be. He wrote a railroad pass for both of them, and for their patient, Chang, in case they needed it, and handed LuAnn a pair of shiny ten-dollar gold pieces, which she refused to accept until he threatened to make her move. Reluctantly, she took the money, promising to return the change to him should she have to use any of it.

This time when he went to Jenkin's corrals, the big molly mule was out with a team, grading rail bed. Jenkins fetched him up a long-loined buckskin gelding that looked not only strong but fast, with alert upright ears and eyes continually searching.

"This one walks like the devil's on his tail," Jenkin's advised. "He's surefooted, but not quite as settled as that ol' mule you rode last time. Sit a little light in the saddle with this ol' boy, and watch that he don't step out from under you. You've stayed aboard that ol' brig you used to handle, through many a gale."

Nolan was not encouraged by Jenkin's comparison. But he said nothing.

"This fella should be a lark for the likes of you, Mr. O'Bannon."

Nolan tightened his jaw with worry, but accepted the gelding.

Rather than take the plateau path up the mountainside, Nolan moved to the railhead and waited for the work train to begin its return to Sacramento. He loaded the buckskin into a boxcar, and went to the engine to make a backward ride back down the track in the company of the engineer. Harold Pettibone, the grizzled old railroader, agreed to stop at Auburn long enough to let him unload the horse, rather than the normal short time to merely pick up passengers and small freight. The horse would require the use of a ramp, but the process would only delay them for a few minutes.

Nolan had learned that there was a mining road from Colfax up to a very few miles below Striker's camp, and it was rumored there was a horsebacker's trail from the road on up to the camp itself. If so, it would take a lot less time than feeling his way up the steep American River canyon side, using only game trails.

They made the trip to Auburn in a little under an hour, rather than the eight it would have taken by horseback.

After Nolan led the animal down the ramp and resaddled the buckskin, he made his way straight to Hanaroy's General Merchandise.

Remembering an advertisement he'd seen in the *Sacramento Union* about Hanaroy being an agent for the Sportsman's Emporium in San Francisco, he knew exactly what he was looking for.

A tool for serious work.

Chapter Fourteen

Nolan studied the flyer hanging on Hanaroy's wall while the clerk waited on a tall woman in a faded dress, with a pair of small children behind her, each sporting a shirt sewn from flour sacking. She bargained hard for a few items, then left in a huff after she'd paid the bill.

The clerk walked over to where Nolan stood studying some implements hanging on the wall behind the counter.

"That a Henry?" he asked the man.

"Finest rifle made today, shoots three rounds a minute, and is said to kill at a thousand yards."

"That could get expensive, three rounds a minute," Nolan said. "Lemme take a gander."

The clerk fetched the rifle down and handed it to Nolan, who was immediately in love. It fit his large hands with perfect balance. He worked the lever action and admired the brass cover on the receiver. It truly was a handsome piece of work. "You feed it right here?" he asked, pointing to the bottom of the receiver.

"Load it once and shoot it all week," the clerk said with a grin.

"How much for it and a box of shells?"

"Twenty-seven dollars, and I'll throw in an extra box of shells."

"You're all heart. Advertisement in the *Sacramento Union* said twenty-five dollars."

"That was at the Sportsman's Emporium in San Fran. This is Auburn, and you're a good long ways from San Francisco."

"Then why don't I go to San Fran and save two dollars?" Nolan asked, but knew the answer, as everything cost more in Auburn and Colfax.

"Cost you that much extra to get there, unless you're going there anyways, and they won't throw in no extra box of shells. Shell's ain't cheap."

Hanging below where the Henry had been was another weapon. "How much for the scattergun?"

"It's a steal at seven dollars."

"Get it down, and fetch a box of shells for it."

Nolan left the store some poorer, but a whole lot more prepared. He went straight to the livery and found the proprietor who doubled as a saddle maker. By the time he'd finished getting something to eat, he'd invested three dollars more for a leather saddle scabbard made to fit the Henry and a case for the scattergun that would hold it when broken down, and that could be tied on the back of the saddle.

With some dried meat and fruit in his saddlebags, along with a box partially full and another completely full of Henry shells, and with sixteen loaded in its long magazine, as well as a box of twelve-gauge brass shells loaded with double-aught buck, he started back to the station to await the afternoon work train to the railhead.

He was getting a late start, but he didn't mind getting to Striker's camp well after dark . . . in fact, it might be better that way.

This time he had to talk the engineer into stopping at Colfax, where he'd begin his climb up the mountain.

He asked directions from a local merchant, and was told to look for a needle rock on a point just below the road and to take the last drainage before he reached that rock. A small but well-used trail should take him right to Striker's camp. The road up the mountain had been well graded and at one time had been a toll road, before the placer gold deposits it led to had played out. Now it was covered with low brush, and higher up by a scattering of waist-high sandpaper oaks, then digger and lodgepole pine. In a very few years it would be totally reclaimed by Mother Nature.

He found where the bank above the road had been cut by the continual passing of horses. He reined the buckskin up the slope, and the big horse put his back legs into the task. After they topped the twenty-foot bank, the trail smoothed out and he found himself following a small creek up a continually climbing ravine. Soon, the lodgepole gave way to Jeffery and ponderosa pine, and the brush to low bear's clover. The forest smelled clean and fresh with only spots of snow left, and he suspected the morning had seen a shower. The red shafts of snow flowers poked up through the occasional snow-bank and rotted undergrowth. By the set of the sun, he figured it was late afternoon when he saw a tendril of smoke in the distance.

He had James Strobridge's mission as his first order of business, but he also wanted to find out if the whiskey drummer was part of Striker's crew, and if the second column of smoke he'd seen was what he suspected.

When he figured he was within a hundred yards of the camp, judging by the smoke he could see, he reined off the trail and staked the buckskin in a patch of manzanita.

The buckskin smelled more of his own kind, and whinnied and snorted loudly a few times. In the far distance Nolan heard the sound of a saw blade biting timber. As Nolan was not interested in the Striker camp knowing he was in the neighborhood, he waited until the buckskin quieted down and he was sure no one was coming to investigate, then made his way on foot, carrying the Henry with his pocket full of shells, until he reached a point where he could see the camp and not be seen.

He had only a couple of hours of light left, and he wanted to make good use of it. Unseen, studying the camp, he noted the Indians he'd seen the first time he was there, again at work in the barn. Three Chinese were working the mill, and trestle timbers were being stacked. A tool rack was covered with saws, broad axes, chopping axes, pickaroons, and tie peelers. At least the man was well equipped.

The big dun Striker had been riding while counting timbers at the bottom of the skid road was among the other stock in the corral.

Then Striker and another man came and went between the mill and the cabins, but neither seemed to be the whiskey drummer . . . although they had the same facial shape. Were they all relatives?

A four-up team of mules stood with heads hanging near the mill; in the chain traces behind them a long ponderosa log rested, after having been dragged down the mountain.

O'Bannon slipped away from his spot in the brush and made his way through a blowdown, carefully climbing over and ducking under a tangle of timber, to where he thought the smoke had originated.

He came to a clearing below a trickling spring, where a lean-to sheltered a copper boiler, coils, barrels, and some crates. A low fire, mostly coals, kept the boiler bubbling, and from the end of the copper coil a steady drip fed a hogshead barrel. Nearby was a stack of sack goods. No one seemed to be about, so he walked into the open to investigate. Cases of bottles and corked crocks were haphazardly stacked with sacks of corn.

The same basic quart-sized bottle that the whiskey drummer had used. It seemed no doubt that Striker was the man providing whiskey. The heat rose in O'Bannon's spine, but there was nothing truly illegal about making whiskey. It was a legitimate trade.

Smacking a bottle across his pate was not exactly a legal pastime, however. He wanted the man he'd confronted, and he wanted to find out just who had slipped up behind him and ruined several days of his time.

The second tendril of smoke had been what he imagined it might be.

"Ain't you O'Bannon?" the voice rang out behind him.

Nolan spun with the Henry leveled at the sound, and stood facing Simon Striker, who also had a weapon, a long finely wrought hex-barreled rifle, hanging at his side. It was a beautiful firearm of a type Nolan had never seen.

"You startled me," Nolan said, and lowered the muzzle.

"Came up to feed the boiler fire and check the batch," Striker said, and walked past Nolan as if nothing was wrong. "You lost, O'Bannon? What brings you to Blood Mountain?" Striker asked as he added a few sticks of wood to the low-burning fire under the copper boiler. He stuck his finger under the end of the coil where it dripped into a barrel, until a drop fell upon it and he stuck it in his mouth, then whistled his satisfaction.

"No, not exactly lost. I'm hunting your place."

"Well, you done found it. You alone?"

"Could'a used a guide to find this place, but yes, I'm alone. I need to sit an' jaw with you a spell."

"Something the matter with the timbers I'm deliverin'?" Striker snapped, his tone almost a threat.

"Let's get a cup of coffee at the camp, and jaw a bit," Nolan suggested.

"Suits me," Striker said, calming down. He strode out toward the camp.

Halfway there, he stopped and turned. "You use shank's mare to get up here?"

"No, I tied my horse back down the trail a ways. Wanted to make sure this was your place."

"Humph," Striker said with a doubting glare. "I'll send a man back to fetch your horse. Gettin' late. You'll want to bed down here until morning. There's a good pile of hay under the shed next to the corral." Striker continued into the clearing that housed his buildings.

"That's neighborly of you, but I need to get back."

"Long dark steep trail."

"Buckskin will find his way."

"You come up the hard way, or you take the old road this time?"

"Got smart and took the road up from Colfax."

"Don't imagine you seen a China boy going down the trail?"

"Didn't see another soul."

"Cook ran off . . . owed me some time."

"What's his name? I'll watch for him if he shows up on the CP." *I'll watch for him, all right, so I can question him.*

"Lee Toy. Got a scar where some ol' boy split his lip. This tall"—he held his hand at his chest—"an' fatter 'n most Chinee. Fool ate most all he cooked."

Nolan nodded. *I'll bet someone gave him a scar. I wonder who that might have been.*

The other white man stood on the cabin step as they approached. "O'Bannon, this be my kin, my aunt's boy, Milo Stark."

Nolan was too far away to shake, so he nodded. Milo Stark was an even larger version of Striker, long-limbed and rangy, with a hard whiskered jaw-line and pork-chop sideburns. His eyes were on the golden side, and his stare intense, reminding Nolan of a Cooper's hawk.

Striker snapped at the man as he pointed down the hill. "Go fetch Mr. O'Bannon's mount and give him some oats." Then he turned to Nolan. "Hell, you folks at the CP are good customers, I can spare you some oats."

Big of you, Nolan thought, but kept the thought to himself.

The man called Milo nodded and headed the way Striker had pointed, Striker paced him a few steps and said something to him under his breath. Something Nolan couldn't hear.

"He's just off the trail, back about a hundred paces," Nolan called after Milo, but the man continued on without turning. Then he turned, but headed for the mill. Nolan noted it, but said nothing.

"I'll have to fire up the pot," Striker said, stomping into the cabin. He rested the rifle on a cot, then turned to an iron stove. "What brings you?"

"You down the mountain yesterday?" Nolan asked.

Striker cut his eyes away, then turned a hard eye back to Nolan. "Just came back into camp this morning. Spent the night at Colfax. Had a meetin' there with some folks out of Sacramento City, wantin' to take all my production."

Nolan studied the man carefully. "Then you probably didn't hear."

"Hear what?" Striker asked innocently.

"New CP mill in Auburn burned to the ground last night."

Striker eyed him in turn, seemingly surprised. "That's a hell of a note. At least for the CP. Y'all must have counted on that mill for a good bit of your supply. I presume you'll be needing even more Simon Striker timbers? Hell, what am I gonna tell these other fellas?"

Striker filled a big twelve-cup porcelain coffeepot from a keg of water as he talked. As the water heated he dropped beans into a grinder and cranked away, then added to the pot a couple of fistfuls from the grinder's little drawer.

Nolan shrugged nonchalantly. "Well, that's why I'm here."

"I guess I could step up production, now that the snow's leavin'." Striker smiled tightly. "Course, that'll mean more men and more equipment, so the price will have to be a little more proud. And of course I'll have to tell these other fellas that the CP gets all my timbers."

"How proud?"

"Oh . . . say fifteen cents a foot. That's what the other fellas agreed to pay."

"Hell, you're delivering them for ten cents now."

"That's now, that's not after having to hire me more help and buy more stock, and havin' to tell these other fellas to forget it. Big investment . . . big commitment."

"I'll talk it over with Strobridge and Crocker. I suspect they'll just slow down the road until we can rebuild the mill."

"I doubt that. But talk to 'em. And another of the companies in San Francisco said they'd take ever'thing I could cut in the way of planks, so I need to know real soon."

O'Bannon was sure he was lying. But he couldn't risk it. They had to have Striker's timbers, as it was time to start the Long Ravine trestle, and he had to have it finished, or at least well along, in two weeks. And the fact was, Crocker and Strobridge would pay damn near any price to see it done.

Nolan downed the coffee he'd been handed. "Well, looks to me like you've got another fifty or so trestle timbers stacked out there. How many you got on the slide road?"

"Not a one. They's all been delivered to the bottom."

"Okay, you send down those fifty at a dime a foot, then I'll see you get fifteen cents for another two hundred trestle timbers, then we'll talk again."

"I got those fifty out there sold to the San Francisco fellas," Striker said, obviously having to fight to keep from smiling.

Nolan clamped his jaw so tightly he feared he'd break a tooth, then relaxed enough to reply, "Okay, Striker, you send us the next two hundred fifty at fifteen cents, and I'll see you get your money. But get them down the slide road by tomorrow night."

"Suits me," Striker said.

Nolan really wanted to break the man's prominent beak of a nose, but instead, he smiled tightly and extended his hand.

As Striker took it, Nolan gave him a hard look, and asked, "You not sellin' any whiskey down our way, now are you?"

"Strobridge told me whiskey wasn't allowed in the CP camps. All I sell you folks is timber."

"Good," Nolan said, dropping his hand. "Keep 'em coming. I got to get back down the trail."

He found the buckskin outside the cabin with a nose bag still in place. He jerked it off and hung it from the hitch rail.

Striker stood in the door, smiling like a toad eyeing a horsefly.

Nolan tipped his hat. "Thanks for the coffee and the horse oats."

"Think nothin' of it," Striker said.

Nolan gigged the big buckskin and the animal single-footed out of the camp, found the trail, and Nolan headed him a quarter mile back toward the road before he again reined him off the trail. This time he worked his way up the hill and into the ponderosas. In a new, well-protected spot, he tied the horse and again made his way back to overlook the camp.

When he arrived, another man was in sight. He worked to unhitch the drag chains from the big lodgepole log dragged there by the team of mules, then drove them away back up the mountain.

Nolan was sure, absolutely sure, he was the man who'd acted as the whiskey drummer.

Chapter Fifteen

When the man Striker had introduced as Milo had walked away, Striker had whispered to him and instead of going straight to fetch Nolan's horse, he'd gone to the mill, probably to warn the whiskey drummer to stay out of sight. That meant that Striker was well aware the man had been the one he'd confronted, and that Striker was a part of it.

He wondered if Striker had been the one who'd cracked him across the head with the whiskey bottle.

It was all he could do not to track the man who'd been selling whiskey and beat him to a pulp, but he calmed himself. He knew where the man hung his hat, that he'd lied about not working for Striker, and that Striker was behind the whiskey that kept finding its way into the CP camps.

However, the timbers were far too valuable to the CP at the moment.

Frustrated, angry, Nolan worked his way back to the buckskin and, as the sun settled behind the far mountains between Blood Mountain and Sacramento, gave the horse his head.

He had more important fish to fry at the moment.

The buckskin had a good nose, and a bent for the barn. It was well after midnight when he arrived back in Colfax, but the work train wouldn't arrive until early morning. It was another six miles to his tents, and he wasn't up to it after a trip up and down the mountain. And he could use a good boardinghouse breakfast, and Colfax had one of the best. He found the livery stable, and put the horse up and bedded down in the hayloft.

The hostler was raking out stalls, his morning duty, and the sound awakened Nolan. He paid the man a quarter for the horse and a quarter for the use of the loft.

When the work train arrived, he felt a lot better, having filled his belly with pork chops, eggs, biscuits, and gravy at the local boardinghouse.

Almost two hundred new Chinese employees rode the flatcars. Crocker's agent had been busy. Nolan decided he would have to campaign for a raise for Ho, as his responsibilities were growing geometrically. Soon, Nolan's Chinese crew would be as large as his Irish one.

When they arrived at the rails' end, it was now only a mile from Nolan's tent camp. The rails would reach him in a couple of days at the most. It was time to move his camp past Cape Horn and near his new primary responsibility, the Long Ravine trestle. He needed to be close to his work, and it didn't hurt his feelings to be as far from Ana Bochevski as possible, and that meant being away from the spiking crew. Nolan had plans for Bochevski, but it needed to wait until after the Long Ravine trestle was finished.

Beyond Long Ravine, the road was again fine-graded for almost two miles, and the rail spiking would continue there, but the rails would have to be hauled by teamster and wagon past both Cape Horn and Long Ravine.

He sought Ho out and asked him to find the man Lee Toy, and gave him his description. Ho said if the man was in California, he would be brought before Nolan.

In addition to the Chinese, the train carried two other new CP employees. Haywood Harrowsmith was the chemist Crocker had hired to concoct nitroglycerin. A small thin man with a prominent Adam's apple, Haywood was balding and bug-eyed, but a nice enough fellow. Cooder P. Tolliver was an Eastern-educated engineer. Nolan did not take to him quite like he did to Haywood. Cooder seemed a little mad at the world. It was either because of his name, or the fact that he was short, pudgy, and pig-eyed. Where Haywood had little hair, Cooder had an abundance that stuck out from under his high-crowned, narrow-brimmed hat like a porcupine's quills, and he was dressed in a city suit with a fancy silk cravat. Not Nolan's picture of a man on a construction job.

By the time they'd boarded the train, Tolliver had given Nolan his life story, a life, if Cooder could be believed, that was full of successes and accolades due to his wide in-depth construction expertise and extensive education. And it was a soliloquy. He failed to ask Nolan a single question, other than if he'd attended a place of higher learning. When Nolan said no, Tolliver had merely glared at Nolan as if he was something the dog had left behind.

Tolliver and Harrowsmith rode in the engineer's cab with Nolan and Harold Pettibone, the man responsible for driving the train.

As it turned out, Pettibone and Haywood Harrowsmith were from neighboring towns in England, and had plenty to talk about. Which left Cooder P. Tolliver to converse with Nolan, which he now seemed happy to avoid. In fact, it seemed to Nolan that Cooder felt it was beneath him to engage in a conversation with a mere uneducated division boss. It was just as well, as Nolan was just as happy to watch the country roll by and contemplate his coming construction project. Besides, Cooder had a voice that alternated between cackling hen and crowing rooster, and at the moment seemed happy to keep it to himself by pursing his little mouth and staring out at the country.

At least the obnoxious little man didn't talk *all* the time.

It didn't give Nolan much encouragement as he would have to work side by side with Cooder P. Tolliver for a good long time. Cooder's first job, as he had been happy to point out, would be to oversee the construction on Long Ravine. Nolan hoped he meant oversee the *engineering*. Otherwise, there was some definite head-butting in their future.

He led the cadre of Chinese, Harrowsmith, and Tolliver the last mile on foot, after having returned the buckskin to Jenkins, the hostler, and having stored Harrowsmith's cases of chemicals to await a pack string to take them on up to near Cape Horn.

Nolan had complimented Jenkins on the horse, and come near to bragging that he'd had no problem sitting the animal, even though the buckskin had sidestepped nervously a few times. He'd pitched nowhere nearly as much as a brig in a squall.

With a knowing smile, Jenkins had assured him he hadn't seen the horse's worst.

When they arrived, Nolan was disappointed to

find LuAnn gone, then remembered he'd instructed her to take Chang to Sacramento to the hospital if need be. When he reached the base of Cape Horn he found Ho, who assured him that LuAnn could handle the job all by herself, and that she'd refused to take Ho from his responsibilities just to accompany her. She and the big unconscious Chinaman had gone down on yesterday's afternoon work train, riding an empty flatcar, as Chang had still not stirred. She would find other Chinese to help her get him to the hospital, where the only facilities for him would be in a latticed back porch where the laundry was done. Then, when she had some word on his condition, she'd return.

Strobridge was waiting at Long Ravine when Nolan and Cooder P. Tolliver strode up. Strobridge extended his hand to the little man, who returned the shake. But his greeting was succinct and limp-wristed. Then Tolliver spun on his heel and strode to the edge of the foundation abutment, where the Long Ravine trestle was scheduled to begin.

"This won't do. This just won't do," he mumbled, then turned to Nolan. "Have them tear this down immediately! I want flying buttresses coming back at forty-five-degree angles—"

"Hold on," Strobridge said. "There won't be any redesign of this trestle. It's scheduled to be finished in two weeks."

Cooder P. Tolliver pursed his lips and reddened as if he'd just suffered sunstroke. He began to tremble, then spat out, "I am the engineer here. I am the one who will be blamed for a failure. Get Crocker here immediately."

James Strobridge couldn't help but smile, but turned to hide it. Then he cleared his throat. "Mr. Tolliver, I don't order Mr. Crocker around. If you want to see him, I'd suggest you climb on the afternoon work train and go down to Auburn, where he's overseeing the cleanup on one of our projects—a lumber mill—that burned night before last."

"Fine," Tolliver snapped, then stomped away.

"Don't count on us changing a whole lot," Strobridge called after him. Then he turned to Nolan, shaking his head. "That's the damnedest thing I've ever seen."

"I guess I didn't get his whole name," Nolan said, with a smile.

"What is it?" Strobridge asked.

"Cooder 'P'—for Pompous—Tolliver, emperor of engineers."

"Sounds about right. He'll be less pompous when Crocker gets through with him. Don't slow down, Nolan. Proceed as planned."

"Yes, sir," Nolan said, and did.

It was just after the work train arrived the next morning when Charles Crocker and Cooder P. Tolliver rode up to the Long Ravine project on a pair of horses.

Crocker dismounted, and Tolliver began to, but after being spoken to by Crocker, remained ramrod-straight in the saddle. Nolan kept waiting for him to shove one hand into his lapels, emulating Emperor Napoleon.

Charles Crocker paused long enough to bite the end off, spit it out, and touch a sulfur match to a big cigar, then walked over to where Nolan was directing the setting of the second tier of timbers on the westerly foundation.

"Mr. Crocker," Nolan greeted him, somewhat apprehensively.

"Nolan, seems like you and Mr. Tolliver didn't exactly get on."

"Didn't hardly have time to get on, Mr. Crocker. He took one look at the work, said tear it down, and when I didn't, he got his hackles up and stomped off to find you."

"It's a bit of a problem, Nolan."

"How's that, sir?"

"Collis Potter Huntington, my friend, partner, and a major stockholder in this road, hired Tolliver back in Washington. And for good reason, so it seems. Seems Tolliver's brother-in-law is Farrell Bolton . . . Senator Farrell Bolton from Massachusetts. Which in and of itself is bad enough, but the fact he's the chairman of the railroad committee . . . well, that makes it a lot worse."

One at a time, Nolan pointed to the four massive stoneworks that were the foundations for the Long Ravine trestle. "If we tear these foundations down, we won't even have rebuilt foundations to show in two weeks when your brigade of bigwigs arrives. Rocks and mortar take a lot longer than sticks and bolts and tie rods."

Crocker shook his head in agreement. "Still, we've got to placate Tolliver in some way. Hell, I'd like to send him to Pennsylvania to count spikes when they're out-loaded for us. . . . But I can't. Not yet, at least." He waved Tolliver over.

The man dismounted and approached with a haughty self-satisfied look on his face.

Nolan felt like slapping his prissy mouth, but rather, greeted him, purposefully using his odd first name, and withholding the courtesy of addressing him properly. "Cooder, how are you this morning?"

The little man began to redden again. "I'll be fine if—"

Crocker stopped him with an outstretched hand. "Nolan agrees totally with your assessment." Tolliver looked skeptical, and it was a good thing he couldn't see Nolan roll his eyes. "However," Crocker continued, "we will continue with the work. You will go back to the drawing board and give us some revised plans . . . using the existing design and improving upon it until it satisfies you. We'll continue on the course we're on, then bring it up to your much-improved design after we've finished the original one. I'll personally appreciate your help in this."

"That is unsatisfactory. I can't—"

"It will take a great talent, such as yours," Crocker said, clamping down on the cigar, but laying a meaty paw on the much smaller man's shoulder in a fatherly manner. "I know if anyone can do it, Cooder, it's you. It'll be a great challenge."

"Well, I suppose—"

"Good, then that settles it," Crocker said.

"Still, I'll have to have some input as the project goes along. Connections, spans, such things as that . . ."

"Of course," Crocker said, and Nolan cringed. "You come down and check the work daily. Nolan here will do his best to adjust the project to your suggestions, so long as it doesn't slow the process. Won't you, Nolan?"

Nolan had a knot in his throat, and he almost choked getting the words out, but he said, "Yes, sir. You bet. So long as it doesn't slow the work."

"Then that settles it."

Nolan again cringed as the two rode away. Crocker looked over his shoulder, unseen by Tolliver. Looking sheepish, he shrugged his shoulders.

Sighing deeply, Nolan returned to the work at hand. Then he laughed as they rode out of sight. He'd seen a lot of Crocker, but had never seen him with a political bone in his body, and had certainly never seen him sheepish.

Nolan returned to his tents early, and again was disappointed not to find LuAnn. He brought a couple of teamsters and a wagon with him, as it was moving time. While they were breaking the tents down, James Strobridge rode up.

"You got a good site to move to?" he asked Nolan.

"Not as nice as this, but it'll do."

"I understand Crocker backed Tolliver up?"

Nolan grinned. "In a way, I guess he did. Crocker's a lot more politician than I'd ever given him credit for. I imagine he'll find something productive for the man to do long before he'll be much of a problem at Long Ravine."

"Humph," Strobridge managed. "I hope Crocker finds something . . . something in San Francisco would be just fine. Did you find Striker?"

"I did, and he's going to gear up to ship us all he can produce. However, it's at fifteen cents a foot. It's the best I could do, with him claiming a Sacramento City company would take all—"

"That's fine, Nolan. We won't have to put up with him forever. He's a slimy sort."

"Worse than that, if my guess is right, but I'm not quite ready to talk about it. The fact is, he's got some fair tie hackers, and the product's good. We should have enough timbers for Long Ravine by the end of next week."

"That's all that counts right now," Strobridge said, then added, "Good work."

Nolan acknowledged the compliment with a nod.

Strobridge looked all around, then turned back to Nolan. "The girl's gone?"

"Yes, sir," Nolan said, not mentioning that her absence was temporary, and that a satchel of her personal items lay tucked in a corner of the tent . . . at least he hoped her absence was temporary.

"Good." Strobridge's tone turned fatherly. "You set a bad example for the men, Nolan."

"Oh?" Nolan's tone hardened. "I didn't notice that any of them seemed concerned in the least." Nolan had never been angry with James Strobridge before, but he was on the verge now.

"It was a bad example, Nolan. These men are without women, and you can't hold yourself above your men if you expect them to respect you."

"Oh, and how's Hannah?" Nolan said, his tone a little on the accusing side. He regretted it as soon as he'd said it.

Strobridge reddened. "Hannah's my wife, Nolan. She's not just some woman I moved into my quarters."

Nolan was quiet for a long moment, then turned away. When he turned back, his jaw was knotted and he spoke between his teeth. "I didn't mean that the way it sounded. I have all the respect in the world for Mrs. Strobridge. You know that." He took a deep breath before continuing. "LuAnn needed the help . . . and to be truthful, James, she's not just 'some woman.' And there was nothing untold about her being here. It was a place to stay, safe from the men, and that's it. Ho stayed here most of the time."

"She's a Celestial," Strobridge snapped, still hot even with the apology.

Nolan spun back to his boss, and eyed him angrily. "I've long known how to tell a Celestial from a white woman, James. Right off, I noticed that she was a Celestial. I treated her as a lady, Celestial or not, and she acted like the lady she is."

Strobridge sighed deeply, calming himself. "Well, the important thing is she's gone."

"That's true, she is gone," Nolan agreed.

Strobridge reined away, then gigged the horse into a trot.

"Let's get this done," Nolan snarled at the two teamsters helping him.

So far, it hadn't been his best day.

As they loaded the wagon, Nolan hoped LuAnn would have no trouble finding him and the new tent location when she returned . . . if she returned.

Chapter Sixteen

Simon Striker reined his tall dun gelding carefully down a steep rocky cliff side. The horse stumbled and clattered, tripping and almost losing his footing several times.

Striker leaned far back in the saddle, giving the horse his head, letting him pick his own way. Below them a pristine dead-still mountain lake reflected some barren aspen and pines, and much higher, still-snow-covered peaks on the other side. Now the snow was patterned, like the white on a paint horse. A pair of mule deer does drank of the far side of the lake, saw Striker and the horse, and began to work their way up into a patch of aspens. On the far end of the lake, water-surface diamonds sparkled brightly enough that you had to shade your eyes where the sun announced the clear day.

The lake lay in a large basin with a natural dam of granite boulders created by a huge avalanche, possibly the result of an earthquake. The level of the lake was even higher due to a hundred-foot-long beaver dam that had been built over many, many generations of the little industrious beasts.

It had stood so long that aspen trees sprouted from the bank of aspen limbs impacted with soil.

Occasionally concentric rings dotted the lake where fish fed veraciously on the first real insect hatch of the spring. Occasionally the plop of a jumping fish rang over the basin, and the ripple-rings were more pronounced. As Striker reached the lakeside, a bald eagle passed overhead, a fish flopping in his talons. Nearby, a beaver slapped his tail in warning to others of his kind that an interloper was near at hand.

But Striker noticed none of this.

Striker made his way down the lakeside toward the dam, having to work his way back up the hillside more than one time to skirt thick growths of river willows.

When he reached the beaver dam, he dismounted, tied the dun, and went ahead on foot. The beaver dam was only a half-dozen feet high, but the escarpment upon which the limb construction rested—the boulders now mostly dirt- and brush-covered—was at least twenty-five feet high.

Striker stood on top of the natural dam and looked down at the lake. It was at least a mile long and a half mile at its widest. Even if this was the deepest part at twenty-five feet, it must have retained many, many thousands of acre-feet of water.

And not four or five miles down the small creek that gathered from water spilled over the beaver dam lay Long Ravine and the site of the proposed trestle. Four or five miles as the crow flies, and a thousand or more feet lower in elevation.

Striker estimated it would take four kegs of black powder to do the job right. He could get them down here with a small pack train.

But he would bide his time. He might as well get

a finished product, might as well destroy as many timbers as possible.

A wall of water crashing through the narrow valley below the natural dam would be a thing to see by the time it reached the trestle site. He estimated it could be a wall twenty feet high by the time it reached the trestle site, if he could get all the kegs to detonate at the same time.

A hell of a thing to see.

He'd used fire too many times.

This time, he'd use water.

It didn't take Nolan long to set his camp back up, but he slept the restless sleep of dissatisfaction. He knew the coming job would require the utmost tact and restraint if Cooder P. Tolliver was to be looking over his shoulder.

He was nervous about LuAnn being gone, virtually alone in Sacramento. Whites seemed to think all Celestial women were whores, and would take liberties they'd never take with a white woman, knowing there'd be little or no punishment for their actions.

After he was settled and had taken his supper, he filled his pipe and sat on one of the new timber rounds he'd had sawn. The night was sharp with chill, but not so much that he was uncomfortable in his shirt sleeves.

He had constructed a small fire ring outside the tent, and built enough of a fire so as not to waste wood, but enough to provide a little warmth. A crackling fire warmed the soul, if not the body, and his soul seemed to be in need of some warmth at the moment.

At this high elevation, the stars shone brilliantly, the Milky Way a virtual slash of light. Busily Nolan studied the constellations—he needed to keep busy—trying to determine how many stars and planets he could name, an old habit from his days at sea when the stars led the way, when Ho sauntered up.

Nolan smiled and waved him to take a seat. "You want a smoke, a chaw, or a sip of the Irish?" Nolan asked, happy to have the company.

"A smoke would be good."

Nolan disappeared into the tent and reappeared with the makings, and handed them to Ho, who took a seat on another timber round.

"LuAnn is gone?" Nolan asked the obvious.

"At your suggestion, O'Bannonboss, she took Chang to Sacramento."

"I hoped you'd be going with her," Nolan said, unable to keep a tone of accusation out of his voice.

"She would not have it. She would not allow me to leave the Horn."

"She is strong-willed."

Ho smiled. "That is so."

They sat in silence for a moment, drawing on their smokes. Finally, Nolan glanced at him.

"What made LuAnn take the identity of a man?"

"I asked Chang the same question," Ho admitted.

"And?"

"She came here as we all did, in hopes of finding something better than we had in China. In hopes of returning to China with some wealth, to care for ourselves and for those near to us."

"And the man thing?"

"When Lu Ang arrived, unlike she had been led to believe, she was taken directly to the barracoon in San Francisco. You know of the barracoon, O'Bannonboss?"

"I've heard something about them. They have done away with them now, haven't they."

"Yes. When the white ladies of San Francisco

learned of the practice, they demanded the politicians shut them down, and they did so. But that was many months after Lu Ang arrived."

Nolan took another long draw on his pipe before he continued his questioning.

"I understand the women there were auctioned off, like horses or cattle. Supposedly sold into servitude to pay for their passage, but as I understand, most were made prostitutes."

"Yes, concubines of the lowest order. Mostly to Chinese men, but some to white devils. Many of them ended up with the rotting brain death."

"So LuAnn was sold?"

"Not so. Before that could be done, Lu Ang escaped. The women were kept locked up, but they had Lu Ang on kitchen duty, bringing food to the others. The night before the auction of that group of women, dressed as a cleaning boy, she was able to leave without discovery. She ran from the place with her things in a laundry bag, hid on a lighter, and found herself in Sacramento. She is tall, and could pass easily, and no one knew her, so she continued to work as a man. She had to tolerate the occasional slap and kick, as all Celestials do, but she would, at least, not be raped."

Again Nolan was quiet for a moment. "So what made her leave China?"

"She was the third daughter in a house of ten children. She had little future there, other than being sold to slavery should the family come upon hard times, or sold for a sum to a man needing a wife or even concubine. It was lucky for her that she wasn't drowned as an infant, for girl children are of little value. As Lu Ang became more and more beautiful, her father negotiated her fate with an interested man of property, a wealthy man, who had many wives. But, as you say, she is strong of will, and Lu Ang decided she did not wish to be the sixth or seventh wife of any man, and she fled in the night."

"And LuAnn and Chang?"

"Merely compatriots. Birds of a feather if you will, as Chang was also escaping China, and his past." Ho took a long drag on his cigarette. "Mr. Strobridge inquired as to Lu Ang this day."

"And you told him?"

"I told him I knew nothing of her, or her relationship with you, since I left your tent. He continued to question, and I continued to answer the same."

"Thank you, Ho. It's no one's business but LuAnn's and mine. And for your information, our relationship is the same as it was when you were staying here."

"Ah," he said, his expression Chinese-inscrutable.

They both sat and smoked until their tobacco was used up, then each found his way to his bunk.

LuAnn was smiling.

Chang had come around enough to squeeze her hand when she'd called his name, then to choke down some broth.

Even though the hospital had been much too full to accept Chang, LuAnn had managed to find him a place under a weeping willow tree at the rear of the brick edifice. She managed to find a piece of well-vented scrap canvas, and with the help of a Celestial washerwoman, repaired the holes and rigged it in the tree so it would provide some shelter should it rain.

When the hospital administrator discovered his new patient, LuAnn managed to negotiate Chang's stay, for a nominal sum, with the provision that one of the hospital doctors would deign to look in on him at least once a day, and that he would be provided with linens and blankets, and broth at least twice a day.

The washerwoman also agreed to care for Chang, feeding him at least twice daily, and making sure he had blankets and clean bedclothes. Now that he was eating, he would be more of a problem, and a bedpan and its attendance would be necessary.

After the hospital care was arranged, LuAnn made a trip to Sacramento City's Chinatown to accomplish three chores, all of which she found to be pleasurable. A Chinese herbalist was employed to call on Chang daily, and to treat him as he thought necessary. Even though Nolan trusted the white-devil doctors, she did not, and she hoped the Celestial would repair any damage done by the white-coated ones.

The second chore took much longer and much more negotiation, and required her to employ a young Celestial to carry the resulting large package to the railroad station.

The third was to visit a number of Chinese groceries, to find some special treats for Nolan O'Bannon-boss.

When she returned to the hospital's rear yard, Chang was awake, if weak and in great pain, and she was greatly encouraged.

She stayed with him until it was time to catch the late train to Colfax, where she would find shelter and await the morning work train.

She had worn her male clothes and confining breast-wrap to make the journey, then had done her hair, and makeup, and changed into her green silk once it became necessary to negotiate with the males of Sacramento, then had re-strapped her generous bustline and re-donned her ragged work clothes and removed her makeup—in fact she had smeared some dirt smudges on her face—for the return trip.

She used her pass, which was readily accepted, and was able to ride in the rear of a passenger car as it was less than half full and no white devil would require her seat.

Simon Striker, with his youngest brother, Efren, stepped off the boat onto San Francisco's quay, just as the sun topped the Oakland hills across the bay. It was time to collect from the two companies he felt owed him at least five hundred dollars apiece.

He'd brought Efren as he didn't want him to have a run-in with Nolan O'Bannon. He'd managed to keep him hidden the last time O'Bannon had visited the camp. When it was time to set up shop again, which would be soon, Efren would again become a whiskey drummer, but until then, why ask for trouble?

He wouldn't ask for trouble, but he would be prepared for it. He wore a revolver strapped to the right side of his hip, and a scabbard holding his Arkansas toothpick on the left side. The knife hung its full fifteen inches, reaching almost to his knee. And Efren carried older brother Simon's fine Whitworth .45-caliber long-range rifle.

Efren was there not only to avoid running into O'Bannon. Simon considered that he might need some backup in this effort, just in case these two city boys tried to welsh on him again.

This time he brought proof, copies of articles published in the *Sacramento Union* and the *Auburn Register* regarding the mill fire. Both of which mentioned that it was a serious setback for the CP, and that the equipment would take months to replace.

If they hurried, they'd have time for breakfast

and still be able to catch that fat city dandy on his way into his fancy office.

This time, Striker would take no excuses.

They found a pushcart vendor across California Street from the three-story offices of the Northern Currents Ice Company. The German tending the cart offered hardboiled eggs as well as fat German sausages. There was also a large pan of strudel. The strudel, the German claimed, was the best on this side of the Mississippi, and his wife had made it fresh in the early morning hours.

Juston Wellington rounded the corner, coming from a business breakfast, and from the opposite direction he'd come from the last time Striker had accosted him on the street. He saw Striker, watching the other way, shoving a fat sausage into his mouth near a pushcart across California Street was from his office.

He'd decided, after the last meeting with the crazed Striker, that the company had made a bad and dangerous bargain with the man and it had to be ended. He was willing to pay something, and had set a limit in his mind.

Wellington spun on his heel and made his way down a side street to where a copper, in a black uniform with a high helmet with the narrowest of brims, leaned against a coal-oil street lamp, swinging his nightstick with one hand, polishing his copper badge with the other, watching the morning traffic of drays and buggies. Colin Farrigan, the cop, was well known to Wellington, as he was often seen sauntering down California Street.

Juston, a good friend and supporter of the mayor and the chief of police, spent a few minutes informing Farrigan that the last time Striker had been outside his office, he'd been accosted by him. Striker, he said, was a madman who thought the Northern Currents Ice Company owed him money.

Wellington made arrangements with the brawny cop for what he was sure was a coming confrontation with Striker. Before he continued back toward his office, he pressed a two-dollar gold piece in the man's large palm.

The Striker brothers barely got through an egg and a sausage apiece, and would miss the strudel as Simon happened to glance back the other way on the street and spotted the dandy, Juston Wellington, strolling briskly, tapping his walking stick on the raised boardwalk. Simon threw his remaining chunk of sausage into the gutter, and quickly told Efren to wait on this side of the street, unless he saw there was trouble.

When Wellington was slightly more than a street width from his office, Simon started across the cobblestones to intercept him.

Striker reached the door to the office building just before Wellington did. This time, to Striker's surprise and encouragement, Wellington had a broad smile on his face.

"Good morning, Mr. Striker," Juston Wellington said, extending a fat hand.

Striker shook, eyeing the rotund city businessman with suspicion. Then he decided to make the best of it. "Wellington, have you seen the papers?" He pulled both newspapers from his back pocket and offered them to Wellington.

"I read the newspapers daily, Mr. Striker. What in there is of interest to me?"

"The mill. I burned down the damned mill, and caused a several-month delay to the CP. You owe me a hell of a pile of money."

"Oh, do I?" Wellington said, not losing the smile. "Well, you may have delayed them a week or so, and that would be, let me see, twenty dollars times seven, or one hundred and forty dollars.

Would you accept one hundred dollars, in gold of course, and consider our agreement terminated?"

Striker began to redden, and angled his shoulders forward as he rested his hand on the butt of the revolver strapped to his hip. "Read the articles, Wellington. I figure you owe me at least five hundred dollars, and that will be just a first installment, depending on when the CP gets back into business."

"Don't be insane, man. I'm canceling our agreement. I'm offering you good hard cash, here and now. You'd be a fool—"

Chapter Seventeen

Being called a fool was just too much for Striker, and he jerked the revolver and shoved it under Wellington's nose. The man's eyes flared wide, his mottled red face went white, and he looked as if he was about to faint.

Just as Simon began to tell him what was going to happen to him, and to the Northern Currents Ice Company, if he didn't pay up, he found himself suddenly on his hands and knees, his head swimming. He turned to see who'd attacked him from the rear, and saw it was a copper, as another blow caught him across the eye and he sank to his belly tasting the cobblestones.

His gun hand was stomped on, and pain shot through him as the revolver clattered away. He felt the knife being wrenched from his scabbard, and managed to direct a desperate look across the street to where his brother was. . . . Where his brother stood like a grazing mule, voraciously eating another sausage, at the same time hungrily eyeing a generous-hipped woman walking nearby.

Striker managed to struggle to his knees, and had to make a decision. Would he climb up and knock this copper out, and throttle Wellington, or would he use his head and get out of this gracefully? For the first time in his life, he had much to lose, and there were one hell of a lot of San Francisco coppers. In fact, he could see two more strolling down California Street, headed their way.

He extended his hands, palms out to the copper, as a trickle of blood wormed its way down his face from a gash under his eye. "Hey, what's the problem here? This is a friendly business disagreement."

"The hell it is," the copper said. "Mr. Wellington said you'd be a troublemaker. We don't abide troublemakers in San Francisco."

Striker, still on his knees, glanced at Wellington, who had a revolting smug look on his fat face. Striker decided right then that he would get out of this, and when he did so, he would butcher this pig Wellington.

To his surprise, the copper clasped wrist irons on Striker's extended wrists. "You need to cool off for a few days, then see the judge, and you'll find out what it costs to affront our good citizens."

With his hand grasping the short chain between the wrist irons, the copper jerked Simon to his feet. Out of the corner of his eye, Simon sensed some movement across the street. He turned to see that his ignorant brother had finally bothered to notice what was happening. He was raising the Whitmore, and it appeared he planned to vent the copper's big chest.

Striker violently shook his head no, no, and his brother lowered the muzzle and stared quizzically.

The copper did not see Efren, only saw Striker shaking his head no. "What the hell do you mean, shaking your ugly head at me? I said you was going to the hoosegow, and that's where you'll be a-goin'." As he finished speaking, the other two coppers stopped a few feet from them, and eyed the confrontation, seemingly satisfied that their comrade had everything under control.

"I didn't mean anything by it. Can I speak to my brother first?"

The copper looked across the street where Striker was motioning with his head, then paled. "He the one with the long gun?" the copper said, seeing Efren for the first time, with none of the three coppers carrying anything other than a nightstick.

"He'll cause you no trouble, sir," Striker said, managing to sound civil and convincing.

"Yell at him to leave the long gun over there."

Striker did so, and Efren left the Whitmore in the custody of the German with the pushcart, then hurried across the street, dodging a dray loaded with lumber.

He stopped five feet from them, resembling a whipped dog with fear in his eyes, and certainly offering no threat. Farrigan stood slapping his nightstick in his hand, glaring at Efren. What Farrigan didn't know was that Efren didn't fear him in the least, but rather feared what was going to happen to him for letting his brother down.

But Simon spoke quietly to him. "Get back to Sacramento and the CP office and tell Crocker that I'm in the San Francisco jail, on a phony charge, and if he wants timbers, he'll be getting me out. Until I'm out, no timbers. Then get up to the camp and stop the ties and stringers from going down the slide road . . . until I get there. Understand?"

"Yessir," Efren said. "You want I should—"

"You should get your dumb ass to Sacramento and find Crocker. If you can't find him, go on up the line and find Strobridge, or at least O'Bannon. Tell them as long as I'm in San Francisco, no timbers."

"Yessir." Efren ran back across the street, causing a buggy horse to panic and rear and step back, and the driver to scream an obscenity at him. Recovering the Whitworth, he left at a trot for the quay as the copper dragged Simon away, and as Wellington smugly climbed the stairs to the double doors of the Northern Currents Ice Company's plush office.

Wellington smiled as he entered. He'd delayed the CP at no cost to the company, and ridded himself of the crazed Striker.

With the knot on his head and the eye that would soon be swollen shut, he imagined Striker would be happy to hurry out of San Francisco, never to be seen again.

Nolan returned to his tents at the lunch break, and was surprised to see the canvas floor cover that normally was in his private tent spread in the front tent, where there had only been a dirt floor.

Investigating his private tent, he was even more astounded to find it spread with a fine Oriental carpet. Many of the old California dons had beautiful haciendas with dirt floors covered with fine Oriental carpets.

Suspecting who his benefactor might be, he walked back outside, and met LuAnn returning from the creek with a bucket of water.

"How's Chang?" Nolan asked.

"Chang has awakened. Doctor say he will be fine."

"I see I'm living in high style. Did you bring the carpet back?"

She smiled, hoping she had pleased him. "Yes, I hope it pleasures you?"

"It's beautiful. . . ."

"It will be easy on bare feet, and much easier to keep clean."

"LuAnn, I'm glad you're back, and glad you're okay."

"Thank you, O'Bannonboss."

"Nolan."

"Thank you, Nolan. You have eaten?"

"Yes, I stopped at the cook tent."

"I will have your supper at day's end. I brought something special."

"Good. You didn't need—"

"Aw, but I did. Here." She held out her hand, closed.

He offered his palm, and she dropped the two ten-dollar gold pieces in it.

"Wait. You spent money on the carpet, and on food, and leaving Chang at the hospital must have cost something."

"I had my earnings," she said, bowing demurely.

"Nonsense," he snapped. "You take this money."

"It is not necessary."

Exasperated, he dropped his voice an octave. "LuAnn, you will take money to keep this poor excuse for a household running. You are to keep your earnings, and are not to spend another penny of your money. Do you understand?"

"I understand. As you wish." She bowed her head, keeping her eyes down.

"It is my wish. I'll see you at the end of the day."

He returned to check the progress on Cape Horn, then went on to where timbers were beginning to rise in the two soon-to-be-a-hundred-foot-tall towers that would support the Long Ravine Bridge.

It wasn't long before Strobridge appeared, and waved him away from where he was showing a group of men how to tie a clove hitch in order to join two hoisting lines.

"What's up?" Nolan asked.

"Your Celestial lady is back." Strobridge accosted him with hard eyes.

"Yes, she's back."

"You plan to have her stay?"

"If she wishes."

"You can't do that, Nolan."

"Are you telling me I can't work this job if I have a helper hired for my personal work. Celestials do extra work for many of the men."

"Those are Celestials that work on the CP also, and yes, they do laundry and such. They are men, Nolan, in case you haven't noticed."

"I noticed that LuAnn wasn't a man, James. Even though she did a good job imitating one. And she was welcome here when she did."

Strobridge ignored the comment. "It's distracting to the men for you to have a beautiful young woman sharing your tents—a woman who's not your wife—not that I'd allow you to have your wife up in these rough conditions."

Nolan had given a lot of thought to this anticipated confrontation, and this time did not get angry. Instead, he negotiated. "James, do you think I do a good job for the CP?"

"You do a great job, and you know that, Nolan."

"So I'm a valued employee, is that fair to say?"

"That's fair to say, but I still can't have—"

"The other bosses live a good ways from their jobs. Hell, most of them are billeted in tents down near the main cook's car."

"That's true."

"Then how about I move my tents well out of sight of the men, say as far as a half mile back in the woods, so the men don't see LuAnn . . . ever."

Strobridge studied that proposal in silence for a moment. "It would be better if—"

"If I quit?"

He was risking angering Strobridge, and knew that no single man was above being fired, from this or any other construction job. Nolan truly wanted to reach an agreement amiable to both himself and the CP.

"I don't want you to quit, Nolan. If this is such a big thing to you, why don't you move her back to Colfax or Auburn?"

"I can't do my job running back and forth to Colfax, James."

"And she means that much to you?"

"She means a lot, James. I'll relocate my tents tonight."

Strobridge sighed deeply. "All right, Nolan. But if I hear of any trouble that results from you having this girl—"

"You won't, James. My word on it."

Strobridge extended his hand and they shook. "Your word is good enough for me, Nolan," he said, but his look was still questioning.

That night, as soon at they finished the excellent pressed duck LuAnn had prepared, they moved the camp three eights of a mile up the Long Ravine Creek, to a spot as beautiful as any Nolan had seen in the Sierras. The creek dropped away to an excellent view of the mountains to the north across the American River Canyon, and great granite mountains rose to the south. It was a spot that couldn't be seen from the Long Ravine Bridge until it had risen its 120 feet.

Nolan had heard there was a beautiful lake not too many miles up the creek. He decided that in a week or two, on a Sunday, after the Long Ravine Bridge was complete, he'd get a couple of gentle horses from Jenkins and take LuAnn to see the lake, and teach her how to fish.

He liked this private spot, and was actually glad

Strobridge had taken umbrage at LuAnn being in sight of the men.

She was much better off here.

Much safer here.

Chapter Eighteen

San Francisco Chief of Police Tobin Brannigan was a little surprised to have a telegram on his desk when he got to work. The telegram was from one of California's most prominent citizens, and most successful businessmen, Charles Crocker.

> Please release Simon Striker immediately. He is critical to the success of the CP's operations. I will guarantee his bail, up to five hundred dollars.
>
> Charles Crocker
> Superintendent
> The Central Pacific Railroad

Simon was on the street even before the inmates had been served their breakfast, before the sun was over the Oakland Hills.

Efren Striker awaited him, having made his trip to Sacramento, found Crocker, and returned—a trip that took all day and night. He was fast asleep on the jail steps. Out of deference to a comment made to him by a San Francisco copper, he had wrapped the Whitmore and its accoutrements in a blanket, keeping it out of sight of the general populace.

Simon gave him a hard kick between the shoulder blades, rolling him down a step or two. He scrambled to his feet, rubbing his eyes with one hand and his shoulder with the other.

"I did like you said, Simon," he managed to sputter, then stumbled along behind Simon as he strode off.

The head jailer, at the chief's instruction, had advised Striker that he should seek transportation out of the City of San Francisco with all due haste, as he was no longer welcome there.

Their trek down to the quay took them to within a block of California Street.

Simon turned to his brother, to whom he had barely said a word since they'd left the jail.

"Efren, you get right back to Colfax and get back up to the mill."

"Where you off to, Simon?" his brother asked.

"Not for you to know. You do as I say." He jerked the blanket-wrapped Whitmore out of his brother's hands, and spun on his heel and headed toward California Street.

A block from the Northern Currents Ice Company on the downhill corner, the Regal English Hotel rose in four-story splendor. Simon strode in and had to bang several times on the desk bell before the night man showed up.

"I want a room, street side, up top somewheres."

The desk clerk eyed him with disdain—unshaven, ruffled, in canvas pants and linsey-woolsey shirt, he wasn't the Regal's typical guest. "I believe we are full up."

Simon pushed a five-dollar gold piece across the counter. "Mister, you can take this five-dollar gold piece and keep the change as a tip, and get me the room I just tolt you about, or I can slap you into next week, then drag you out into the street and push your ugly face into a pile of horse dung. Your choice.''

Without speaking, the clerk quickly grabbed the register and spun the book around for Simon's signature. Simon signed "X" then held out his hand for the key. The tip would be more than the cost of the room, and the last thing the clerk wanted was trouble from this rough lout who filled the doorway with his bulk.

"320," was all the clerk could manage; then he held the key well above Simon's open palm, and dropped it in.

"If'n it don't satisfy me, I'll be back to trade," Simon growled, then went to the stairway and began his climb, toting the long gun wrapped in a blanket as his only luggage.

When he got into the room, he went straight to the fine counterweighted casement window, shoved aside the green damask draperies, and raised it. As he suspected, he had a perfect view of the front stairway of the Northern Currents Ice Company.

He wiped the rifle down, reloaded it, pulled up a ladder-back chair, and sat, laid the muzzle on the sill, and waited.

Trying to pass the time, he kept adjusting and readjusting the elevated sights. It appeared to him to be 250 yards or so, which was no challenge for this rifle.

The jail had not offered the best sleeping accommodations, and the noise of drunks arriving at all hours meant he'd been awakened every few minutes. His eyes kept trying to close. When he saw the fat city dandy, he'd almost reached the office steps.

Striker was awake in less than a heartbeat, and had the rifle zeroed in on Wellington's chest as he strolled the last few feet to the granite stairway.

Expelling a breath, and holding it, he carefully squeezed, the rifle bucked, and the big .45-caliber bullet slammed into the fat man's chest.

There was no kicking and withering; the man was blown to his back on the boardwalk, his arms and legs splayed.

Bet you ain't got no shit-eatin' grin on yer ugly puss now, Striker thought as he rewrapped the long gun.

He made his way to the rear stairway, with only one hotel guest peeking through a two-inch crack between door and jamb.

It was several blocks to the quay, where he would get a mug of coffee and some sweetbread, then catch a steam flatboat for the climb back up to Sacramento, where he could catch the train to Colfax.

The next week went smoothly, with the two towers of the Long Ravine Bridge rising nicely, bents and cross-bracing climbing skyward. They hadn't lost a day due to the lack of timber supply, even though the Striker boys had failed to ship for over two days. They'd had enough stockpiled to see them through. And thanks be to God, they hadn't lost a man, even though the towers had now reached the seventy-five-foot mark. The engineer, Cooder Tolliver, had pestered Nolan somewhat, but then again, he'd actually come up with some decent suggestions. He seemed content to spend most of his time in a small office Crocker had provided him, far back down the track in a corner of the Auburn station, madly redesigning the Long Ravine Bridge, convinced it would be remodeled the instant it was finished.

Strobridge seemed content with the fact that LuAnn was not in view of the men—out of sight, out of mind.

Nolan was as content as he'd ever been, with LuAnn satisfied to keep house and cook. However, her sleeping in the front tent, with him in the rear, was beginning to wear upon him. His pressing manhood had almost overcome his good sense on more than one occasion, but rather than rock the boat, he'd restrained himself from making any advances whatsoever. She was very discreet, keeping herself well covered whenever he was near, except for that maddening slit in her skirts, and bathing in the bubbling brook only during the time he was gone.

He had been concerned about her safety, and had taught her to use both the Henry and the scattergun. Nolan was concerned about not only the stray bear or cougar, but the worse danger, the stray Irishman. He left her with the scattergun, but carried the Henry when he went to work, hoping to see the stray deer down in the creek bottom. He'd seen a few, but they were all young does, and he would only take an old barren doe or a young buck, which he'd much prefer, and it was hard to tell the young bucks from the does, as their horns were little more than nubbins this early.

The bears were out of their dens, and were occasionally sighted high up on the mountainside, feeding on the spring tubers near the snow line, leaving great swaths of uprooted soil in their path. So far, Nolan had seen only black bears, although it was rumored there were plenty of California's famous grizzlies about. And he worried that they would soon come down to the creek to fish.

But all in all, the time was an idyllic one.

He had also taught LuAnn how to fish, and what some of the edible plants were, suspecting that she knew more of them than he. The occasional beaver pond on the creek offered great fishing, and more than once he'd had fresh trout, steamed, or fried in bacon grease, or boned and in a broth of green vegetables and dried mushrooms. The only wild thing growing this early was diminutive miner's lettuce, but before long wild onions would dot the few small meadows the Long Ravine Creek canyon bottom offered. Mushrooms would begin to sprout after the spring rains, but Nolan was not confident enough in his knowledge to try them.

Knowing LuAnn as he did, he was sure she'd have some method of testing their safety.

Their only visitor had been Ho, who'd come for dinner more than once, and of course, no females had come, but LuAnn, too, seemed content beyond reason.

During the day, LuAnn wore her man's clothing, but long before he returned for supper, she was cleaned up and clad in one of her silk dresses.

The rail reached Cape Horn, and had skipped it and Long Ravine, and Bochevski and his spikers were beginning again on the far side. They would be able to come back by week's end, and lay a good portion of Cape Horn, if things kept progressing as they were.

Each day teamsters worked their way down a narrow road to the ravine's bottom, then 250 yards across its bottom and back up to the graded roadbed. Their six-up mule wagons were loaded with rail, ties, spikes, bolts, splice bars, and bolts, nuts, and washers seemingly without end. The hauling was tedious hard work, and Nolan was glad he was on the trestle. And each day droves of men from his crews, mostly graders, passed the location of the growing trestle. As did the spikers and tie setters, and their boss, Bochevski.

Another one hundred Chinese had arrived to work the road, and Nolan had sensed some growing discontent among the Irish. A hundred or two among the five thousand was one thing, but now the number of Celestials was approaching one thousand, and there was no sign of the yellow flood stopping. Nolan also sensed some growing jealousy among the other division bosses. He now had two thousand men under his direction, compared to no more than a thousand for each of the other bosses, although they all earned the same wages. Of course, one thousand of his men were Celestials.

He'd not seen Bochevski since the boxing match, and it was just as well so far as he was concerned. Nolan's life was going so smoothly, he was looking for no trouble to smudge it.

Saturday morning, he awoke with a queasy feeling in his stomach. Maybe things were going too well? He left the tents without taking breakfast, much to LuAnn's chagrin, only enjoying a cup of her fine tea.

When he arrived at the bridge site, the Henry in hand, only a few men were on the job. A crew of surveyors was setting up on the west abutment, so Nolan climbed up to jaw with them. He'd requested that they come to make sure his growing towers were properly aligned, a job easily accomplished with their transits and levels.

One of them was Alec Flynn, the man he'd found drunk and who had ferreted out the location of the whiskey drummer as retribution. The morning sickness was growing again among the men, and Nolan feared the whiskey drummer was back at it. He waved Flynn away from his crew.

"How's it going, Alec?"

"Fine, sir. I want to thank you again for letting me keep this job."

"No problem. That's not what I called you aside for. It looks to me like we've got another drummer at work . . . or possibly the same one."

"I'm a teetotaler, Mr. O'Bannon, so I wouldn't know. I haven't touched a drop since that day. . . ."

"Well, Alec, I'm proud of you. We'd all be better off without the demon drink."

Nolan patted him on the back and started away as his erection crews were beginning to arrive.

"Mr. O'Bannon." Alec Flynn stopped him.

"Yes."

Flynn seemed to search for words, then finally just spat it out. "I was surprised that you never went after Bochevski for what he did."

"To Chang, you mean?"

"Who's Chang?" Flynn asked.

"The Celestial fighter Bochevski used the fist-load on."

"No, no, not that . . . for whacking you up aside the head with that whiskey bottle. That was no way for a man—"

"What do you mean? Do you mean it was Bochevski . . . Bochevski who hit me down at the whiskey drummer's?"

Chapter Nineteen

Nolan stared at Flynn.

He'd never suspected that it was Bochevski who'd damn near killed him with a whiskey bottle across the head.

Damn near killed him.

"I thought you knew, you were lookin' right at him . . . or so I thought."

Nolan studied Flynn a moment. "I left you back up on the road and you were goin' back to your camp."

"Actually, I just walked a little way, then decided I wanted to see what was happening, so I worked my way back down through the woods, slipped up on y'all, and watched from a hideout spot."

"And what did you see?" Nolan demanded, the heat beginning to rise in his spine.

"You runned the men off and pulled down on the drummer when he sassed you, and he went to bustin' bottles. Bochevski was back in that patch of willows near where the drummer was set up. He slipped up behind you, but you turned on him, and he whacked you a good one; then he gave you a kick to the ribs when you was down. They loaded up the whiskey—"

"They? You mean Bochevski helped the man load up and get out of there?"

"Sure as St. Patrick drove the serpents out of Ireland. Bochevski helped load the mules; then he picked up your revolver and stuffed it in his belt; then he strode out of there just like he was cock of the walk."

"You mean it was Bochevski who took my Colt."

"Yes, sir. Swear on me sainted ma's grave."

"That rotten son of a bitch."

"Always seemed that way to me," Flynn said with a hint of a smile.

Again, Nolan seemed lost in thought. Then he laid a big hand on Flynn's shoulder. "Thanks, Alec. I had no idea it was Bochevski. As much as I disliked him, I had no idea he was a thief as well as a rotten bastard. You won't have to wonder for long why I didn't go after him."

Nolan again started to stride away, the flash of anger now settled into the base of his skull as a seething smoldering heat. Then he stopped and turned back again. "Flynn."

"Yes, sir."

"Keep this to yourself. I didn't know Bochevski was behind me, and fair is as fair does. I don't want him to know I'm comin'."

"Yes, sir."

Nolan strode away, a man with new purpose. He had been purposely avoiding a confrontation with Anatole Bochevski. Now it was foremost in his mind.

There are just some things a man's gotta do, no matter how comfortable he's been.

When he got back to the base of his towers, a man whom he'd never met awaited him.

The tall, lanky man wore a tin star, and extended

a rawboned hand. "You're O'Bannon, I'm Toby Chester. Sheriff Toby Chester, from down Auburn way."

"What can I do for you, Sheriff?"

"You know a fella named Striker? Got a mill up the mountain."

"Sure I know him. He provides us with ties and, in fact, he cut these bents and stringers you're lookin' at."

"Well, the police chief over in San Francisco sure wants to have a talk with him. And I got to wonderin' if ol' Striker don't seem to be the one with the most to gain from that mill fire you folks had. And he was around when another fire or two happened. I wouldn't mind having a chat with him myself. Where there's trouble on the CP, I'm wonderin' if he has a hand in it."

Nolan studied that a moment. Sure as hell, Striker had plenty to gain from all the trouble costing them ties and timbers. Then Nolan turned his attention back to the tall sheriff. "I heard he was bailed out of jail over that way."

"This ain't about that problem . . . not exactly. There was a cold-blooded murder; same fella that Striker had the earlier run-in with took a big slug to the chest. From a long ways away, as nobody had any idea where the shot came from. Kilt him dead. Happened just after Striker was released on bail. And Striker's man was totin' a long gun."

"I heard that Crocker guaranteed the man's bail. We do have it caught in a crack without his timbers, which I'm sure is why the big boss stood up for him." Nolan sighed deeply. As much as he disliked Striker, he did have to have timbers to do his job. "I haven't seen Striker, but if I do, I'll tell him you're lookin' for him."

"Tell him to drop by my office in Auburn if you see him afore I do, that is, if he wants to get shed of this Frisco trouble. I'm headin' up the mountain since I didn't find him here . . . going to his camp. I'll probably come across him up there."

The sheriff tipped his hat and started away, until Nolan stopped him.

"Sheriff, there's a whole den of snakes up there. If you expect any trouble, I wouldn't go it alone."

"He don't know I'm coming. And besides, I don't have no warrant. We just want to have a little palaver with him. To see if he'll go along to San Francisco on his own." Again, the sheriff touched his hat brim. He moved on long legs to a tall dappled gray, with long black mane and tail. Nolan noticed what a handsome animal he was as the sheriff touched him with the spurs. He single-footed away in a comfortable quick gait.

That afternoon, Nolan got another surprise. Ho had found Striker's old cook, Lee Toy, and at Ho's instruction, the man awaited him at Ho's tent. For this, Nolan would take a little time away from the towers, even though it was only two days until Crocker's entourage of bigwigs was due to inspect their progress. He hoped he'd be working on the impressive spans by the time they arrived.

Nolan asked Ho to accompany him, and they strode the half mile to where one of the Chinese camps was nestled in a fine little meadow. A skunk-cabbage-lined creek bubbled though the meadow's green center, and they found Lee Toy there, picking the first growth of miner's lettuce.

The man looked at Nolan with eyes wide, obviously afraid that Nolan would betray his presence to Simon Striker. Nolan offered him the makin's, and the man rolled a cigarette and seemed to relax a little.

After Nolan lit his smoke for him, he told the man to keep the bag of tobacco and papers. The chubby little man relaxed even more. Nolan smiled with only his eyes, with the thought that Lee Toy was a dumpling of a man.

The scar on his lower lip revealed he'd received a vicious blow. Nolan thought that was as good a place as any to begin.

"Striker give you that scar?"

A flash of anger crossed the rotund little man's face; then he answered. "Yes. Striker smash me with butt of rifle." He bared his teeth like a rodent, and showed spaces. It was obvious he'd lost a front and side tooth to the blow.

"Striker told me he wanted you found. Said you owe him money."

Again fear flickered in the man's eyes. "I owe nothing. He owe me plenty. You not tell him—"

"No, you are safe here. In fact, if you wish a job here, you may have one."

Ho interrupted. "I have already found him position as cook for one of the Celestial crews."

"Good." Nolan hunkered down on his haunches, and the others followed suit. "I need to know some things about Striker."

"Whatever desire, O'Bannonboss," Lee said quickly.

"He sells whiskey. He sells it to the workers of the CP?"

"Yes, brothers and cousin take turns bringing mules with whiskey down mountain."

"Do you know a man named Bochevski, a railroad man?"

"I overheard Striker talk to brothers 'bout this man, but have not seen man myself."

"And what was the talk."

"That this man, Bo . . ."

"Bochevski."

"That name. That he was partner of Simon Striker."

"Partner in what?"

"Whiskey. He full partner with Striker."

"The rotten son of a bitch," Nolan said, shaking his head.

"Yes, all—Striker, brothers, cousin—all rotted sons of bitches," Lee agreed.

Nolan couldn't help but smile at the little man; then his smile broadened. Both Ho and Lee laughed, because Nolan seemed so happy. They didn't know Nolan was happy because one of his big problems was solved. He'd avoided Bochevski because Strobridge would have been very unhappy should they come head-to-head in front of the men. It might have cost Nolan his very good job, and his position was tenuous enough due to his refusal to send LuAnn down the mountain. Strobridge was not a man you crossed more than once, if you got by with once.

As Strobridge had often said of his division bosses, they had an example to set.

He wondered how Strobridge would feel knowing Bochevski was a thief and worse in James Strobridge's eyes, that Anatole was going against the policy of the CP for his personal gain.

Nolan felt as if he'd just been given a free hand to deal with Bochevski any way he cared to.

And he damn well cared to.

It was day's end, and Nolan was on top of the most westerly tower, showing the men how to ready the crown to receive the twenty-foot-thick span, when he saw the crews returning from the rails' end.

He climbed into a cask hitch he'd shown the men how to tie when they'd begun the tower, and lowered himself via a block and tackle. Now that the tower was its full one-hundred-foot height, it required five different block-and-tackle rigs to get him to the bottom. He'd come down much faster than normal, and was slightly winded. But when he hit the bottom, he could see Bochevski in the distance, walking with a group of his spikers, laughing as if he owned the world.

It was almost another hundred feet to where the rough road crossed Long Ravine's bottom. He moved casually across that distance, catching his breath as he went.

When he reached the road, Bochevski and his men were only twenty steps shy of him. He stepped to the center of the road.

When Bochevski saw him, he strode up and stood with his hands on his hips.

"I thought you'd gone down the road and taken a job as a milk maid." He and his men got a great laugh out of this, and roared with great gusto.

Nolan smiled broadly. "I'm glad to see you in good humor, Ana. But your partner won't be so happy to know you've been found out."

"Partner?" Bochevski asked, his great grin tightening.

"Partner. Simon Striker, he's right over there, settin' up your whiskey shop." Nolan pointed down into the meadow.

Bochevski's smile faded completely, and he turned to study the meadow below. "Why, that dumb—"

Just as Nolan had planned. He brought the right from behind his back, catching Bochevski full on the side of his lantern jaw as he was staring into the distance, driving it through him as if he was striking something a foot behind. The big man went down as if he'd been poleaxed with a sledge. Remembering his ribs, and hardly being able to breathe, Nolan immediately kicked him, then again, and again.

Bochevski's men charged forward, knocking Nolan back and grabbing his arms, pinning them against his sides.

"You'll be lettin' the man get to his feet," one of them snarled.

Then they let Nolan loose as Bochevski was struggling up. "That was for comin' up behind me, you bloody coward," Nolan snapped as the spikers released him.

Bochevski shook his head; then his smile began to return. He took a step in Nolan's direction, and Nolan charged forward. They traded blows, hammering at each other, each rocking the other in return.

Charging forward, Nolan ducked under a couple of roundhouse swings and hammered blow after blow to Bochevski's ribs, zeroing in on the spot where he'd kicked the man. Finally, Bochevski spun away, half crouched, holding his ribs, exposing his head.

With all his concentration on Bochevski's wide face, Nolan waded in. Two solid blows opened Bochevski's cheek-bones, and blood flew into the crowd. The larger man reached for Nolan, trying to tie him up, trying to hug him to his chest and crush him, but Nolan sidestepped him and cracked him hard on the side of his head, smashing his ear.

Bochevski went down again. This time Nolan took a step back and kicked him hard in the face, smashing his nose and flipping him over backward.

Again Bochevski's men raced in and surrounded Nolan, but by now, Nolan's tower crews were arriving, and before his arms could be pinned, a dozen fights were under way around him. He spun back to face Bochevski, believing him to be out cold in the mud.

As soon as he turned, Bochevski drove into him, low, his shoulder at Nolan's waist. Then the big man gathered him up and raised him on his shoulder, spinning him, hoping to smash him down on the ridge of rocks lining the road.

Nolan clawed behind him, trying to catch Bochevski's eyes, but the man managed to slam him down into the rocks. Luckily his shoulders hit before his head, or it would have been over.

Rolling off the road, Nolan was able to recover his feet before Bochevski scrambled over the rocks and caught up with him.

The big man roared like a bull as he charged, his arms outstretched, his face blood-covered.

Nolan awaited him, then sidestepped at the last instant and dropped, entangling the larger man's legs with his own as he did so, dropping him flat on his face. Before he'd even bounced, Nolan was up and on his back, pounding, blow after blow to the sides of Bochevski's wide head. Bochevski managed to crawl away, and this time Nolan let him regain his feet.

Bochevski had no men to back him up, as all were engaged in their own battles up on the road.

The huge Pole was on his feet, but wavering. Blood flowed from both ears, from cuts in his eyebrows and cheekbones, from a smashed nose.

Nolan glared at him. "Yer not only a low-life coward, but yer a thief, Bochevski. I want my Colt back, before you pack up and leave."

"It'll be you leavin'," Bochevski managed, and stumbled forward.

Nolan feinted with a left, and smashed another right to the battered nose of the larger man, who was knocked back a step or two.

"You'll be leaving, Ana," Nolan said, stepping into him again, feinting with a right this time, and catching him with a left hook on the smashed ear.

This time Bochevski reeled back, stumbling on a rock, going on his back.

Nolan decided it was time to end this, time to

make sure Bochevski would not again struggle to his feet. He charged forward, driving his lace-up brogan deep into Bochevski's crotch.

The big man managed to sit up, grasping his personals with both hands; what you could see of his face behind the blood coating was now panicked. Nolan put all be had behind the next kick, catching Bochevski on the point of the chin.

His head snapped back, and he flopped on his back, unmoving.

A shot rang out, and all combatants snapped their heads around to see James Strobridge and Charles Crocker astride a pair of large geldings, Strobridge with a revolver pointed into the sky.

All went silent.

"This is a hell of a note," Strobridge said quietly. "All of you get down the road. The next man who raises a hand against his coworker will draw his pay."

Nolan wiped away blood trickling from his mouth.

As the other men stomped away, Strobridge and Crocker reined the geldings down to where Nolan stood, mopping himself up.

Bochevski still hadn't moved.

Strobridge shook his head disgustedly.

"Did you kill him?" he asked.

"No, sir. Not that I didn't give it a hell of a try."

"I think you've done it this time. The men up there said you met Anatole in the road, and started this donnybrook."

"Aye, James. I started this round, but Ana Bochevski started the fight long ago."

Crocker spoke up for the first time. "Is there a reason I shouldn't give you your walking papers?"

"Yes, sir. There's a damn good reason. Bochevski stole from me, and he stole from you and the CP."

Crocker and Strobridge glanced at each other.

"How's that?" Strobridge asked.

"You remember I found that whiskey drummer, and took a rap on the head that damn near took me to meet my maker?"

"Of course I remember," Strobridge said.

"That was Bochevski, rapped me from behind. It was Bochevski who had the whiskey drummer set up there. And to add insult to injury, his partner is Simon Striker."

"Striker? The man with the mill?" Crocker said.

"The man with the mill, and a hell of a big whiskey still," Nolan offered.

"Well, there's nothing we can do about his making whiskey," Crocker said, and Nolan knew he was influenced by the fact it was Striker bringing them most of the timbers they now used.

Then he continued. "But we can do something about one of our own going against company rules. And soon, we'll be able to shed ourselves of Striker. I found a mill up on the American that's been cutting timber for the mines. They've agreed to float it down to Sacramento, where we can load up. And the price is much better."

Bochevski was beginning to stir.

"When he comes to, tell him I want him in my office in Sacramento on Monday," Crocker said.

"Monday?" Nolan asked, more than anxious to get rid of Anatole Bochevski, and seeing his chance to do so.

"Monday, after we get through this weekend. Tomorrow and Sunday, we've got damn near two dozen politicians here, or did you forget?"

Nolan glanced over at the towers. "We've done our best, Mr. Crocker," he said, the heat beginning to crawl up his backbone.

"Yes, Nolan, you have done a hell of a job. But I want this place to look as if the devil's on everyone's tails tomorrow. You get your men buzzing, like that tower was a giant hill. A couple of our illustrious visitors, including Richardson, the vice chairman of the railroad committee, want to see the work while the men are at work, and will be up here tomorrow. Make damn sure things are happening."

"Yes, sir, you can count on me; we'll be swinging timbers out over the gap," Nolan said. His muscles were beginning to bunch up, the soreness already seeping deep as a result of the battle, and his head was beginning to ache as the anger wore off.

"Tell Bochevski the same thing. I want sparks flying off the spikes."

"Yes, sir," Nolan said, but resented the fact he had to tell Bochevski anything, other than to pack up his things.

Bochevski managed to sit up, staring around as if he had no idea where he was.

To Nolan's gratification, Crocker and Strobridge completely ignored the big Pole. As Crocker and Strobridge reined their horses away, up alongside the towers to investigate the progress, Nolan walked over to Bochevski. He rested his hands on his knees, and bent near the bloody man's battered head.

"You want a little more, Ana?"

Bochevski stared up at him through bloody eyes. "I guess I've had about enough."

"Not quite," Nolan said. "You're gonna get a little more from the big bosses on Monday. You're to be in Crocker's office in Sacramento on Monday."

Bochevski's jaw clamped. "You bloody turncoat," he managed, as he was struggling to regain his footing.

"You're the turncoat, Bochevski. I'd suggest you mind your manners, as I am still harboring a hell of a big grudge, and don't know if just pounding your ugly head again would work it out of me."

Bochevski backed away, obviously not wanting anymore.

"Now, let's take a walk back to your tent, as I want my Colt," said Nolan.

Bochevski shook his head, trying to clear the cobwebs, then without saying anything more, stumbled away up the road.

Nolan took a little detour, stopping by a lean-to harboring the plank work desk he had set up to run the job, and gathered up his Henry resting there.

His fists were too sore to take much pleasure from beating on Bochevski again, but he wasn't sure he wouldn't enjoy whacking him with the butt of the rifle, should he get any more misery from the man.

That evening, when he arrived back at the tents, he decided he must look much worse than he thought, as LuAnn treated him as if he had been hit by a train, rather than several times by a big Polish locomotive of a man.

His left eye was half-closed and blue as a robin's egg, and his ear was cut and seeping blood. But the worst of it was his hands, and the lack of knuckles. It wasn't that they were beaten flat, but rather that they were so swollen that the knuckles were almost indentations rather than knots.

She quickly got a bucket of near-ice water from the creek, and had him sit on a timber round to soak his hands as she cleaned and tended his eye and ear.

"You have your pistol back," she said, but didn't question how.

"I do. I found the dirty thief who stole it."

They were silent for a long while as she worked at his cuts and abrasions with a wet rag.

Finally she inquired, "Did you fall from the tower?"

He laughed. "That bad, eh?"

"From high on the tower, you fell?"

"No, I had a little doo-da with Ana Bochevski."

"What be a 'doo-da'?" she asked with interest.

"A fight . . . a Katy-bar-the-door old-fashioned no-holds-barred brawl."

She ignored the part she didn't understand. "The man beat Chang with pipe?"

"One and the bloody same."

She looked at him questioningly. "And you still live?"

"As you can see, battered but not beaten. You should see the other fella."

"What 'other fella?' " she asked innocently, thinking they were talking about Nolan, Ana Bochevski, and some third party who hadn't been mentioned.

Nolan laughed, then grunted as it hurt to do so. In fact, every movement and every breath hurt. "I meant to say, you should see Bochevski."

"You beat him?"

"Like a stepchild," Nolan said, then realized he'd again used slang she probably didn't understand.

"Why you beat stepchild?" she asked as she continued to dress the eye.

"One wouldn't, LuAnn, me love," he said, laughing, then grunting in pain again. Then he realized what he'd said as she stepped back and looked at him with more than passing interest; her look softened.

"I wish knew when you tease."

"Only sometimes, LuAnn," he said, his own voice much softer.

"You need lay down," she said, pulling him to his feet.

She followed him to his rear tent and when he

sat on his cot, she lifted his legs and removed his brogans, as he collapsed on his back and closed his eyes.

"It soon be better," she said, almost in a whisper. "Couple of days, all better."

He felt the light touch of warm lips on his eye, then his ear, but didn't open his eyes as he didn't want to break the spell.

"Do not rest too soundly. I finish supper."

It was dark when he awakened, with her sitting patiently beside the bed.

"Now, you have some broth," she said. "You want in bed, or you want get up?"

"I'll get up," he said, and let her pull him upright.

He walked outside and they enjoyed a trout, mushroom, and vegetable broth, and the stars, blanketing the clear night sky. A nighthawk winged nearby, his wings distinctively cutting the night air, and bats flew just close enough so the firelight reflected on their wings, attracted to the bugs that were attracted to the light.

They ate in silence, Nolan again content with himself and with their circumstances. Had he not been so bloody well beat up, this might have been the night when he offered to kiss her, but as it was, he went to bed.

Who'd want to kiss this ugly Irish knotted mug? he thought.

The last thing he remembered before falling asleep was her voice from the outer tent. "Nolan, thank you for beating Bochevski. Thank you for me, more for Chang."

He smiled in the darkness of his tent, and fell contentedly asleep.

The next morning, he knew it would be one hell of a day, as they had the politicians to prepare for. Not only did he need to get as much of the impressive span constructed as possible, he had to spit-and-polish the job site so his crew looked like something other than louts.

Strobridge told him the pair of prominent politicians were to arrive in Crocker's personal railroad car sometime in the early afternoon, and that Crocker would delay them along the way as long as he could, so Nolan could get as much accomplished as possible before they reached the site.

As he left the tents and waved good-bye to LuAnn, he wished every bone in his body wasn't aching.

He would have to be out on the spans with the men, making damn sure every bolt and tie bar was well and properly placed. And every foot they progressed from the landing would mean they were higher and higher off the ravine's bottom. At the same time, the span would be begun from the west tower, reaching both toward the landing, or west end of the bridge, and equally toward the next tower. The span would have to remain balanced from the tower, so equal loads were distributed, which meant a careful advance until it looked like wings from the main tower. When the tower was finally anchored by the span from the landing meeting the span from the tower, then the distribution of the load would not be so critical, but until then, it was a virtual pile of matchsticks that could be brought down with a small miscalculation. Then the process would be repeated from the east landing to the easterly tower.

Both operations would be equally dangerous, but this first even more so, as they were being hurried.

He brought every man who he'd trust to work the height to bear on the job. By midafternoon, when Crocker and the politicians arrived, they had almost twenty feet of the spans constructed. So the first span had an open gap of only 110 feet. It was enough that any fool could see how impressive the span would be . . . even a politician.

Crocker called Nolan down from the tower to join him, Strobridge, and the politicians, and to explain the work.

When the politicians were ready to return to Sacramento, Crocker gave him a pat on the back, an unusal gesture from the big man.

For a moment, Nolan didn't ache in every muscle, as his swelling pride seemed to offset the pain; then they left, and the aches returned.

Only a couple more hours, and he could get back to LuAnn, supper, and his cot.

He'd be more than ready.

Early on Saturday morning, Simon and Jed Striker, the middle Striker brother, had worked their way carefully down the rock cliff to the lake, with three mules in tow, each loaded with two kegs of dynamite.

Two nights before, Simon had been in Colfax, and had heard rumors that Crocker had made a deal with another mill located on the American River. A mill that could easily float timbers down the river to Sacramento, where they could be loaded on the train.

A deal that Crocker had reputedly made at seven cents a foot, delivered in Sacramento. A deal that Simon knew would cause Crocker to bargain hard to lower the price on Striker timbers when they next negotiated. And that would have to be soon.

He knew the beginning of the end was near, at least for the high price he was receiving. It was his plan to drive the price even higher over the next couple of months. He'd hired another half-dozen tie hackers and teamsters to step up the production on the mill, and now, as he'd feared he would, Crocker was sabotaging their agreement.

Well, he knew a thing or two about sabotage.

They had placed the kegs of powder in strategic locations, and connected them to a central fuse location well above the lake level on the cliff-side.

Even though the deal in San Francisco had fallen apart, he still could guarantee the sale of many more timbers by destroying those in place. And this was a chance to do so in grand style.

Simon was content as he reviewed their work. He pulled his pocket watch from his canvas pants, and checked the time.

He'd been worried that he'd never ridden the canyon, and had decided that if they finished soon enough, he'd do so this afternoon, just to make sure nothing would deflect the wall of water he was about to send down on the Long Ravine Bridge.

He sent Jed back up and around the mountain to their camp, with the instruction that he was to push the tie hackers hard the next morning, even though it was Sunday. Simon would need no help lighting the fuse the next morning. He'd picked Sunday as it was not his intention to drown the crew of the CP, particularly those who were busy in the utilization of timbers. If he killed them, timbers would not be used as quickly. He only wanted to wipe out and bust up the timbers in use, and float the remaining supply on down the Long Ravine canyon so far it would be uneconomical to try and recover them.

Of course, if an Irish lout, or a heathen or two or even twenty, drowned, it would be no skin off Striker's backside.

As Jed and the mule team picked their way back up the cliff-side, Simon set out to ride the canyon until he was in sight of the bridge, and until he was assured nothing would impede the mountain of water.

Not that he truly thought anything could.

This was the first day he'd ridden this animal, and he was more than pleased with the gelding. It stood seventeen hands, was a well-marked dappled gray, with black flowing mane and tail. It would bring a good price when he took it down to Sonora to sell. It was a pity he couldn't keep it, but he knew the Auburn sheriff's horse would be too well known. And too closely tied to the late Sheriff Toby Chester.

When, and if, they found the body that he'd had Efren haul many miles from Blood Mountain, they'd presume the gray had run off.

They were all plenty busy, he and Jed here at the natural dam, Efren getting rid of the sheriff's body, and Milo Stark, their cousin, on his way down the mountain with three mules loaded with whiskey.

Simon picked his way along the canyon bottom for over three miles, having to climb up out of the stream bottom twice where it narrowed and the creek pooled deeply. He passed several beaver dams, every pond with the concentric rings of feeding fish. Once an osprey passed overhead, with a fifteen-inch trout clasped in its talons, heading for his nest and mate high in some tree—but Striker noticed none of this.

He was picking his way around a huge boulder, then drew rein sharply, causing his mount to step back. Dismounting, he pulled the Whitworth from its saddle scabbard and stalked forward. There, fifty yards or so downstream, was a sight he would have never guessed he would have stumbled upon. A woman. A practically nude woman. A fine-hewed shapely chemise-clad woman.

He chuckled quietly, and backed away. He led

the horse back a few steps to a small open area covered with grass, and staked him out.

Then he made his way down closer to the stream and picked his way through the boulders, the Whitworth hanging loosely in hand. When he was only ten yards from where the woman sunned herself, dozing on a wide flat boulder, he was surprised, and overjoyed, to see she was a Celestial.

Fair game for any white man.

As he neared, he realized what a catch this would be, as she was shapely and flawless. Full breasts, and a handsome flare of the hip. Not pudgy, as were many Celestial women, but taller and slender. His luck was unbelievable.

He was within ten feet of her when she opened her eyes, they flared in fear, and she screamed like a banshee. Charging forward, he clambered for her, but she was quick and dropped off the boulder . . . and came up with a double-barreled shotgun. He was still boulder-high and she three feet lower, so his kick easily found its mark and the shotgun flew away.

She tried to bolt, but he dove, catching her by the ankle as she went down, and he smothered her.

"Stop, stop!" she screamed.

"There ain't gonna be no stoppin', Chinee girl," Striker said with a cackle.

Suddenly, her look changed, and her voice dropped to a low tone. "Stop, stop! I like."

"You like?" he said, a bit surprised.

"I like, but rocks . . ." she said, and he realized she lay on the rough stream-side.

"Grass," she said, pointing up the slope to a grassy area.

"Sure, why not," he said, grabbing her by the hand and leading her to the grass, which was only three paces from where the shotgun had landed.

She smiled demurely at him as they reached the grass, and slunk onto her backside, looking up and batting her eyes at him. He set the Whitmore aside, and reached for his belt buckle. Just as he'd loosened the restraint and began to drop his trousers, she dove for the shotgun.

But he was too quick, and dove right behind her, again catching her ankle. He jerked her back, rolled her over, and slapped her, and slapped her again, snapping her head back and forth, until he'd knocked her almost senseless.

Picking up the shotgun, he fingered the lever, broke the gun, ejected the two shells, spun the weapon around and clasped it by the barrels, then smashed it on the rocks.

Then he turned his attention back to the girl.

She was staring at him with hatred glowering in her dark eyes.

"O'Bannon kill you," she said with a catlike growl.

He moved closer, his pants again to his knees, then realized what she'd said.

"O'Bannon?"

"Nolan O'Bannon. Big boss of CP."

"Nolan O'Bannon ain't no big boss. Crocker is the big boss."

"O'Bannon kill you, you touch me."

"I take some killin', Chinee girl. You O'Bannon's woman?"

"I O'Bannon's woman." She glanced at the sinking sun. "He due home any minute, an' he kill you dog-dead."

Striker chuckled, but he hoisted his pants. He glanced over, seeing the rough clothes she had in a pile near where she'd been sunning herself.

He snatched her up by the wrist and slung her at the clothes. "O'Bannon won't be off work for a couple of hours. By that time, he'll think a bear done et you, if he even gives a damn." But looking at the girl, he knew O'Bannon could well give a damn. "Get your damn clothes on. We'll be halfway back to my camp before he knows yer gone. I need me a cook and a bed-warmer."

Slowly, she began to dress.

He kicked her and she went to her knees. "By God, I said get dressed. You'll learn to mind Simon Striker, Chinee girl, or by God you'll die of the effort."

She dressed quickly, until she reached for the sandals.

"Leave the footgear," he said, and she looked at him questioningly.

"I said, leave the damned shoes. You'll be less likely to be trying to run off if'n you got no shoes."

Then he dragged her the fifty yards back to the horse, stumbling through the rocks and brush, and made her swing up behind him.

It would half kill the big gray getting them up and out of the canyon if he pushed hard, but hell, he was going to sell the nag anyway.

Besides, he would be stopping at the lake, and spending the night.

A very pleasant night, if he had his way, and he damn well meant to have his way.

Besides, he could see the trail for a half mile behind him when he was on the dam, and if anyone followed, he'd have a clear shot.

Nolan took his time on the climb back up the creek to his camp, having to use the Henry for a walking stick part of the way. He'd treated the Henry as if it was his firstborn, and so far it didn't have a smudge, much less a mark, and he hated to even put its butt in the sand.

But he was dog-tired, bone-weary, and sore to the marrow.

Still, he had the hint of a smile on his face. The day had gone well. Crocker and the pair of fat politicians had left singing the praises of the crew and their progress. Nolan knew he would sleep the sleep of the truly contented this night. All he needed now was a good meal and a kind word, and he would go down with the sun.

And tomorrow was a blessed day of rest.

The men had scheduled a Sunday clogging contest, to see who was the lightest of foot, and to entertain the entourage of politicians. There would be at least two fiddlers, a pair of mouth harps, a mandolin, a flute, and a banjo to provide the tempo. Nolan had heard these boys play, and knew it would be little more than tempo, but that was all cloggers needed.

But Nolan was taking the day off; he was no clogger, and the politicians, sure as hell's hot, didn't need him. Hell, Crocker could spread enough bullshit to obliterate any small amount Nolan might lay down. Besides, he was too damn tired to make useless palaver.

It would be a day of rest and recuperation, maybe a day to suggest to LuAnn that their relationship take a new tack.

When he reached the tents, it was too quiet. LuAnn was nowhere in sight. He yelled for her, but got no answer. *Maybe the fish aren't biting today and it's taking her some extra time to fill the frying pan.*

He went to the keg, flipped back the hinged half lid, and drank directly from the dipper; then he fetched his pipe, filled it, and perched himself on a timber round out beside the fire pit. He'd give her time enough for one pipeful before he went looking.

When he'd sucked the last of the flame from the

pipe, he began to truly worry. Entering the tent, he checked to see that all of her dresses were there, thinking she might have dressed, then taken a stroll. But they all hung on the tent frame. She was always dressed in finery by the time he returned from work.

The shotgun was gone, so wherever she was, she was at least safe from the critters.

Finally, he resigned himself to the fact that he should go looking for her, as badly as he wanted to curl up on his cot and rest.

He was over two hundred yards upstream from the camp, at the first deep pond, when he noticed her sandals lying askew in the sand. LuAnn was neat to a fault, and nothing was ever askew when she was in charge. A deepening dread swept through him, knotting his stomach, and racking his backbone.

Then he calmed himself. *Hell, she's probably just gone wading and has gone farther than she meant to.*

He called to her again, and again heard no answer, only the bubbling brook and the screech of a hawk overhead. Kneeling near the sandals, he carefully studied the sign. The sand was disturbed, but he could make out nothing that was clear enough to tell him anything else.

Thank God, at least no bear or cougar prints.

Just a few feet up the creek bed, he found the busted and bent shotgun.

Sweet Jesus, what has happened?

He shouted as loudly as he could—this time his voice shuddering with the desperation he felt. He shouted until his throat began to hurt as much as his back and shoulders.

Moving only a few more steps, he spotted tracks in the mud. Her bare feet, and the tracks of a predator, a low-life critter that at that instant he realized he should fear most. Boot tracks. He was no tracker, but he could surmise by the scrapes in front of her bare footprints that she was being dragged part of the time.

He moved quickly up the trail, skipping from rock to rock. Then he stopped, and dread covered him like a shroud.

Hoofprints. They replaced the foot prints and bootprints.

Hell, they were on horseback.

Unless he was worse at reading signs than he thought, there was only one horse. Could he move fast enough on foot to catch them riding double? Moving up through these rocks would be a tough job for a horse carrying double. The horse would have to be moving much slower than normal.

Then again, he had no idea what time the prints were made.

Hell, they could have set out on the horse at noon, or even this morning.

No, he had to have a mount if he was going to catch up.

Without further contemplation, he spun on his heel and ran. It was almost two miles to where Jenkins had set up his new corral and blacksmith and separate harness lean-tos. But it would only be one way on shank's mare; then he'd be mounted on the way back.

He left the Henry in his camp, figuring he'd pick it and the Colt back up on the way back through. Running, glancing at the sun, he estimated he had only an hour and a half of true light, then maybe a half hour of twilight.

What's the stage of the moon? he wondered. *How much light will I have after the sun's down? Was it a full moon last night?* He cursed himself for not knowing. If he was at sea, he'd know the stage of the moon, if it be full or fingernail or blacked out, if it waxed or waned.

He responded to none of the men who spoke to him or waved at him as he passed, single-mindedly pounding away down the road—slowed to a jog by lack of breath—then alongside the rail.

More than just a little winded, he reached Jenkins's corrals, and cursed his luck when he found the man gone. Hell, all of the men were at chow or on their way.

But the buckskin was there.

He caught the big horse and trotted with him to the harness lean-to, and saddled and bridled him, then had another thought.

Finding the big mule, Perch, he led her to the lean-to where Jenkins had the harness neatly laid out, and saddled her also. He fitted a lead rope to her, and tied her reins to the saddle horn, mounted the buckskin, and set out back the way he'd come at a canter, leading the big strong mule.

With two mounts he could trade off without resting the animals. Without losing time.

He would catch them . . . he had to catch them.

To his surprise, he came upon Ho and Chang on the track. He reined up.

"Ho, someone has taken LuAnn. Someone on horseback took her on up the canyon above where my tent is. Tell Strobridge I might be gone for a while." He started away, then reined up again, and turned. "I'll not come back without her." Then he gigged the horse and jerked the mule into a trail-eating canter.

He hadn't even taken the time to tell Chang that he was glad he was out of the hospital. But that could wait until a better time.

If any time would ever be better again. . . .

As he had reined away, he heard Ho explaining to Chang what he'd said, and even over the pounding hoofs, he could hear Chang roar with anguish.

When he reached the camp, Nolan flew from

the saddle, dropping the reins to the ground. He strapped on the Colt and hung the Henry's saddle scabbard on the buckskin, sank the weapon home, put a box of shells in the saddlebags, then was off again.

When he reached the place he'd found the hoofprints, he slowed, picking his way, eyeing each print. Then he glanced at the sun, which had long disappeared below the canyon wall. The shadows were deepening.

Sure his prey followed the creek, he gigged the buckskin.

Dragging the mule was no easy task, as the gait of the buckskin was faster than that of the mule, and he was continually leaning back in the saddle to jerk on the mule's lead rope, to hurry the animal. But logic told him it would eventually be worth the effort. He figured he'd covered at least three miles. But he had the very last of the sunlight.

His back and shoulders were already aching from the effort, from the fight the night before, and from the very hard day on the tower. But no one ever died of a shoulder and backache.

Just as the last of the light flickered in the canyon, he glanced up and noticed the sky tinged red. Red sky in the morning, sailor take warning; red sky at night, sailor's delight. At least it was a promise of good weather, which was a good thing as he'd left without his slicker.

There was one more boulder pile; then he could see that the canyon widened out, almost level for the better part of a half mile before it reached another rocky escarpment.

When he reached the last of the boulders, something appeared in the rocks, not five paces from the buckskin. The marmot that had popped up in the rocks chirped loudly, and the buckskin reared and sidestepped so quickly he almost left Nolan in the trail, at the same time that the mule sat back, jerking Nolan flat out in the saddle.

Something sang off the rocks behind them, and he heard a loud report. A shot. He still fought the animals, fighting to regain control. As Jenkins had warned, the buckskin liked to buck, and it was all Nolan could do to stay mounted. Another ricochet sang off the rocks, and another loud report of a shot echoed down to him.

Hell, some bastard was shooting at him.

He dragged the Henry from its scabbard, and dove from the pitching saddle.

Shed of his load, the buckskin charged forward up the trail, and released, the mule went back the way they'd come.

Thank God for the marmot; thank God for the marmot who disliked his territory being invaded. And thank God for the spooky buckskin. Otherwise he'd be stone dead. The little people were smiling on him this day, even if they'd taken the form of a marmot.

Nolan hunkered down behind a boulder and waited, catching his breath, composing himself, working out his next move.

Things were both bad and good. The bad was that the sunlight was now only a hint in the sky; the good was that whoever was shooting at him would not have any idea where he was in less than a quarter hour.

Of course, he would also have a hell of a time finding the shooter.

He was sure of one thing. Wherever the shooter was, he'd find LuAnn.

Hunkering deeper behind the rock, he waited for total darkness.

When he figured it was safe, he rose and started back down the trail. He only went fifty yards before he found the mule. The dragging lead rope had tangled in the brush, and the molly mule was tied as soundly as if Nolan had tethered her.

He untied her, loosened her reins from the saddle horn, and mounted up. Moving back up the trail, he was more than a hundred yards farther along before he heard the buckskin nicker quietly. The big gelding had stepped on his reins, busting one, and was grazing contentedly near the trail.

Nolan switched the lead rope to the buckskin, remounted the molly mule, and again set out letting the wise molly pick her own way.

It could prove to be a long night, or a very, very short one if the shooter was waiting in the rocks ahead.

Still, he moved forward.

He remembered a saying his ol' da used to use, usually when he was in his cups. *Every man to the devil in his own way, and in his own good time.* Well, his way was going to be trying to save LuAnn, and his time was now, if it had to be. Straight ahead, even if into the jaws of Satan.

One thing was for damn sure. He wouldn't find LuAnn by hiding in the rocks.

Simon Striker had reached the top of the ridge over the lake in the darkness, the woman astride the horse behind him. The gray was blowing badly, his sides heaving, and Striker had no interest in killing the animal, no interest in walking back to camp.

The bitch had clawed for the revolver at his waist, but he'd caught her wrist and wrenched it until he thought it broken, then told her if she tried that again, he'd kill her slowly.

She'd stopped, and he'd been able to gig the horse on ahead.

It was too damn dark for this foolishness. When

he reached the level atop the ridge, he reined off the trail and threw his leg over the horse's neck, dismounting in one motion, dragging the woman after him.

He shoved her to the ground and told her to stay there. Digging a short rope from his saddlebags, he used a foot to turn her on her belly, then tied her wrists tightly. Then he removed the horse's lead rope and used it to bind her to the trunk of a thick ponderosa pine.

The moon was just beginning to peep over the ridge to the east, and he knew that in a very few minutes there would be light enough to see the man tracking him as he came up the narrow trail on the cliff-side. This time he would make it end. He had work to do with the sunrise, and no time for this foolishness.

The Whitworth's sights were adjustable to one thousand yards, and the man should come into sight at some less distance than that.

With luck, he wouldn't have to even take a shot; the wall of water would do the job for him.

He remounted and put the spurs to the gray, reining him back down the trail until he reached a spot near where the fuses ended. Springing out of the saddle, he scurried around in the darkness until he found the fuses, wound together. As quickly as he could, he got a sulfur head burning, and touched it to the black cord. It sputtered, and he spun on his heel and ran it back to the gray, mounted, and spurred the animal up the trail.

He found a spot at the trailhead, far enough that he wouldn't be killed by the rain of rock that was sure to come, crouched behind a boulder, and waited.

Hell, this was as good as Sunday. The men were off work, and the towers were far enough along that he'd destroy hundreds of timbers.

And with luck, he'd destroy the man tracking him.

Nolan managed to cross the big flat without being shot. He got a tight smile when he saw the hint of strong moonlight caressing the top of the east ridge. Thank God, he'd have enough light to go on. There was a good chance it was near to a full moon.

He topped a tall escarpment, the molly carefully picking her way, the buckskin following obediently. Then he heard hoofbeats behind him.

What the hell?

He dismounted after finding a cleft in which he could leave the horses. Moving back to the trail, he climbed atop a boulder larger than the mule was tall, and hunkered down.

By the time the rider was within fifty paces, the moon had reached half-mast over the ridge, and features in the hillside were again discernible. When he pulled even, Nolan relaxed. It was Chang, the warrior, to Nolan's great surprise and pleasure.

Hanging from his waist was a thick sword, which he reached for when Nolan hailed him. Then he relaxed when Nolan rose up on the boulder so Chang could see him.

He, too, rode a solid-looking mule.

He had little English, but used what he did have. "Lu Ang? You find?"

"I'm still following track."

Chang shook his head, then motioned ahead, and Nolan agreed.

By the time Nolan mounted, Chang was twenty yards up the steep trail.

With the moon now just touching the ridgeline with its bottom rim, Nolan could now see its reflection shimmering across a large lake below them.

He suddenly had the nostalgic wish that he'd taken LuAnn there.

He gigged the horse to catch up with Chang, but the big Chinaman was moving fast, pushing the mule up to the top of the ridge.

Just as Nolan thought they were near to topping the steep incline, flame licked out of the rocks above, and Chang did a backward somersault off the back of the mule. Nolan's mule reared and spun in its tracks, leaping, slipping, sliding back down the trail, almost trampling Chang in the process. There was no room for two animals on the narrow trail, and the molly mule, as steady as she had been, sat back, trying to turn herself. She stepped off the downhill side of the trail, and Nolan sprang from the saddle, pulling the Henry at the same time, crashing down into a pile of rocks below the trail.

As soon as he recovered, he laid the Henry across a rock, and fired at the spot where he imagined the shot had come from.

Another lick of flame shot from the rocks above, and the bullet twanged off a rock near his head.

Now he had a target, and he fired as fast as he could lever them in; a dozen shots splattered into the rocks above.

He heard a yell, then the clatter of stones. The sound seemed to be moving away.

Changing his position so he'd be away from where he'd sent his own tongues of fire, he waited for another shot to ring out, so he could answer it accurately. But nothing came.

Finally, after what seemed an eternity, he worked his way the dozen steps back up to the trail, and moved up it until he found Chang. The big man had pulled himself off the trail into the shelter of the rocks.

Nolan sat the Henry aside, and felt until he found

the man's wound. It was just under his left shoulder, and seemed to be clean through and through. It had probably smashed a rib, unless Chang had been lucky enough to have it pass between. It was only a couple of inches from the outside of his rib cage, so it probably had not hit anything vital.

Nolan whispered to Chang as he was binding the wound with a large part of Chang's shirttail that he tore away.

"I'll hike back down and get the animals, if I can catch up with them. Then you can head back down the mountain."

"Lu Ang," he said, pointing up the mountain.

"I'll get the horses, then you go down the trail," Nolan said, then pulled his Colt from his holster and handed it to the big Chinaman.

"Stay here," Nolan commanded, then turned and hustled down the trail after the stock. He only made a few paces when he came upon Chang's mule, where the animal stood on a precarious rock ledge ten feet below the trail.

Nolan carefully made his way down to the animal, then led him back up to the safety of the trail. Only then did he realize the animal was badly lame. He could barely gimp along; he stood with his right forefoot held up above the trail. Nolan stripped away the saddle and bridle and set the animal free, hoping he could find his own way back to Jenkins's good hands.

Then Nolan strode out to find the buckskin and molly.

He walked almost back to his camp before he found the molly, standing with head down in a small grass meadow on the streambed.

Tying a Spanish hackamore with the lead rope, as both her reins were broken, he remounted and rode to just beyond the camp, where the buckskin stood with canted hip, his head down, sleeping.

Nolan and the molly startled him, but he only bolted for a few yards; then Nolan caught up, holding the mule's lead rope.

Again, they were on the trail, after LuAnn and the man who wanted any pursuers dead.

The moon was well up by the time he again sat beside Chang, checking his wound. Nolan helped him into the saddle of the molly, and started to lead the mule around so he could head back down the mountain. But Chang jerked the reins, shaking his head no.

"You'll bleed to death, friend, if you don't get down where someone can properly help you."

"Lu Ang," he said, his voice earnest.

"LuAnn," Nolan said, and smiled tightly. He guessed there were two of them who truly cared about LuAnn.

With the Henry across his thighs, Nolan led the way to the top of the ridge. As he'd suspected, the man was long gone, and LuAnn was nowhere in sight.

All he could do was hope the buckskin would follow where another horse had gone, and he urged him ahead.

This time, if the shooter was waiting, it would be Nolan in the lead, and he probably wouldn't be as lucky as Chang had been.

Every man to the devil in his own good way, Nolan repeated to himself. *Let's see if I can send this shooter to the devil in my own good time.*

The trail had leveled out, seemingly working its way around the mountainside. The cover was lodgepole and Jeffery pine, and the occasional stand of ponderosa.

They rode for an hour. Then Chang fell out of the saddle. Nolan dismounted and went back to the man, unsaddled the molly, and made Chang comfortable leaning against the saddle covered with the saddle blanket.

Then he studied the trail, desperately trying to find the hint of horse tracks. Nothing.

Damn if the buckskin hadn't taken a trail other than the one the shooter, and he hoped LuAnn, had taken. For the first time he worried about the possibility that LuAnn was not astride the horse. The animal had done well for carrying double. Maybe he didn't carry double at all. Maybe LuAnn had escaped and run off into the woods, and he'd missed the sign. He couldn't possibly see it in this feeble light.

Or maybe, God forbid, she had been used and murdered and thrown off the trail far behind where they now rested. She wouldn't be the first Celestial woman to meet such a fate.

Damn, he was disgusted with himself.

Damn, damn, damn.

He went back to where Chang lay, and saw that he was asleep, or had passed out, so he stripped the saddle and bridle from the buckskin and made a bed for himself. Luckily, it was a warm night, and dry.

He'd pick it up in the morning, when he could see the damn trail.

He tried to sleep, but he was so tired, and so worried, he could not. He merely dozed until the moon had been down for hours.

It was Chang who shook him awake with the sky in the east just changing shades. Nolan managed, as beat-up and sore as he was, to get to his feet. Then he remembered that Chang was wounded, shot clean through. Fresh blood streaked his shirt.

Nolan made his way to the big man. "Let me rebind that," he said, and Chang stood obediently as he did so. The man seemingly had little use of his left hand, but had managed to get his blanket and saddle into place on the molly. Nolan finished saddling the molly, then saddled the buckskin.

Long before the sun topped the ridge, they were backtracking, Nolan, in the growing light, carefully studying the ground for sign of a track heading off in another direction.

Damn the bloody flies, Simon thought, *the by-God lousy fuse had gone out. The explosion hadn't gone off, the water hadn't killed the man who followed, or wiped out the trestle.*

Damn the bloody flies.

Now he would have to come back to the lake, and set it off Sunday as planned. What the hell, it would do the job on Sunday or any damned day, and the men wouldn't be working tomorrow.

Simon had given the horse his head, sure he'd find his way back to camp, and he did, even though this was the first trip he'd made out of that camp. *Smart horse,* Simon thought, *pity to have to sell him.*

Still, it was well after midnight when they plodded into the timber camp.

And Striker was far too tired to use the woman as he'd planned. Rather, he tied her and locked her in the storage shed, warning her that showing her head outside the shed would cost her that very same head, and went to the main cabin.

His two brothers were asleep, and Cousin Milo was down the mountain, selling whiskey. He shook Efren awake and made him dress, as he slept in the same long underwear he'd worn all winter.

"Stand guard outside with your rifle. If anyone rides into camp, shoot them off'n their horse. You wake me at first light."

"What the hell is going on, Simon?" his brother asked with a yawn.

"Did Jed get rid of the sheriff?"

"Said he dumped the body in a mine shaft three or four miles south of here."

"Good, now get out there and stand guard, and don't you be dozing, 'cause if I catch you, I'll skin your hide and tack it to the outhouse wall."

"Yes, brother," Efren said, yawning again.

Then Simon found his own bunk, and fell into it.

Efren, as ordered, shook him awake at first light. And as usual, Efren's first comment was a complaint. "Sure wish we had us a cook," he groused. "I hate makin' the coffee, and all y'all do is complain when I do."

"You don't have to," Simon said, remembering the girl. "There's a new cook tied up and locked in the storage shed. Fetch her."

Efren did so, and had a bit of a bewildered look on his face when he pushed her into the cabin. "This here's a woman," he said.

"I swear," Simon said, shaking his head, "I should'a sent you away to university. Of course it's a woman, you damn fool. Now get back on guard. We'll bring you a plate." He walked over and kicked his brother Jed's bunk. "Get up, shirker. It's daytime, and we might got trouble a-comin'."

Jed sat up in his bed. "What kinda trouble?" he said, rubbing his eyes.

"Gun trouble. Sum'bitch either got a weapon fires a lot of shells, maybe a Spencer, or they be a lot of 'em. Get loaded up and get outside. I done put a new bunghole in one of them, or leastways think I did." He pointed to the stove and growled at LuAnn. "Cook, woman," he snarled. "Coffee, bacon, an' beans. Beans is in the pot and need heatin' up."

Jed was pulling on his boots, having slept in his clothes. He eyed the woman with great interest.

Simon turned his attention to him. "Get loaded, take the Spencer, shotgun, and pistol, and get out along the trail somewheres. They be coming from the east, if'n they can track. Shoot down whoever comes a-callin'. I'll have Ef fetch you up when the grub's done."

Jed stretched, then asked, "What was all that shootin' we heard 'bout sundown?"

Simon slapped him on the head. Jed stepped back, and balled his fist. Simon snatched the big knife he wore on his hip out of its scabbard, holding it at arm's length, and snarled, "You want to eat this pigsticker?"

Jed relaxed, lowering his arm, undoing the fist.

Simon again snarled, "You sum'bitches heard me in a by-God gun battle and jest went about your business?"

"We didn't know—"

"This time, you hear any shootin', you don't let yer shirttails hit yer ugly backsides while you get on down there. Understood?"

"Understood." Grumbling, Jed made his way outside and disappeared toward the forest, heading into the morning light above the camp.

Simon yelled after him, "I'm headin' back down to the lake soon as I grub down, but I'm gonna circle around the fools, lest I stumble on them. I got a damned-fool fuse to relight. You retie this woman after she cleans up, and keep your hands off'n her or I'll chop 'em off at the wrist. You tell Efren the same." He got a yelled acknowledgment, then turned to LuAnn. "Woman, you get that grub done. I'm goin' outside to shake the dew off'n my lily." He laughed at his feeble joke, and stomped out.

* * *

LuAnn's throat had gone dry when she heard Simon say that he'd shot one of his pursuers. *Could it be that Nolan had been shot? Who could be with him?*

She wished she had some snake or puffer-fish venom to put in their food, but she had nothing. Walking to a wax-paper window, she tried to make out where they were, but she could only see the one who had been called Efren. He was up on top of the mill building, a rifle in hand, keeping his eyes on the forest above the camp. A pair of men she hadn't seen worked in the mill, and another three were harnessing up some mules to a drag line.

How many are they? she wondered.

She went to a door in the rear of the cabin, but the man who'd dragged her up here was standing only ten paces away in a privy with the door open, his back to her. *Could she sneak by him?* No, he turned, stretched, and started back toward the cabin. She would bide her time, then make her escape.

She had to get away.

She had to find out if Nolan was all right.

They only had to backtrack for a half mile before Nolan could see where tracks led away from the game trail the buckskin had followed. He pointed to them, and Chang nodded his big head in acknowledgment.

Nolan reined the buckskin up the new trail.

Striker finished his meal, yelled at Efren to come and retie the woman, then grabbed her by the arm and shook her until she winced. "You be a good Chinee girl. I'll show you what a real man's like when I get back from this little errand."

Then, when Efren arrived to take the woman to the storage shed, he went to the corral and had one of the Indians saddle the dun he normally rode.

He took a higher route around the mountainside, back to its north side, which fell away into the rift that cradled the lake that he'd begun to think of as Mirror Lake. He hadn't ridden two miles when he came to the head of a cliff. He had started to rein the dun along the cliff to see if he could find a way down, when he spotted two riders in the distance to the east, coming up from the direction of the lake.

Instead of riding around them through the high woods, he led the dun back into the woods, tied him off, slipped the long rifle from its scabbard, and returned to the edge of the cliff. This was too good an opportunity. The riders were at least three hundred yards away, but that was no reach for the Whitworth. Still, it might do to let them get some closer.

Nolan led the way, glancing back on occasion to make sure Chang was still in the saddle.

The big man seemed to be doing better. The bleeding had stopped, and the wound seemed to be sealed over. Still, Nolan worried that he wouldn't live to get back to see a doctor.

The mountainside opened up to a timberless escarpment, with a cliff up ahead of them. The trail seemed to work its way up to and around the toe of the cliff to where the country again leveled out and was tree-covered.

As they got closer, Nolan studied the rocks at the base of the cliff, then the cliff's top, probably a hundred feet above.

He caught a reflection off something. The sun was at his back and—

There it was again. He turned in the saddle. "Dismount, Chang, and find cover."

Chang looked at him curiously, not understanding.

"Boom-boom," Nolan said, then pointed to the top of the cliff, over two hundred yards away.

Chang seemed to understand. Nolan leapt from the horse and found cover in the boulders, as Chang managed to dismount, the molly between him and the cliff above.

A lick of fire spat from a high spot ahead of Nolan. He ducked, and heard the distinctive whap of a big rifle bullet striking flesh.

"No," he shouted, thinking the big Chinaman had taken another hit.

He scrambled toward where Chang had been dismounting, and met him coming his way.

Both of them sank down into the boulders. "You all right?" Nolan asked.

Chang shook his head, then said two words. "Mule dead."

"Damn him, that was a fine mule. She deserved better," Nolan said, and reaffirmed the fact that he was going to get this shooter.

He moved away from Chang, snapped the Henry up over the boulder, and began to fire at the spot where he thought the sniper to be hiding. Loosing a half-dozen rounds, he then scrambled to another spot and fired three more.

He'd only grabbed one box of shells from the tent, and decided he'd better start picking his shots. These repeating rifles ate a lot of ammunition. He made his way back to where Chang was hiding, and found the man gone.

Maybe he's come to his senses? Nolan thought. *Maybe*

he's making his way afoot back to the railroad and help for that wound?

Jed stood in the woods, his head cocked to the side. *Damn that older brother of mine, done got his'sef in trouble.* He counted the shots, over a dozen. As he made his way back to find Efren, he considered letting Simon handle this little problem by himself. Jed hadn't appreciated the slap, just because he'd failed to run off and find out what some shootin' was about. His older brother treated him like he was still a younger, and he weren't no younger no more . . . that slappin' would have to stop.

Hell, Simon might already be shot dead.

He thought it, but then shook his head. Not Simon. There wasn't a man who could shoot Simon dead.

But by the time he found Efren and they'd saddled up and spurred the horses out of camp toward where the shots had come from, he'd forgotten about the slap.

Another shot twanged off the rocks, kicking shards over Nolan, and he flattened himself. The man definitely had the advantage with the high ground.

In order for Nolan to get at him, he would have to work his way to one end of the cliff or the other, as the cliff itself was far too steep to try to ascend; besides, it would be sure death to try.

If the shooter didn't get him, the cliff probably would.

Nolan got his head up enough to study his situation. On both ends of the cliff, he'd have to scramble across wide-open areas in order to reach a copse of trees and gain enough cover to work his way up the mountain and be able to flank the shooter.

He was in a bad situation.

Hell, he had to try. Snapping the Henry up on the rock top, he waited until the man fired at him again. With the light of morning, the lick of flame from the rifle was no longer such a marker, and he had to track the sound and look for the black powder smoke. This time rock shards splattered his neck, drawing blood.

Nolan aimed carefully, shooting slightly above the target. Then he scrambled again, gaining another twenty feet of the hundred yards he had to cover before he must make a mad dash in the open to reach the copse of lodgepole.

The man's weapon seemed to be a single-shot, as Nolan's rate of fire was much greater than the shooter's. When he thought he knew the man's location, he snapped off a shot, then scrambled again, eyeing the cliff top. But the shooter had again changed location. Nolan decided he had to be more careful. He'd already gone through half a box of shells, and he had a long way to go.

He tried to slip to the next boulder without firing at the man first, and paid as the shooter creased his side with hot lead. Flattening himself against the boulder, he inspected the wound. Nothing but a burn from hot fast lead. And a pair of holes in his shirt.

He decided to wait, let the sun rise a little, let the man maybe think he'd killed his pursuer. After what seemed to be at least a half hour, but was probably half that, Nolan again swung the Henry to the top of the rock and watched for the shot.

To his great surprise, at least three shots rang out from different locations on the cliff top, and lead peppered all around him. Sweet Jesus, the shooter had friends. Now what would he do? He couldn't possibly pin them all down before he tried to scramble to the next rock.

What the hell could he do next?

When his brothers had arrived, Simon sent one of them to each side, telling them to find a good spot at least thirty or forty yards from where he perched.

Jed took off to the left of him, and Efren to the right. After they fired the first volley, he then decided if they spread out even farther, one of them would surely reach a spot where a man behind a boulder couldn't possibly hide from all of them, and at some time one of them would surely have a clear shot at him.

Yelling at his brothers, he told them to keep moving until one of them had a clear shot. They were already out of Simon's line of sight, but that didn't matter. His brothers could take care of themselves.

Simon figured he'd killed one of the pair with the first shot, hearing the distant thump of the big .45-caliber bullet strike flesh. But then he realized the mule was down and not moving. Had he hit the man also? He couldn't tell, but he'd seen no sign of that man since.

Efren moved until he saw what he thought was the man's pants leg. But he had the worst of the Striker weapons, a cap-and-ball Harper's Ferry muzzle-loading rifle. And he wanted to be sure of his shot. He kept moving. The head of the cliff began a gradual downslope as he moved farther east, and got not only lower but somewhat closer to the man behind the rocks.

Finally, Efren reached a spot where he could see the man's lower torso, and he estimated the distance at only 150 yards. Hell, he could hit a deer in the heart at 150 yards with the Harper's, and he was confident he could hit this man.

He licked his finger and wiped the front sight of the rifle, then laid it up alongside a scraggly manzanita stump, and squeezed off a shot.

Damn, he'd hit at least a dozen feet in front of the man in the rocks. He fished another bullet out of his pocket, fed the muzzle with a shot of powder from his flat brass powder horn, put a patch on the end of the ramrod, and started to tap it home, when he heard a scream so close it chilled his backbone.

He jerked to his knees, as a huge ugly Chinaman bolted up in front of him, a thick sword lifted over his head in both hands.

Far below in the rocks, Nolan, too, heard the scream. He rolled back away from his boulder and stared up at the top of the cliff where the scream had come from.

Chang stood, the sword raised high in one hand, a man's head held high in the other. He gave another spine-rattling yell, then threw the head end-over-end out into the void. Then he dropped the sword, reached down, picked up the headless torso high over his head, and flung it out into space.

Another shot rang out, and Nolan turned to see another man, this one as far from Chang as Chang was from where Nolan hid. He stood atop the cliff in plain view of Nolan, and was snapping a rifle to his shoulder, his attention on Chang.

Nolan scrambled to his rock, rested the Henry there, heard a shot, then fired at the man himself with his rifle; again and again he levered and fired, until the man disappeared behind the cliff's edge.

The first man who'd shot at them fired again,

the shell passing so close to Nolan's ear he felt the slap of wind.

One down, thanks to Chang.

Maybe another, if he'd hit the man who was firing at Chang. He hoped the big Chinaman was all right. Nolan took the opportunity to scramble another twenty-five feet, where he found a boulder, then rather than sitting up to fire again, bolted to the next boulder large enough for cover.

This time shots seemed to come from both of the men on top of the cliff. If he'd hit the second man, it wasn't serious enough to keep him from firing back.

Nolan took a deep breath, and tried to settle himself. Fear and anger pumped through him, but LuAnn was still out there somewhere.

This time he raised up and snapped a shot off at the man he'd hoped he'd hit before, then ran like hell for the last big boulder before he had to cross the forty yards of open space to reach the trees. If he made that, he'd be convinced that the little people of Ireland's bogs were truly looking out for him.

Just as he was about ready to fire again, and bolt through the true test, he caught a movement on the cliff top. He started to swing his rifle a little to the right, then realized it was Chang, on the attack again.

Jed, the middle and largest of the Striker brothers, had been surprised at how accurate the man's fire was from below, and he'd almost been hit.

He'd been more surprised to look far down the cliff face, and see his brother's head being lopped off by some crazed man who was at least as large as himself.

He was about to decide that Brother Simon could

have the rest of this battle to himself, when he heard something behind him, and spun around to see the big man, a Chinaman, coming at him, a Colt revolver in one hand, an ugly sword in the other. The Chinaman was no good with the Colt, and although he was firing as he came, the shots went wild.

Spinning on his back, Jed snapped a shot off and the Spencer bucked in his hands. A red spot billowed on the big Chinaman's chest, dead center.

Jed's mouth started to form a smile, then grimaced, as the man stumbled, but kept coming. Jed managed to lever in another shell and fire again, before the man was on him.

Jed screamed, kicked, and gouged, but the big man dragged him to his feet, then enveloped him in a great bear hug, rendering his arms useless.

Nolan managed to keep behind the rock, hidden from the first man, but could still see what was happening with Chang and the second man.

Nolan watched, unable to do anything. To fire at the man was to risk hitting Chang. The huge Chinaman dragged the man to his feet, enveloped him in his big arms . . . and plunged over the cliff.

He didn't release his adversary until they hit a rock outcropping halfway down the drop, which had to be in excess of a hundred feet. Then Chang spun away one way, and the man the other.

Nolan changed direction, and broke from his cover, running about two hundred yards to where Chang had fallen. To his surprise, no shots rang out from the location where the first shooter had been.

When he reached Chang, it was obvious the man was dead, but from the two bullet holes in his chest, it was obvious he would have been dead nonetheless.

Still, no shots from above.

Nolan walked the twenty-five yards to where the other man had landed, and stared down at one of the Striker brothers.

"Two down, one to go," he said under his breath.

He walked back to Chang. "I'll be back, good friend, and we'll take you down so you can go home," Nolan said. Then, his jaw set, he went to find the buckskin. It was obvious the first shooter had fled, and more obvious that he was another one of the Striker brothers.

After he found the buckskin and remounted, he made his way to where Chang had flung the first man. He found the body quickly, then had to hunt for the head.

Jed Striker and Efren Striker down, he concluded. The other man, the first man to have shot at them, the man who had have LuAnn . . . That man had to be Simon Striker.

And Nolan knew where Simon Striker hung his hat.

He gigged the big buckskin, looking for a game trail that would take him west.

Simon Striker had a decision to make. Should he head for the dam and the powder he had set and ready to go, or should he head back to camp and retrieve the money he had hidden there?

No one had really seen his face to connect him to any crime, no one could prove he'd had anything to do with taking O'Bannon's woman, and no one could prove the powder kegs at the dam had been placed by him.

But O'Bannon would surely discover two of the

men shooting at him were Striker brothers, and he would surmise the rest.

The woman back in camp could be done away with. Then nothing would tie him to the problems the CP had been having. Of course, he'd still have to deal with O'Bannon, proof or not.

Then there was the matter of the Auburn sheriff, and the matter of the city dude, Wellington, with the Northern Currents Ice Company, and what he was sure would soon be a warrant issued by some San Francisco judge.

He should have killed the desk clerk before he left that hotel.

Hell, altogether, it was probably a good time to cut his losses.

He decided he'd head back to his camp, kill the woman so she couldn't testify against him should he be caught up with, dig up what money he'd put away, which was considerable, ride the dun and lead the gray, and head out for Sonora. The gray horse would probably fetch a hundred dollars in the old gold town of Sonora.

Cousin Milo was down at the rails setting up to sell some more whiskey, and what he got from that load would be more money than he'd ever seen. He could take care of himself.

That was the plan. It was a good plan.

Simon put his spurs roughly to the dun's side, and the horse leapt forward.

Nolan rode until the country became familiar, then reined higher up the mountain until he crossed the flume that he knew led down to Simon Striker's camp. He pushed the buckskin hard, swearing to him that he would make up for the misuse when he got LuAnn safe under his wing.

Coming upon two men dragging a big lodgepole

behind a six-up mule team, he eyed them carefully, but they doffed their hats and waved.

He yelled at them. "You fellas seen Simon?"

"Went by here a few minutes ago, headin' out like he hadn't had chow in a month of Sundays an' there was an apple pie where he was headin'."

Nolan waved, and spurred the buckskin into a canter, crashing through the occasional low pine bough trying to sweep him from the saddle.

Smoke in the distance, then the sounds of the mill.

He slowed the horse and moved until he was fifty yards from the group of buildings, then dismounted.

The dun Simon Striker normally rode was tied outside the cabin, its sides heaving.

Nolan was twenty-five yards from the side of the cabin when he heard the front door burst open and slam against the building. He snapped up the Henry expecting Simon Striker to round the corner with gun in hand, but the man dropped off the porch and was crossing the yard heading for an outbuilding. He did carry the long rifle in one hand, a satchel in the other, and had a pistol jammed into his belt.

Nolan tracked him, not thirty yards behind, the Henry hanging at his side.

Striker reached the outbuilding, and was fumbling with a padlock, when he obviously heard Nolan's footfalls, and spun. Nolan was now only ten yards away.

"O'Bannon," he said, his voice normal. "What brings you up the mountain?"

Nolan motioned at the dun with his head, without taking his eyes off Striker. "Followin' that dun horse."

"Cousin Milo just rode in on that'n," Striker said, then yawned.

For a fraction of a second, Nolan had his doubts; then a voice rang out from inside the outbuilding.

"Nolan, help!" It was LuAnn.

Striker scrambled for the Whitworth, leaning against the building, but he wasn't fast enough.

As he was bringing the big rifle up, Nolan centered the Henry on his chest, cocked, and fired.

The slug blew the big man back against the door, and he bounced off, managed two or three steps, trying to cock the long rifle, then fell on his face in the dust.

Nolan swept the rifle around the yard, where men stopped working in the mill and the corrals.

But no one made a move toward him. Finally, a man walked out of the mill and strolled toward him, but the man was unarmed, wiping his hands with a rag.

"Nolan," a small voice again rang out from the outbuilding.

Nolan recovered the key where it had fallen, unlocked the door, and LuAnn leapt into his arms. He couldn't help but smile, even as the strange man approached from the mill.

The fellow stopped ten paces away. "You the law?"

"Nope, I'm the fellow he stole this beautiful woman from."

"We figured the law would be here soon, as one of the boys saw him shoot down a man with a badge. Shot him down in cold blood, then led his horse off like he'd just made a bargain."

"You run this mill?" Nolan asked, LuAnn still clinging to him.

"Sure do."

"Well, I'm a division boss with the CP. You keep 'em coming down the slide road, and you fellas will get paid."

"That's fine with us," the man said, then he smiled. "Looks like you're in good hands."

But Nolan ignored him, as LuAnn had his cheeks in both hands, and was kissing him so hard his lips hurt. Hell, he realized, they were the only part of his body that hadn't been hurting for the past two days.

But somehow, this hurt seemed just fine.

With LuAnn astride Striker's dun, and Nolan leading the sheriff's gray, they made their way back to their canyon the way they'd come.

When he reached the cliff face, he dismounted, and with LuAnn's help, loaded Chang's body on the sheriff's horse. LuAnn shed a few tears, but composed herself. Nolan promised her that Chang's body would be returned to the Celestial homeland, with enough money to bury him properly and send his spirit on the way to meet his ancestors.

When they reached the lake, Nolan noticed the black singe of a burnt fuse near the trail. He instructed LuAnn to stay on the trail with the horses and Chang's body, and followed the mark until he found unburnt fuse, then on to where he located a keg of powder in the rockfall dam.

That son-of-a-bitch, he thought. *Striker was going to blow the dam and wipe out all of their good work. All to sell a few more timbers?*

Nolan had had some remorse over shooting the man, and would have over shooting any man. Striker had been the first man he'd killed who was looking him in the eye. Others maybe, in the heat of a sea battle with pirates, he was sure he'd shot, but never a man at not much more than arm's length.

His remorse was considerably lightened when he found the kegs of black powder.

Clearing the kegs away from the dam, moving them well below, he worked for over an hour before he and LuAnn continued the journey.

The next morning, he left LuAnn in camp, went down the creek with Chang again tied to the gray, and followed the rail to Strobridge's private car.

His boss stepped out of the car with two cups of coffee. "You come down to see the clogging?"

Nolan motioned to where he'd tied the horses, Chang's body wrapped in a tarp. "Not today. Striker killed the Celestial Chang."

"How'd that happen?"

"Striker carried off LuAnn, and I went after him. Chang followed, and probably saved our bacon, but it cost him dearly. He and LuAnn were old friends."

"And?"

"And I killed the bastard . . . and we shot his low-life kin."

"My God, Nolan—"

"You'd have killed them too, John. Striker had set some charges to bring down a lake full of water and wipe out all of our work on the new trestle . . . guess he thought he'd sell more timbers. But I shot them because they shot at us, to Chang's bad luck. He was a hell of a man."

Strobridge shook his head in wonder. "I never did much take to Striker. But I'd never have thought—"

"I'll have some of the Celestials take care of Chang; then the company can haul him over to San Francisco and ship him home?"

"Just like we did the others," Strobridge agreed.

Nolan finished his coffee. "I'll be missin' for a while tomorrow. I'm taking LuAnn and Sheriff Chester's horse down to Colfax. I'll be finding a place to live . . . for the both of us . . . then I'm going on down to Auburn to see the sheriff, if we've still got one. His horse was in Striker's camp, his help reported seeing Striker shoot down a man with a badge—likely as not it was Sheriff Chester."

"That's a hell of a note—"

"I'll find someone to tell about what must have happened, and to turn the sheriff's horse over to."

"What about our timbers?"

"I struck a deal with the men working the mill. They'll keep them coming."

"Jesus, Nolan, sometimes it seems like this bloody rail is never going to end, and we just got started."

"What did you do about Bochevski?" Nolan asked, a little apprehensively.

"Sent him packing. We got a tough enough job without some division boss working at cross-purposes."

"Good. I'd have hated to have to keep banging his hard head. I'm still sore as a boil all over." Nolan took a deep breath, then sighed and began to move toward the horses. Then he stopped and turned back, speaking with a half smile. "Five men to a five-hundred-sixty-pound rail, three blows to a spike, thirty spikes to a rail, four hundred rails to the mile. Hell, John, that's only a quarter million pounds of iron to the mile. That's no hill for a stepper. My Celestials have to move ten times that much rock."

Strobridge waved at Nolan O'Bannon, yelling after him. "Then get on down the mountain and get back here. We still got some steppin' to do. We've got another thousand Celestials arriving next week, and you all got a mountain of rock to move."

Nolan mounted, and yelled something to him in Chinese as he gigged the big buckskin.

Strobridge had absolutely no idea what he'd said, but he laughed nonetheless.

For a sneak preview of
L. J. Martin's
next Western novel,
Stranahan,
coming from Pinnacle Books in
August, 2003
just turn the page . . .

Chapter One

To say being awakened with the cold ring of a muzzle pressed between your eyes rattles your backbone, would be like concluding that the sun rises in the east.

Sam Stranahan was no tenderfoot, having trapped furs and hunted buffalo, been a herdsman and occasionally a freighter, and even panned a little color now and then. And all this before he had thirty years, which were behind him as of yesterday, if he had his days right.

He was no stranger to guns, but this was a first for him.

He lay flat on his back on his bedroll, his saddle for a pillow, the morning sun just cutting the horizon and somewhat blinding him.

"Is there something I can do for you fellas?" he asked, afraid to flinch, afraid to raise a hand to shield his eyes from the sun. His breath roiled in the morning cold.

"You were in Bozeman yesterday?" The question came from the gravelly voice behind the cold steel still resting between Sam's eyes.

He couldn't bring himself to move his head to

see, but he sensed there were more men present than the three he could make out beyond the obstructing gun hand.

"I was not," he offered quietly. "I've been dodging redskins for the last week, coming up the Yellowstone. I figured I'd be in Bozeman tomorrow sometime."

"Track said you come into this camp from the southwest."

"I backtracked to the river late yesterday, wantin' to camp by water . . . I was startin' to whiff myself."

The man with the gun cackled.

Sam was beginning to feel the heat rise in his backbone, having to explain his personal ablutions to a bunch of strangers. Still, he kept his voice low and constant. "You're getting my hackles up, mister. Take your damned weapon off'n my forehead."

"Or what?"

Sam could sense some humor in the man's voice. It was clear the man accosting him thought he had nothing to fear.

"Do as he says, Rusty," another voice rang out. This one seemed to have some authority behind it.

"I ain't convinced," the voice behind the cold muzzle said, the cackle belonging to the man referred to as Rusty. Sam could see he'd turned to glance at the voice of authority.

Sam slapped the gun away with his right hand, catching the man's wrist with his left, and backhanding him hard across the mouth as the right came back.

Although he knocked the one he could reach momentarily senseless, the rain of blows and kicks that fell upon him made him curl up in a fetal position, before getting his legs under him. As he drove up to his feet, he caught the flash of a descending rifle barrel out of the corner of his eye, and heard the crack of iron on bone before everything went black and whirlpooled as he slunk back to the cold ground.

"Thacker, what do you think?"

The man speaking was a ruddy-complexioned redhead with hatchet features, his hat now on the ground six feet away. He backhanded a trickle of blood from the corner of his mouth, a result of the blow from the now-unconscious man on the ground.

The one the redhead referred to as Thacker wore a star on his vest; a vest encircling a barrel of a torso. His head was a keg atop no neck, set on wide shoulders, with a hat large enough that it had to have been custom-made. He pulled a gold pocket watch from his vest pocket by its gold chain and checked the time before he ordered, "Search his bedroll and pack. I'd guess he'd be who he says, as he's only one and we been trackin' three, but it's worth a gander."

There were six of them. They'd come into Sam Stranahan's cottonwood-protected camp just before sunup. Two of them, Cree Indians, had moved Stranahan's weapons out of reach before the redhead had shoved the muzzle between his eyes.

They were a posse from Bozeman, who'd come downriver in pursuit of a gang of stage robbers. Robbers who, as a result of their last of many holdups, were also murderers, as they'd shot the man riding shotgun dead center in the chest. The shotgun guard was the redhead's brother, which, to the casual observer, explained the man's eagerness to get a pound of flesh in return.

That they were tired and impatient was an understatement. All of them were dusted from head to boot, and sweat had trailed down their cheeks and foamed the withers and muddied the flanks of their mounts, even in the morning chill. They'd been riding hard all night, only pausing at the Big Timber stage stop for a quick breakfast of beans, fried hens' eggs, and side-pork. Even the two Cree trackers were tired and eager to get back to their women.

As three of the white men, including the redhead, searched through the bedroll and pack, Stranahan began to regain consciousness.

Just as he sat up, rubbing the goose egg on his forehead, the redhead held up a money belt triumphantly. "By all that's holy, this is the son of a bitch that shot Howard."

Thacker still sat quietly astride his tall gray Tennessee Walker. "Pacovsky, it ain't no sin for a man to have a little money."

Something about the tone of their voices and their attitude told Sam they knew he wasn't the man they sought. Then why were they harassing him? Unless they wanted his rig and whatever else he had.

The redhead called Pacovsky thumbed through the wad in the money belt. "A little, hell. There's ten thousand here at least. Some gold coin and a hell of a bunch of scrip."

Sam tried to get to his feet, but one of the other men shoved him back to his butt. Sam spat blood, backhanding his mouth again, then managed, "There's just a little over thirty-eight hundred of my hard-earned there in scrip and coin, but it don't surprise me that this brindle-topped fool can't cipher."

The redhead took a step forward, but Sam spun and got his legs between them, threatening a kick, and the man held up.

"Let him stand," Thacker said.

Sam pulled on his boots, then slowly climbed to his feet.

Thacker eyed him. "You're ever' bit of six feet.

Hair color's black and down to your shoulders, and the blue eyes seem right. You got a name?"

"Stranahan, not that it's any of your by-God bloody business."

"More Irish trash," the sheriff mumbled. The man with the badge seemed to be making up his mind; then he motioned to the one he called Pacovsky. "Bring me the money, then shackle him in the saddle."

"The hell you will," Stranahan spat.

Thacker slipped a scattergun from a scabbard alongside the gray with the whisper of cold steel on leather, leveled it on Stranahan's midsection, then ratcheted back the hammers. He growled, "Son, we can do this my way, or your way, but it seems your way is the bloody way. This ol' ten-gauge is loaded with cut-up box nails. Do you want a taste? If you do, the last thing you see'll be your guts on those rocks behind you . . . or do you want to come along easy-like and see what the judge has to say?"

"I didn't do nothing to give you call—"

"Judge Talbot will sort it out."

Rusty Pacovsky gave him a boot to the backside, and Stranahan stumbled forward, in the direction of his horse. "Git over to that ugly grulla, and we'll shackle you after you're mounted."

Sam Stranahan thought again about how pleasing it had been to slap this redheaded fool, and it would be to do so again, but the scattergun still lay trained on his midsection. One of the Cree had saddled and tied the reins to the saddle horn of the grulla by the time he reached where his stud had been staked amongst an island of green grass in the sage. As he came alongside the animal, he made up his mind.

No highbinder Montana territorial judge was going to hang him for something he hadn't done, and no fat sheriff was going to confiscate money he'd worked over five years to save. And he'd had a hangman's noose rasp his Adam's apple once before, and had sworn then it'd never happen again.

He'd rather have it all end here and now.

The sheriff let down the hammers on the shotgun, remounted, and was sliding it back in the scabbard as the redhead shoved Sam up alongside the horse. A pockmarked Cree in filthy leather leggings held the horse's lead rope, with the bridle tied to the saddle horn.

As Sam swung up, he gigged the animal hard to the ribs and gave a rebel yell. "Yeehaw . . . gid'up, Blue." The blue grulla, never the bashful one, charged directly into the Cree, knocking him flying.

The redhead tried to hang onto Sam's leg, but with great pleasure Sam drove a left hand back time and again into the man's hatchet nose, and after three leaps, he dropped away, rolling in the dust.

Sam bent low in the saddle and grabbed up the trailing lead rope, and stayed low in the saddle as a handful of chopped-up nails sliced the air over his head.

In five jumps he was in a sage-lined ravine, and pounding up away from the river bottom and the wide Yellowstone.

He was a long way from free, but he knew the blue grulla stud, and unless there was some horseflesh there he'd underestimated, or unless one of them got off a lucky shot, it was only a matter of time before he'd leave them in the dust.

The bad news was his money belt, his weapons, and his bedroll were left behind.

But Last Chance Gulch, and his brother's gold

claim, was up ahead of him. That was his first goal; then he'd worry about getting his money back.

His first thirty years had been fairly tough, but it looked like they'd been a cakewalk compared what might be ahead.